Romancing Miss Stone

Romancing MISS STONE

M.C. VAUGHAN

Recycling programs
for this product may
not exist in your area.

ISBN-13: 978-1-335-04166-1

Romancing Miss Stone

Harlequin Enterprises ULC
22 Adelaide St. West, 41st Floor
Toronto, Ontario M5H 4E3, Canada
www.Harlequin.com

Printed in U.S.A.

To Dad,
who showed us every '80s adventure flick
and would have been so proud.

One

Bo Ferguson snuck a glance at the clock tacked onto his home office's exposed brick. Seven, and this should-have-been-an-email meeting was *still* going.

He fought the urge to rub his eyes.

His promotion to senior algorithm engineer six months ago came with an anchor to his desk. The responsibility was worth it, since it meant he could shave his mom's and sister's money worries down to a manageable level. The lone luxury he'd allowed himself was his ergonomic masterpiece of an office chair to support his clench-prone back muscles.

Actually, scratch that "lone luxury" bit.

He didn't pinch pennies when it came to his newfound cooking hobby, either. Before his fiancée left for an archeological dig in Belize in January, she'd teasingly encouraged him to eat more than PB&Js and string cheese. He could take a hint and used their time apart to beef up his chef game. To his surprise, cooking was fun.

The kitchen was low-stakes, unlike everything else in his life.

"Bo, what's the ETA on your code?" his project manager asked.

The door's squeaky hinge signaled his cat's arrival. Where

had she gone? Shit. He had maybe thirty seconds before Lorelai yowled for dinner.

"Bo, if you're talking, you're muted."

"Sorry," he said. "What was the question?"

"Is your code on track? Any blockers?"

"No blockers. I'll check it in later tonight. Early tomorrow at the latest."

"Great." She noted his response in the task management system. "Anyone have new agenda items?"

Silence, as expected.

He and his teammates had a pact not to prolong meetings. They'd rather spend these much-needed minutes grinding toward their go-live deadline at month's end. An on-time delivery would earn them sweet stretch goal bonuses, and his would go straight into his and Destiny's wedding fund.

"Okay." His project manager flashed a thumbs-up. "See you at our morning stand-up."

Lorelai pounced on his lap from the antique shelves next to his desk.

"Uhngf." Bo clicked the bright red Leave button. Hopefully his team hadn't heard his pained grunt. "Why are you like this, Lore? We had a truce."

The orange cat licked her paws, then settled onto his thighs.

"I know, I know. You miss her." He scratched under her chin. "Me too. But don't take it out on me. She'll be home tomorrow, and we'll be back to normal."

If their past disagreements were any indication, they'd work this out fast. He'd pick her up from the airport with a bouquet of her favorite tiger lilies, they'd come home to his Victorian-era fixer-upper and they'd finally talk things through.

He leaned back in his chair to give Lorelai room to stretch.

Talking would be great, actually. Destiny had punted their eight-o'clock calls every night this week. She'd texted that there were farewell dinners, research closeouts, documentation for her dissertation…all of which was true, but the distance nagged at him.

It had started over the holidays. After his promotion in the fall, he was in a secure financial position. They'd been dating for seven years, so it couldn't have been much of a surprise when he popped the question as the ball dropped at midnight. She'd said yes without hesitation. The next day, they'd gone shopping for a ring, she'd picked out the one she'd liked best and they'd been happy.

For a week.

Then, she'd confessed she wasn't sure. About him, or marriage, or both, she couldn't say.

Before they could hash things out like rational adults, the Ch'ooj Creek archaeological research site in Belize had invited her to participate in a dig. This was too good for her professionally to pass up, so they'd agreed this would be a good break. They'd use the time to take a breather, then figure things out when she returned.

"Ready for dinner?" he asked the cat.

The two-hundred-year-old floorboards creaked under his chair's weight as he rolled back from the desk. Lorelai leaped from his lap and followed him down the stairs, tripping him as she twisted through his ankles.

He caught himself on the railing. "Every time, Lore?"

She meowed and dashed into the kitchen. Tonight's fare was honey-glazed salmon, blanched green beans and saffron rice. The whole thing took twenty minutes to cook, less time than delivery and twice as delicious. He divvied the meal onto plates for him and his sister, covered hers with a lid, then flicked a smaller, unsauced portion into Lorelai's bowl.

She chowed down without a second glance.

"You're welcome." He scratched her behind the ears, which she ignored.

As he flicked on the television to catch up on the news while he ate, his phone buzzed with a text. He sighed. Was Destiny seriously canceling on him again? How could he pick her up from the airport without her flight info?

He unlocked his phone and tapped the text.

Babe, this is difficult to write.

He dropped his fork on the coffee table.

We're not meant to be a forever-couple, and it's not fair for me to jerk you around. I'm happy here, happier than I've ever been, and I want the same for you, so I'm ending our engagement. Please have a good life.

Wait, what? A single text threatened to shatter his heart and future. His trembling thumbs stumbled over the keyboard, typing and deleting garbled words until he strung together a coherent message.

Des, this doesn't make sense. You're supposed to be on a plane in the morning.

He clutched the phone, waiting. Seconds stretched into torturous minutes, and he got...

Nothing.

No response—no confirmation that his message had been delivered, much less read. Was she on the other end of the phone? Belize was only two hours behind Baltimore. She should be awake and have time to talk.

He poked her profile, then clicked Call.

A half ring, then, "Hi, you've reached Destiny Richards. I'm on a date with my trowel, so please leave..."

Voice mail. He rubbed the tightness in his chest, waited a beat, then called again. Same result. Dread thickened his throat as he paced the length of the town house. She couldn't mean what she'd texted. He was humble enough to admit they weren't in a perfect place when she left, but a few tense months shouldn't mean the end of seven years together.

Unless... Could he have misread their relationship that badly?

Oxygen came fast and shallow, forcing him to take a knee. The nap of the Turkish rug bristled against his palms. He closed his eyes to focus on his breathing, to calm it with counting, the way his doctor had coached him to when panic attacks came on.

The darkness was a mistake.

Now he was reeling, tumbling through milestone memories. Asking Destiny to marry him at the top of the Harbor Court hotel... Adopting Lorelai at the BARCS Animal Shelter... Dinner with Dad at the casino buffet when he'd blown through town for a poker tournament...

He couldn't pinpoint where things had gone off track.

Candy-colored light from the front door's stained-glass panel skated across the floor as his sister let herself into the house. A crisp April breeze whipped through the room, and the piercing squeal of an MTA bus's brakes made him wince.

"You won't believe the day I had." His sister, Delilah, wheeled her bike in, folded it, then hung it on the rack he'd installed when she moved in to help with the rent. "The new guy who runs my lab is the *worst* piece of patronizing garbage. He actually asked me—"

She paused, mid-un-clip of her helmet.

"Bo?" Fear edged her voice. "What's wrong? Is Mom okay?"

He sank back onto his heels, then riffled his hair.

"Bo. Seriously, you're scaring me. It's seven thirty. You should be eating dinner and watching the news, but you're on the floor."

"Mom's fine." He exhaled. *One, two, three.* Might as well rip off the bandage. "But I'm not. Destiny sent me a breakup text. Then I think she blocked me."

Del's windbreaker swished as she hung up her helmet. "Oh."

His sister's face, a feminine version of his own, was inscrutable. This was bad. He'd been able to read her like an instruction manual since the day they were born. Even before her diagnosis and the meds that had balanced out her irrational whims, he'd understood her on a chromosomal level.

Not today, though.

"My fiancée breaks up with me, and 'oh' is all you've got?" Bo pushed up off the floor. "You gave me more sympathy when my freshman girlfriend cheated on me with my roommate."

"Because that was a complete surprise."

Delilah brushed past him and into the kitchen. Wordlessly, she grabbed a bottle from the top of the fridge and two shot glasses from the cabinet of random glassware.

"What's that for?" he asked.

"If we're doing this, I need to take the edge off your mood."

She set the glasses on the corner dinette by the back door, then poured two shots. "Sit."

There was no arguing with Del when she took that tone.

He sniffed at the glass. "Rum?"

"It's either that or Grape Pucker. You have a shitty liquor cabinet."

"Because I don't drink."

"You do today." She gestured at his shot glass. Once he held his aloft, she tapped her empty one against it. "Drink."

His eyes watered as the rum burned a path down his throat. "There." He coughed. "Now what the hell?"

"Uh, uh, uh." She wagged her finger. "You know the rule."

He pursed his lips. Twinhood meant he and Delilah told each other truths that no other humans on the planet would dare to. After all, they had the full context of their shared life together. It did not always make for a peaceful home life, however. So, at sixteen, their birthday gift to each other was a promise to keep their opinions to themselves unless invited to share.

He'd never invoked radical candor about Destiny because they'd all known each other since middle school. He knew what his sister thought about his fiancée.

Didn't he?

"Delilah Jane Ferguson, please tell me what you think about this situation."

"I would be happy to, Boaz Jasper Ferguson."

She shed her windbreaker, revealing her black lab tech scrubs. He loved those scrubs. They represented how far she'd come, how hard she'd worked to catch up after everyone but him and their mom had given up on her. They'd always been each other's best friends, fiercest defenders and biggest cheerleaders whenever life was too much.

"You *swear* this won't make things weird between us?" she asked.

"We're twins. Things have always been weird between us."

"Fair. But I have been sitting on this for years, so remember that you asked for it." She pointed at him. "Maybe Destiny breaking up with you is for the best."

That thumped him in the chest. He furrowed his brow. "Go on."

"Do I have to?" She rotated the shot glass on its base.

"Yes."

The seconds ticking on the kitchen clock pecked at his patience.

"Del," he prompted. "Don't hold back."

"She's not right for you. She might've been when you two started dating. You helped each other get over a heartbreak. But…" Del blew her dark hair out of her eyes. "Please, Bo, don't make me say this."

"Oh, you're saying it." He poured himself another shot.

"She's kind of a jerk. Selfish."

"No she's not, she's—"

Del held up a finger. "Stop. You invoked radical candor, so I'm coming clean. You had a crush on her since we met her. Fast-forward to when she strung you along and used you as a backup date for formals. You even took dance lessons so you could surprise her in case she asked you to prom."

The truth of what she said itched.

He scratched his jaw. "That's not exactly how it was."

"Dude, I was *there*." She poured him another shot. "When

that guy smashed her heart after college, who white-knighted his way into picking up the pieces?"

"Me," he grudgingly admitted.

"You. Good old reliable, predictable Bo."

"That's not all I am." He knocked back the rum. He'd embraced reliability and predictability to keep his family intact. Left to his own devices, though, who knew? Maybe he was a secret swashbuckler.

He nudged the empty shot glass toward his sister.

"Of course that's not all you are. You cook a mean salmon, too."

"Is that why Destiny sent me that text?" Lorelai buffed his ankles, so he picked up the cat. "Because she's off having the adventure of a lifetime and I'm boring?"

"No." Del laid her hand over his. "She sent you that text because she's an asshole who doesn't deserve you. Bo, seriously, you're the best. You helped her get into grad school, navigated the financial aid system to get the best benefits—"

"I helped *you* navigate the system too, then invited you to live here during your post-doc to split expenses. I help the people I love."

"And I adore you for it. You did nothing wrong. Appreciate the silver lining here. Destiny's a fun hang, sure, but lacks in basic human consideration. Did she pitch in with the housework? The grocery shopping? Ever take care of you when you were sick?"

He thumbed the divot in his chin. "No, but I never asked her to."

"You shouldn't have to ask. Caring people do that stuff." She held up the bottle. "Want another? This next part might hurt."

"Jesus. The *next* part?" His vision wobbled. Uh-oh. He should not have had that many shots. He waved her off. "Just hit me with it."

Del took a deep breath, then let it out long and slow.

"Okay. You've always treated Destiny like one of your algorithms. You put kindness, support and love into your relationship, and you expect you'll get stability back. It's a reasonable expectation, but Destiny's not like that, Bo." She squeezed his hand. "She's all take, and no give. You've always…waited for her to come to her senses. Some might call it patience, others might call it masochism. You deserve better. Someone who sees you, loves you for all your quirks, and allows *you* to be the one to take chances."

Ouch. Delilah added ghost peppers to the salt she'd tossed into his wounds earlier.

Through her eyes, he might be boring. Risk averse. It had suited him for most of his life, helped keep his family afloat through dark times. But here was his twin, his best friend, telling him that particular trait was no longer required.

He shooed Lorelai from his lap. "You're wrong."

"That you deserve better?" Del leaned back. "Oh, brother mine, we have got to talk about your self-esteem."

"No, about me waiting, and being predictable, and having no sense of adventure." He shoved back from the table. "I'm going to Belize."

Two

The soft Caribbean breeze dancing through the palm fronds around the Belize Dreams's pool contrasted with the brittle tension between Alex Stone and the man seated at the resort's bar. If she didn't phrase this next sentence perfectly, her tourism company would be dead in the water, and her father's legacy along with it.

"Mr. Belisle." She slid a rum punch, the first of a hundred she'd make today, toward the man in the short-brimmed fedora. Despite the gentle reggae pumping through the speakers, she kept her voice low to avoid eavesdropping. "I promise I'll pay off the debt."

He cracked a peanut. "Chula, I know you *want* to pay the balance. But you owe everyone in Azul Caye. You must be running out of options."

Her stomach squeezed the cocktail-fruit breakfast she'd gobbled before her shift.

Belisle's assessment was correct. Stone Adventures was on the brink of collapse, but she stubbornly expected a miracle. She had to, because even if she sold the business, the people she owed wouldn't get their full due. *That* was unacceptable. Azul Caye was, at its heart, a small town. The people she owed—except for Belisle—were her father's friends. Regular attendees at birthday parties, barbecues, holidays. They helped take care of him when he was dying so that she could keep leading tours. She'd make them whole, every last one of them.

"I'll pay them all back."

"How?" He sipped his cocktail. "It's almost the wet season, which means fewer tours. Do you plan to sling drinks around the clock at every resort in town?"

She crossed her arms. "If that's what it takes."

Beyond the pool, a handful of kayakers splashed into the calm cerulean bay. She wished she was leading them out onto the water instead of dealing with Belisle. But as he was the biggest investor in town, she had no choice but to stay put and humor him.

"You could tend bar for a thousand days and not equal what you owe, never mind the mounting interest. Give up, chula, and sell the business to me. I will work wonders with it, and your father will still adore you from heaven."

With acid dripping from her smile, she said, "Mr. Belisle, please don't tell me you left your private island and came all the way here to tell me about all the things I *can't* do."

"You're new here. You don't know how things work."

Polite, polite, polite. She must stay polite, even though she wanted to stab his pinky-ringed hand with her corkscrew. She jammed her twitchy hands into her pockets to keep up her calm facade.

"With all due respect," she said. "I've lived in Azul Caye off and on my whole life. I know how things work."

Belisle shook his head. "Then how did your accountant boyfriend steal your capital?"

Because she'd been grieving and distracted—and math made her queasy.

Her opponent did not wait for an answer. "You're a spitfire and smart, but you have no college education, if I recall? No formal training in business. I do. I could hire you on as employee number one, and you could learn from me. But if you won't sell, maybe we can figure out an alternate agreement."

She pursed her lips. Nothing aboveboard followed a statement like that.

"And what might that be?"

He cracked another peanut, then dropped the shells onto the small pile forming in front of him. Great. She'd have to clean those up after he left.

"My boy, Rodrigo." Belisle leaned forward. "He's awkward around women."

Alex had run into Rodrigo here at the resort and in many of the city's night clubs before her father fell ill. The friendly distribution rep for Belize Gold Barrel Rum wasn't awkward around women. Far from it. He was just asexual, and perfectly open about it.

Maybe not with his father, though? Tread lightly...

"I'm sorry," she said. "I'm not seeing the connection to an offer."

Belisle lowered his sunglasses. "You're a pretty girl, he's a handsome man, you're already friends. Go out with him, and see what happens. If you hit it off, I could talk the other businesses around to forgiving some of your debt. Or, at a minimum, offering you our friends-and-family repayment terms."

Alex coughed to hide her heaving stomach.

Ew, ew, ew. Belisle was asking her to pimp herself out to his kid. Except she couldn't pimp herself out to someone who didn't want her. She'd have to call Rodrigo and warn him that his father was brokering these kinds of deals, even though he would be mortified.

She'd decline the offer with a truth that didn't out Rodrigo. Belisle might take it as an insult to his family, but she had few options.

"No can do, sir. I made a promise to myself never to mix business and pleasure again."

"My son is not like that boyfriend of yours—"

"Ex," she corrected.

Belisle nodded. "And good riddance. Rodrigo would not embezzle all your money and leave you holding the bag."

The strong scent of imitation coconut wafted through the covered bar. More patrons had entered the pool area. Chances were good they'd be interested in pre-lunch cocktails.

"I believe you, sir, but the answer is still no."

"Then that's that." Belisle knocked twice on the bar, then sipped his rum punch. "Your first payment of ten thousand dollars will be due on Monday."

Alex pinched her thigh to keep her face from giving away her panic.

"In six days? Belisle, come on. Be reasonable. I need more time. The police said they have a lead on Peter's whereabouts."

"We've all been patient these last few months. Even if the police find your thieving boyfriend—"

"Ex." Her cheeks heated with frustration.

"They may not find the money. And then where would that leave your friends and neighbors?" He spread his hands wide. "I understand you do not care for me, but surely you care about them and their futures."

Her heart squeezed. The people from her father's hometown were more of a family to her than her blood relatives back in the States. She hated that her romantic blindness to Peter's shadiness had put them in financial jeopardy. Tourism-based businesses lived on razor-thin margins, and her inability to pay their bills cut everyone's bottom lines closer to the bone.

She'd pay those bills, or die trying.

"You'll get your money, Belisle." In her periphery, she caught a glimpse of a resort guest at the end of the bar. Perfect. An escape hatch from this uncomfortable conversation.

"Don't say I didn't try to help you, chula. I'll pray for you. But if you don't pay, I have it on good authority the courts will liquidate your assets—including the house and the additional hectares—to satisfy the amount owed to each of the vendors."

The dishtowel was rough against her hands as she twisted it.

The land was the asset that kept her father's dream, his legacy, alive. She'd rather eat a fistful of blinding tree leaves than lose it. Without the pristine beachfront property, she wouldn't have collateral for development loans. She and her younger sister, Julia, wouldn't be able to build the small resort they'd envisioned, and worse, she'd likely sour their relationship. When Dad got sick, Julia offered to defer college to help, but Alex insisted she'd had things under control. If she'd accepted Julia's help then, things might be different.

But she couldn't dwell on what-ifs.

"If you'll excuse me." Alex tucked the towel into her back pocket. "I need to tend to another patron."

Though her father had warned her never to do so, she turned her back on Belisle. She couldn't hold her icy smile. As she stalked toward the guest at the other end of the bar, she did her best to squelch her panic.

Alex Stone, solver of problems, refuser of reality, would not give in to fear.

None of this was how she'd pictured her life when she moved back to Belize. She was supposed to start an adrenaline junkie tour line while Dad handled the light family trips and the business side of things. When he got sick, he'd brought Peter aboard because he knew how much she hated invoices, budgets and billing. She handed the Stone Adventures numbers grind over to him without a second thought.

Now here she was, losing it all because she'd allowed a handsome man to fool her.

But she still had hope. A blueprint for how to extract herself from this mess would be better, but luck had always served up solutions in the past. She'd jump on any opportunity that came through in these scant six days.

Not a great plan A, but it was all she had.

So, you know. Tick tock, luck.

"Hi there, sir," she said to the back of the patron's head.

As the resort guest rotated on the barstool, she hid a gasp.

A man possessing wavy dark hair, a white shirt rolled up to his elbows, glasses tucked into the vee of his unbuttoned collar, and eyes as bright and magnetic as the Great Blue Hole off the coast of Belize City sat before her. He was alone, but that didn't mean he was here solo. His person could be elsewhere enjoying one of the resort's many amenities.

She placed a cocktail napkin on the bar. "Something I can get for you?"

Please let him be ordering a round of Panti Rippas. The coconut rum-and-pineapple juice cocktail was her least favorite drink, but the most expensive thing on the menu. The big tip would line her pockets.

"Yes." He hit her with a crooked smile that must separate

women from their clothes like a magic trick. "I'm told you can help me."

Oh, he gave good voice, too. Low and rumbly and full of mischief. The thing that caught her off guard, though, was the meaningful eye contact. Most guests stared slightly past her as she made their boozy dreams come true. This guy's attention felt like a spotlight.

"Is that so?" she asked through a grin.

Shit, what was that? She didn't flirt with customers, especially not after a polite shakedown from the town's main developer. But this guy... Maybe he'd make a good distraction from her financial woes.

"Could I have a water, please?" he asked.

Dammit. Water wouldn't pay the bills.

"Sure thing," she said through a tight smile.

Not his fault he didn't plan to get blitzed in the late-morning sun. Responsible, actually, since the temps were supposed to hit ninety by noon. Most guests didn't show that level of self-preservation and passed out like dried mangos in the loungers surrounding the pool. Still, he could have ponied up for a fresh-squeezed lemonade instead of a freebie.

As she scooped ice into a plastic tumbler, the current from the fans lazily spinning above the bar played with tendrils of her hair. She thumbed them behind her ears. Try as she might, she never completely secured the rebellious curls. They were the only feature she'd inherited from her mother. With a sigh, she fired a blast of water into the cup.

"Here you go, sir." She set the water on a Belize Dreams coaster, then turned to address a group of caftaned women who'd sidled up to the opposite side of the bar. Pineapple-scented privilege wafted from them. *There* was the potential for tips.

"Hang on," he called. "There's something else."

What, a bowl of free peanuts?

"Do you want a menu, or..."

He shook his head. "No. I need information about a guide."

She swallowed hard. Had luck delivered this bookishly handsome maybe-client? Her hopes had a bad habit of being dashed harder than a coconut against a rock, so she'd better confirm they were speaking about the same thing.

"There are tours associated with the resort, sir. If you ask the concierge, he'll help you."

"I did. They only have prepackaged tours. He sent me out here to find a guide who can assist with a more...bespoke... tour."

Hell yeah. Good job, Luck.

"Oh, okay. I've got you. What's your name?"

"Bo," he said.

"Hang tight one second, Bo."

She took the Caftan twins' order—Panti Rippas, natch— mixed and delivered them with a compliment on their outfits, then returned to Bo and his luscious forearms.

"Where are you headed?" She wiped down the bar to hide the fidget in her hands. "The Mayan temples? The forest re- serve? Jaguar preserve?"

Please let it be the temples, all the way on the other side of the tiny country. She'd be able to eke out a few days' fee for that one.

"Um, I'd rather talk to the guide. Alex Stone?"

Ah, cool. Casual misogyny.

She nodded. "Yep, hang tight one sec."

She circled the stand of booze in the middle of the U-shaped bar, then reapproached Bo, hand outstretched.

"Alex Stone, at your service."

His wrinkled brow smoothed out, and he took her hand. And, *whoa*. The electricity his firm grip shot through her was enough to knock her heartbeat out of whack.

"Sorry about that," he said. "I should know better."

"Yes, you should." She flexed her fingers to shake off the spark. "The question stands—what's your destination, and how can I help?"

He slid his phone across the bar. "It's an archaeological dig site up north that's off the beaten path, so I'd rather not chance it on my own. Think you can get me there?"

A thrill bubbled in her belly. The spot he'd touched was on the other side of the country, near the ruins, but terrain she knew as well as the gemstones tattooed on her inner arm.

"I can help, but it'll cost you."

"What are we talking?" he asked.

She ran through the routes in her head. "If the weather holds, a day to get there, but we'll probably have to stay overnight before venturing into the forest. Then, a couple of hours hiking in and back. Should be two, three days max round-trip."

"And all that adds up to…"

She dragged her gaze over the big gold face of his watch… the designer clothes…the artfully cut hair…

Yeah, he could afford it.

"Ten thousand."

He spluttered, then took a deep breath. "There's no one cheaper?"

"Sure." She lifted a shoulder. "But there's no one better."

He adjusted his glasses, assessed her, then nodded like he'd settled something.

"If that's what it takes, then that's what it takes. I don't have time to haggle. Five thousand dollars American to start, then five thousand when we return." He extended his hand once again. "Deal?"

With trembling fingers, she reached out to shake the hand of her salvation. She'd meant ten thousand Belize dollars. Under current exchange rates, the US dollar was worth twice as much.

But she wouldn't correct his misunderstanding.

With that money, she could pay most of her debt *and* kick-start the relaunch of her adventure tour company. This time, *without* a shady boyfriend waiting to drain her bank accounts.

"Deal," she said.

Three

Bo lugged his gear to the hotel's shaded pickup area. Given the hour, the tropical sun hadn't yet kicked in full blast. Hopefully it would burn off the clouds. He tucked his baseball cap into his back pocket, then sat on the bench by the entrance.

No sign of Alex, but he was early.

A powerful mix of adrenaline and worry had kept him up half the night. Was he a creep for coming here? Or was it the right thing to do? Delilah had urged him to let the whole thing go, but his sister didn't want him back together with Destiny. He needed an unbiased opinion, but those were thin on the ground. He'd lost touch with his college friends when he and Destiny coupled up, and he wasn't close enough with his co-workers to ask them.

He jiggled his knees.

Without an impartial jury to tell him this was a bad idea, here he was in Belize, possibly on the brink of the cringiest moment of his life. He palmed the back of his neck. He still had no idea what he'd say to her. *Hey, fancy meeting you here?*

"Need a cab, sir?" the valet asked.

"No thanks. I'm waiting for a tour guide."

Something rushed toward him. Instinctively, he ducked, and a big black-and-yellow bird swooped past him and back up again. It flapped its wings to slow down, then landed on the portico's crossbeam support.

It pointed its machete-length beak at Bo.

Bo could identify orioles and ravens courtesy of his life-long Baltimore residency, but his favorite childhood cereal had taught him the name of this one.

"Is that...a toucan?" Bo asked the valet.

The bird opened its beak. The portico's roof amplified its loud, horrible call, which sounded like a blend of a frog's croak and a pig's snort.

"Yes sir." The valet spun a key on his finger. "He's called Rocko. That noise means he sees something he does not like."

Bo refused to take that as a sign. He recorded a video of the bird, then sent it to Delilah with the message, *Rise and shine!*

Next, he opened his office's chat program to check in on their project. He shouldn't give people the impression he was around, but he had a tough time setting work boundaries. His project manager okayed his last-minute request for personal days, but he'd still worked three twelve-hour days before his flight to finish his deliverables.

He'd hate to cost the team their stretch bonuses.

As he worked, the dull roar of high tide crashing into the beach echoed in the distance. He'd caught a glimpse of the ocean from his room's balcony as he prepped contingency plans for this journey. Just a few more emails and messages, and he'd be at inbox zero. Nameless birds chirped high in the trees, but an approaching engine drowned them out.

He lifted his head. Alex?

Nope. A staff member zoomed past in a golf cart.

Where was she? They'd agreed to meet at seven, sharp.

Bo shoved his phone in his pocket, then paced in front of

the resort's entrance. According to his watch—and the sun that peeped between the slate gray clouds—it was 7:16 a.m.

He could text, but he didn't want to seem pushy.

Maybe she'd bailed on their deal because he'd flubbed things when he assumed she was a dude? His mistake said more about him than it did her. When the concierge described Alex Stone as the best guide in the region, Bo had expected a SEAL Team Six, Brad Pitt type.

Instead, he'd gotten a woman with coffee-black hair and eyes to match, tanned skin dotted with freckles, and a no-nonsense attitude. Not to mention distracting curves he *really* shouldn't notice. The whole point of this trip was to figure out his situation with Des—

The low rumble of an ancient red Jeep Wrangler cresting the hill interrupted his train of thought. The thing sounded like it hadn't been tuned since 2004. He kept his gaze fixed on the road leading to the resort as the mud-spattered jalopy stopped in the drop-off area.

Now his watch showed 7:18 a.m.

Where was Alex?

The Jeep's streaked passenger window rolled down.

"Good morning, sunshine," a familiar voice called. "Ready to hit the road?"

He shaded his eyes. No, no, no. This could *not* be Alex's car.

"You're late," he said.

"Are you kidding? By Belize standards, I'm early."

Alex hopped out, then circled toward his pile of luggage and supplies. The morning breeze tugged at the curls she'd secured in a ponytail and flattened her white tank top and chambray shirt to her belly. She'd worn hiking boots, but he'd chosen sneakers.

Maybe he should change into his boots?

"What *is* all this?" She gestured to his stuff. "Are you moving to Ch'ooj Creek?"

"The basics."

"The basics for what? Invading a small country?"

"For all the contingencies." He lifted a shoulder. "I have one bag of clothes, and the rest is stuff we might need in the rough."

In the week before his flight, he'd read travel blogs and ordered the most highly recommended items for the most likely emergency scenarios. For his first trip outside of the United States's mid-Atlantic region, he wanted to cover his bases. His gear included reasonable items—first aid kit, tent, camping stove, waterproof lighter, shelf-stable food, spices, water purifying chemicals, a crank radio and a deck of cards.

The basics.

"It's an eight-hour drive, sixteen with traffic. We're staying at a hotel near the dig site. Nobody's roughing it."

"I like to be prepared. Obviously you do, too." He gestured to the attachment on the back of her rust bucket. "You've got a dirt bike in case your Jeep breaks down."

"That's not what it's for. Dig sites don't usually have roads big enough to accommodate cars, and I'd prefer not to hike for hours." She jammed her hands into the pockets of her cargo shorts. "You'll be fine without all this. Trust me."

His dad had used that gem one too many times. *Trust me, bud. I've got a system. It's a sure thing.*

"I never trust anyone who tells me to."

She batted her eyes. "But you should. I can handle anything this trip dishes out."

"Does that mean you're a mechanic?" He slung his backpack over his shoulder. "Because your Jeep's an antique."

"How dare you insult Betty? She's a 2011, which was a great year for this make and model." Alex patted the hood. "We'll take whatever fits. You can leave the rest with the concierge."

Challenge accepted. He hadn't blown most of middle school on *Tetris* for nothing.

The backpack stuffed with his valuables would stay with him up front, but the rest could go in the back. First his duffel bag of clothes, then the box of supplies. Next, he wedged a zipped canvas bag of dried goods between the box and one of Alex's paper grocery bags, from which three different flavors of chips poked out.

"Big fan of junk food, eh?" He returned the passenger seat to its upright position, then climbed inside.

"Yep." She lifted a shoulder. "It's the only way to road trip. Let me guess. You swiped apples and oranges from the breakfast buffet?"

He patted his backpack. "Protein bars, too."

"Glad you're prepared for an apocalypse." She suppressed a laugh. "Now, let's go."

Storm clouds churned overhead, engulfing them in shadow. The area's pleasant earthy smell intensified as palm fronds danced in the wind. The chatty birds had ceased their chirping.

None of these struck him as good omens.

"Should we be worried about rain?" At home, a sky like this meant a downpour was imminent and he should check that his sump pump was working. Hopefully dark, shifting clouds were different in the tropics.

"Nah, that'll blow over." She slipped her keys into the ignition.

Zero digital indicators appeared on the faded dashboard. "Where's your nav system?"

Alex tapped her temple. "Right here."

His stomach sank. "You *cannot* be serious."

"I'm always serious about navigation." She twisted toward him. "What's the problem?"

"It's just…" Bo gestured to the dashboard, the road, then the universe at large. "Everyone uses navigation systems."

"I'm not everyone. Service is spotty in the forest. I have a satellite phone for emergencies, but it's better for me to know the roads than be dependent on GPS. Otherwise we'd be up shit's creek when the tree canopy interferes with the signal."

She leaned over to open the glove box. As she rummaged in its open maw, her silken forearm, the one that featured tattoos of three gemstones, lightly skimmed his knees. He wanted to trust her, but all he knew about her was that she wasn't punctual, and all he knew about Belize was that its toucans hated him for some reason.

That left an awful lot to chance.

"I can tell this is making you twitchy, so quiz me." She tossed a handful of maps at him. "Pick two places and I'll tell you how to get there."

"You don't have to prove anything."

"I do, because I don't want you to be a doubtful asshole the whole way." She tapped the map resting on his thigh.

He ignored the tingle that shot straight to his cock. Fast as that toucan had charged at him, he unfolded the map to cover his lap. He'd been without any contact like that for ages, and he did not need her to make things uncomfortable with inadvertent dick twitching.

"Pick." She twisted toward him. "I'm not leaving until you do."

"Only because you're holding me hostage." He dropped

his finger on a place at random, then leaned closer. Clearly his glasses prescription needed an upgrade. "How do we get from here to Middlesex?"

"A couple of nice dinners and a night of dancing."

Another jolt to his cock. Thank God he'd spread out that map.

"Ugh, you don't get jokes, either?" Alex groaned. "Anyway, you couldn't have picked an easier destination. Take Hummingbird Highway straight there. Next?"

She was a hundred percent right. "Hopeville."

"Easy. Southern Highway, exit at the shore. Give me one more. Make it hard this time."

He should not have this strong of a reaction to this woman saying *hard*.

Bo cleared his throat. "Tabasco, Mexico."

"Ah, an international adventure?" She tapped her fingers on the steering wheel. "Okay, so we'd take Hummingbird Highway north, then pick up Coastal. We'll be on that for about sixty kilometers until we merge onto Western, then Burrell Boom Cut, and then pick up Northern Highway. We might take the Orange Walk Bypass, but this time of year, I bet we could stay on Northern and make the same time."

Step for step, he traced his finger along the easiest, cleanest path between the two locations. Alex nailed it. Maybe he *could* trust her.

"Well?" She raised an eyebrow. "How'd I do?"

"Perfect. I'm impressed." Bo was a sucker for competency, especially in skills he lacked. His shit sense of direction annoyed the hell out of him. He could carry complicated data models in his head, but he couldn't get from his house to his Mom's place in the county without Google bossing him around. "Sorry I was a dick about it."

"You're not the first."

"There aren't many highways in Belize, huh? At least, not on that map."

"Good eye." She started the Jeep. "There are four highways, and lots of tricky side roads winding through cities and national parks. I'd bet a full third of our roads aren't even on a map, hence the need for personal knowledge. Any other proof you need to allay your concerns, sir?"

"Knock off the *sir* stuff." Bo shoved the map in the glove box.

"Don't be salty that my brain is superior to satellites."

"I'm not. I told you, I'm impressed." The Jeep's tires kicked up dust as they merged onto the dirt road that would take them into the city. "I'd love to be that confident about anything I do."

"Oh, I'm sure there are things a handsome man like you is *very* good at."

He couldn't tell if her tone was flirty or teasing. Not that it mattered. He cut a glance toward her. Well, it sort of mattered. Flirting was an ego boost. Considering why he was here…his ego could use the boosting.

She shifted gears smoothly, her long thighs pumping the clutch and gas as elegantly as a maestro conducting a symphony.

Eyes on the road, Ferguson.

"Lighten up, Bo. That was another joke."

Destiny had said that same thing a million times—*lighten up, Bo*. She teased him that his nonstop worrying stemmed from a desire to be in control. But standing on guard for problems was how he prevented them from happening.

He blew out a breath.

Couldn't he cut himself a break for a day, though, and enjoy being in paradise?

Just look at that gorgeous tropical scenery. Lush green trees in foreign shapes and sizes, mountains rising in the distance… Hell, even the shape of the clouds was different than the ones at home in Baltimore. The fresh novelty of everything outside Alex's windshield stirred Bo's sense of adventure. For the past four years, he'd been staring at the same four walls of his home office, in the same neighborhood, the same city.

He'd forgotten what it was like to experience something new.

Although…new meant unpredictable, and that could be dangerous.

As they merged onto the highway, Alex flicked on the radio. Upbeat steel drums filled the car. With a wide smile, punctuated by a dark freckle over the left corner of her mouth, she took her hand from the gearshift and pointed at him.

"Bo Ferguson, I dedicate this song to you. Hard."

Her use of his first and last name felt like roll call. He wasn't sure he liked it.

She cranked it louder and joined Bob Marley. "I said don't worry about a thing…"

For the next few minutes, she sang along—badly and loudly—to "Three Little Birds." As the song wound down, traffic thickened around them.

He lowered the volume. "Ha ha, I get it. You've known me for all of twelve minutes and you've decided I'm chronically tense and should relax."

"Shouldn't you?" Alex glanced at him. "Besides, I'm not the only one making snap judgments. And—whoops, hang on."

Four

Alex swerved onto the shoulder to bypass a poky chicken truck bumping along twenty kilometers an hour below the posted speed limit. Bo white-knuckled the grab bar above the glove box, giving her an excellent view of his corded forearms.

"You almost hit that truck," he said.

"Oh, I did not." She upshifted, then merged back with the speedier traffic. "I missed it by a kilometer. I couldn't veer left, so I took the shoulder. That's what it's there for. Emergencies."

Alex's head throbbed. She'd been up late packing, rearranging her schedule and texting Rodrigo a heads-up that his dad was trying to set up dates for him. Any one of those things might've caused a tension headache, but none of them were the culprit this morning.

Since puberty, shifts in barometric pressure triggered her migraines. Living with her mother in unflinchingly sunny Southern California during the school year wasn't so bad. The rainy season in Belize, however, was a different beast.

When Dad was alive, she'd close the curtains, go to bed and curl into the fetal position while she waited for it to pass. As the sole proprietor of Stone Adventures, however, she couldn't afford the luxury of a day off. Nope. Instead, she swallowed a fistful of meds at sunrise to dull the stabbiness. She nudged her sunglasses back up her nose. Pain like this meant the darkening storm clouds weren't an idle threat.

A deluge was coming.

As much as she'd like to cleave off the aching half of her head, her migraine superpower came in handy. For example, she'd never take a snorkeling group to a picturesque caye while her head pounded like this. Road trips, however, were fine.

"No, it's not." Bo shook his head. "It's there for disabled vehicles."

"What is?" She snapped back to the conversation. "Oh, the emergency lane. Listen, I'm sure everyone who didn't get in a pileup a second ago is *very* okay with me using the emergency lane to pass the chicken truck."

"Can we just…" He let go of the bar, then crossed those luscious forearms across his chest. "Make a deal that you drive the speed limit?"

"Absolutely not." He was lucky she enjoyed the way his blue T-shirt clung to his shoulders. "Let's get something straight, my guy. You're a guest—"

"Client."

She ground her teeth. Throttling him would probably get her a one-star review.

"Fine. You're a *client* in my Jeep, but it's still my Jeep, and my rules. I swear on a stack of whatever you believe in that I'll get us to Ch'ooj Creek in one piece. But to get you there in the timeframe you requested, I will occasionally need to speed."

She slowed and downshifted to allow a school bus to merge onto the highway. There, see? She wasn't a speed demon all the time. The adorable kids in the back waved like maniacs, so she waved back.

Bo, killjoy extraordinaire, did not.

"Getting pulled over will add time, not save it."

"The cops won't pull us over," she said. "The rules here are squishier than wherever you're from."

"That'd be Baltimore, Maryland. North of Washington, DC, south of New York, and stuffed with seafood, charm and weirdness."

She chuckled. Tempting as it was to ask him a follow-up question, Alex held back. She was already attracted to him, which was a giant blinking neon sign that she should keep things professional. Since her taste in men was not to be trusted, it would be better to remind herself of his annoying characteristics.

Like…

In twenty-four hours, he assumed she was a dude, chastised her for being late, overpacked, chastised her *again* for speeding and doubted her navigational abilities. Okay, fine, he'd apologized for the first and last thing. But she'd be wise to hold on to the grudge, keep her distance and *definitely* ignore the flutter in her stomach whenever she contemplated spending the next two days in his handsome company.

"Let's listen to music instead of talking." She tuned the dial to a punta rock station. "Enjoy the local culture."

He gestured toward the radio. "We'll be lucky if the station lasts thirty miles. I foresee more conversation in our future."

"Nah." She upped the volume. The loud, fast beat of the music might inflame her headache, but it would also keep him from talking.

"Are you from here?" he shout-asked. "You sound American."

Apparently, Bo Ferguson did not take hints easily.

"My mom's based in LA, so I split my time between California and Belize growing up."

He lowered the volume on the radio. Rude. He had obviously never been properly trained as a passenger. Control of the music was sacred and belonged to the driver.

"So you *are* American."

He said it like he was accusing her of something.

Alex furrowed her brow. "I have dual citizenship, but I consider myself Belizean."

Mostly because she associated all things American with her mother, and wow, did she not want to be anything like her mom. When her parents split, her mom had yanked her from this place against her will, all so she could pursue a more luxurious life than Dad could offer. There were *so* many things wrong with that. Like, marriage was for better and worse, richer and poorer, sickness and health, 'til death do you part.

Not until the urge for an upgraded lifestyle hits you.

The day Mom loaded Julia into the SUV to cart her off to college, Alex packed her bags, scribbled a note for her mother and hopped a plane to the international airport in Belize City. Mom was pissed, but Alex had never looked back. Why would she? Belize was the only place in the world where she fit in, just as she was.

"What's your favorite place to visit?" Bo asked.

Alex chewed the inside of her cheek. Each of the destinations in her roster of tours was special. The beaches could be calm or rough depending on the time of day, but were beautiful no matter what their mood. Mayan ruins stood tall despite time's attempt to scrub them down to rubble. Caves granted access to the country's depths, and the lush jungle was home to amazing creatures. And the breathtaking world below the ocean's surface was both gorgeous and protective, since the Belize Barrier Reef buffered the shore against storms.

"That's impossible to answer."

Therefore, she didn't. The horns from the punta rock music filled the silence.

"I'm just trying to make conversation," he said.

"Why? Look at all this." She gestured at the emerald landscape and the sapphire sky. "When will you ever be here again? Drink in the majestic view while you can."

"I am, but conversation passes the time."

"Depends on the topic." She shifted into a higher gear. "Like, if you were to tell me about the intricacies of the tax code, I bet time would stand still."

"You're in luck, because I have no interest in tax codes." He adjusted his glasses.

She licked her lips. Today was full of surprises. She'd had no idea that professor-style hotness was her kink.

He lasered his blue gaze on her. "I mostly like to learn about people."

"Why? Most people are terrible. Natural wonders, on the other hand, are awesome."

She cut around a sightseeing tour bus, likely headed to the San Mateo Spice Farm and Botanical Gardens. That was not one of her listed destinations. Why tour curated gardens when there was wild nature to enjoy?

"*You're* not terrible. You're helping me."

"For a fee." She bit her lip.

A fee that was a total rip-off. If he kept her talking, she'd probably admit as much, and then guiltily refuse to accept the overpayment she desperately needed. To keep from discussing finances, she swigged water from her insulated bottle.

"Do you always undercut compliments?"

Jesus, he was relentless. "Do you always ask this many questions?"

"Sorry." He riffled his hair. "Professional hazard. I develop shopping algorithms for a living. The more I know about a person's history, their interests, the more context I have for correctly making suggestions they'll appreciate today. Like, a person buying a fishing lure might also be interested in a fishing rod, or hiking boots, or waterproof matches."

They were steadily cruising in fifth gear, so she could safely take her hand off the gearshift to massage her temple.

"Is that your way of saying you'd like to get to know me better?"

"Yes," he said.

"Why? Do you want to sell me something?"

He laughed. "No, because I'm curious about you."

She almost gasped at the sincerity in his voice. And boy oh boy, sincerity was not a vibe with which she was familiar. The guys she was normally drawn to were fun-loving charmers with secrets that made her want to explore them.

Not men who said what they meant, even if it sounded corny.

Like her Dad.

Grief ebbed through her. The Jeep's cab was too tight. Between Bo's big frame filling the seat next to her and his unasked questions, she felt trapped. Which was silly. If she wanted, she could feed him a hundred lies.

Alex lowered her shoulders to ease her bunched muscles. "I'm not that interesting."

"I bet that's not true." His crooked smile was obvious in his voice.

Her face heated. Lying wasn't in her nature, but she wouldn't
go deeper than what she'd share with the average barfly at
the resort.

"Okay, if you insist, here are the scintillating details. I'm
twenty-eight, and I have a twenty-five-year-old sister. Julia and
I are both named after emperors, and I'm semi-estranged from
my mother, but not because she named us after emperors. My
dad had a lot of friends, but no close family. I love chocolate and
hate pineapple, and I want to get a pet but I shouldn't because
I'm rarely home. I didn't go to college, my middle name's Ruby
and…" She drummed her fingers against the steering wheel.
"My dad died three years ago and I inherited his tour business,
which I'm hoping to expand."

After a beat, Bo said, "I'm sorry for your loss."

His consolation came fast and easy.

It sounded genuine, too.

A lump formed in her throat. *This* was why she didn't like
getting personal with people. She could do an A+ job of ignoring her feelings until someone expressed sympathy. Kindness triggered a fresh dive into awful memories she'd much
rather avoid, thank you.

"Yeah," she said. "Me too."

She pumped up the volume to drown out further conversation.

The solid hour of punta rock didn't help her aching head.

As they followed the highway through the Deep River Forest Reserve outside of Medina Bank, scattered drops devel-
oped into steadier sheets of rain. Brake lights flared around
them, and her wipers left smeared trails against the windshield.

"When's the last time you changed the wiper blades?" Bo asked.

"A few—"

Lightning forked across the sky, followed by a car-rocking clap of thunder. The skies opened and the rain pounded against the roof of her car. Hazard lights blinked like fireflies all around them as traffic ground to a halt.

"I can't see around this truck," she said. "Can you?"

He craned his neck. "Yeah. There's police activity on the shoulder."

"What's causing it?"

Three motorcycles zipped between the lanes of traffic.

"No idea, but everyone's getting off the highway."

"Seriously?" Alex blew out her lips. She inched forward until they reached an officer in orange-and-yellow emergency gear. He was directing traffic to an off-ramp.

Alex rolled down her window and shouted, "What's the problem?"

"Sinkhole," the officer shouted back. "Northbound lane's shut down. Likely for weeks."

"We don't have weeks," Bo said.

No kidding. Not when she needed to make a payment in five days.

The cop shrugged, then waved them through.

Bo opened the glove box and found the map. "Guess we'll take a longer way 'round."

Alex glanced at the clock. "Nah."

Bo gestured out the window. "If the road's gone, we don't have much choice."

"*That* road is gone. I told you, there are lots of side roads, and fighting traffic on the same route as everyone else is a no-go, I promise you." Alex put her Jeep in Reverse, then twisted in her seat and gripped the back of Bo's headrest.

"What are you doing?"

"Taking the last exit."

Alex edged out of their lane and onto the shoulder, then punched it. Bo yelped. What was he complaining about? Time was of the essence. She had to beat everyone out of this mess before their map apps redirected them to the same route and clogged the side roads.

After a tense half kilometer, she arrived at the exit ramp she wanted. A quick downshift and they were on the main road in a sleepy village adjacent to the highway.

"We're almost there," she said.

After a rapid series of turns, they arrived at the forest reserve's entrance. The poster-sized brown welcome sign was covered in ivy, and the roadway was obscured by lush ferns and vines. Perfect. She'd hoped the Forest Department hadn't cleared away the overgrowth. If Betty could barrel through the first curtain of vegetation, they'd be golden.

She rumbled forward.

"Alex, stop," he said. "You can't be serious. That's a gateway to hell."

She hit the brake. "Sure, if your idea of hell is green and leafy."

"Green and leafy is fine. *That* is a kingdom that a sorceress cursed for a hundred years." He thrust his hand toward the windshield. "That's ax murderer territory."

She sighed, put the Jeep in Park, then twisted toward him. Her annoyance transformed into reluctant empathy when she clocked the concern etched on his face. Looking at the forest through his eyes, his description was fair.

"I get that it makes you nervous, but here are your options." She held up her thumb. "One, I can take you back to Azul Caye, and you can find a guide who'll do whatever you tell them to do. That'll add three days to your journey." She flicked her index finger up. "Or two, you can trust me. We'll take this alternate path and get to Ch'ooj Creek tomorrow."

She was gambling.

Ninety-eight percent of her did not want him to take the first option, because then she'd lose out on a life-changing amount of money. The other two percent saw the upside in ridding herself of his unrelenting curiosity.

He shifted his gaze between her and the entrance. "Have you done this before?"

"Yes." Which was true. Well, true-ish. She, her dad and her sister had camped at this reserve twenty years ago as part of a group hiking trip. She'd never actually *driven* through the park, but come on. There wouldn't be a road if you weren't meant to drive into it.

His gorgeous, deep blue eyes searched hers. She forced herself to maintain eye contact. The intimacy made her skin crawl.

"Okay. On one condition."

She blinked, then rubbed her eyes. "What's that?"

"We test out standing water before we drive through it, and we don't drive after dark."

Both were reasonable requests, but she resented that he thought she'd be dumb enough to risk Betty in unmeasured waters. The icing on that resentment was he doubted her genius shortcut and thought that it might take them all day to complete a three-hour drive through the reserve.

"That's two conditions." Alex tightened her jaw. "The first

is a no-brainer, and the second one doesn't apply because we've got hours and hours of daylight ahead of us. There's no way we'll still be in the forest after dark."

Bo lifted a shoulder. "Then it shouldn't be a problem for you to agree."

"Okay, if it calms you down, I agree to your terms."

They inched into the darkness.

Five

Bo vised his grip around the grab handle above his passenger window. As they edged toward sunset, the atmospheric river was letting up, but the damage was done. The all-day rain had transformed the dirt roads into muck. They should've stuck to paved highways like he'd wanted, but the time to argue about that was at the start of this journey.

Also…he valued his life. After crawling through the forest for eight hours, Alex might murder him if he *well, actually*'d her. He doubted she'd need any help hiding his body.

So, yeah.

He preferred slow over dead.

Since their protein bar lunch, the only sounds in the Jeep had been the grunts and rumbles of the engine and the patter of raindrops that slipped through the dense tree cover. But in the last half hour, the daytime gray had deepened to a dark grizzle, which meant he needed to speak up.

"So," Bo said. "About that second condition."

Alex pursed her lips. "It's not *that* dark."

"It will be soon. Sun sets in Belize at 6:12 p.m."

She glanced at her dashboard. "Uh, it's 6:12 now, and there's still light, so maybe your research is wrong."

"Your clock is inexplicably twenty-four minutes fast." He tapped his watch. "It's 5:48."

Alex downshifted to climb over a rotted fallen tree. His teeth rattled as they thumped down on the other side, but they were no worse for wear. This Jeep was sturdier than it appeared, and Alex's command of it was masterful. Throughout this journey, she'd coaxed the vehicle through divots and over bumps like she had a magic wand instead of a gearshift.

"We should keep going," she said. "We've already racked up three hundred kilometers. The main road *must* be a little ways up ahead."

"But we don't know how close we actually are, or if conditions will hold. It would be better for us to use the last bit of light to set up camp. Any place that isn't potentially leading us off a cliff is a good choice. Like there, maybe?"

Alex surveyed the relatively clear spot to which he pointed. After a few beats, she sighed.

"Fine." She crept into the carve-out. Branches popped and snapped under the Jeep's tires. "It won't take long to set up camp."

"The tent I brought's only supposed to take ten minutes."

She raised an eyebrow. "Why'd you bring a tent?"

"I like to be prepared." He cracked open his door, and the loamy scent of the forest greeted him.

He took a deep, lung-expanding breath.

New situations normally made him anxious, hence the copious research to tease out the contingencies for which he should be ready. He would've bet that he'd be freaking out, but he was calm. The hypnotic sway of the enormous trees, the rain drumming against broad leaves, the occasional chirp

of an unidentified creature, the lack of alerts from his phone…
all of it was meditative. Pine, dirt and potential.

If this was what "being in the moment" meant, he understood the appeal.

"That's super weird." Alex shifted into Park and shut off
the Jeep.

"Preparedness is weird?"

"Preparedness is good, *if* you know what you're doing. But
you don't." She raised the emergency brake. "Let me ask you
this—is your five-star reviewed tent a hammock tent?"

"No." As he slid out of the car, a fat drop of water pelted his
neck.

"Too bad." She exited, then extracted a lumpy bag of nylon
from behind the driver's seat. "The good news is, *I* have a
hammock tent with an insect net *and* a rainfly."

She circled around the Jeep, then thrust the bag into his
hands. "Bad news, I only have one. But it is a double."

Yeah, he agreed with her. This was definitely a good news/
bad news situation.

"So we're…"

"Bunking together, yep. Don't worry. I don't bite unless
asked." She widened the drawstring closure on the bag, then
withdrew a strap. "Cinch this to that pine tree over there,
about six feet off the ground. Any lower and our asses will
be in the mud."

He did as Alex instructed, while she wrapped straps to
two other trees, swearing at one of them for sliding. He bit
his lips to stop his laughter. Unclear why he found her short
temper funny, but he did. Not just funny, though. From her
toned calves to the color rising in her freckled cheeks, she
was adorable.

He stopped in his tracks.

What was *wrong* with him?

He was on his way to visit his fiancée—ex-fiancée—to ask why she'd found it so easy to ditch the future they'd planned. The last thing Bo should be thinking about was another woman's freckles, the mischievous glimmer in her sparkling brown eyes, her wide smile, or her delightfully perky breasts.

Ferguson, no.

He lifted his cap and ran his hand over his hair. Jesus, he was acting as if he'd never been near a woman. Of course, Destiny had left three months ago, and they hadn't been getting along before that, so it had been…a while.

He turned back to his tree and fiddled with the perfectly cinched strap. If he'd known he'd be bedding down with an attractive woman, whose legs he'd been staring at for the better part of the day, he would have jerked off this morning. The fact that she found him irritating did nothing to kill the twitch in his dick. If anything, her attitude made him want to win her over.

"You done yet?" Alex asked.

"What? Uh, yes." Rain spattered his glasses.

Good. The less he saw of her, the better.

"Then grab this."

Their hands grazed as he took a nylon corner of the crumpled tent. The rough of her fingers did not help him keep his imagination in line. To distract himself, he buried his attention in her instructions. After ten minutes, they set up a double-wide hammock covered by a bug net and tarp that resembled a sail.

"So, that's the shelter." She dusted her hands together. "What's for dinner?"

"Um, we already ate the protein bars, but if we start a fire—"

"Kidding. I've got it covered." Her dark hair was plastered to her head. "Let's eat in the Jeep. Less rain, fewer bugs."

He could offer to cook the food he'd brought, but he'd follow her lead here. His three days of research couldn't compete with her practical know-how. She'd made the best of a tough situation without losing her cool, and he respected that. Aspired to it, actually.

Inside the Jeep, she twisted to rifle through the bag in the back. Her hip nudged against his shoulder, and hell, her ass was *right* there.

She plunked back into her seat.

"Okay, for your dining pleasure this evening, I've got beef jerky and crackers, and you've got apples." She divvied out the food as she spoke, then snapped her fingers. "One last thing to make it a perfect meal."

She reached across his lap to open the glove box. He pressed back into the seat to avoid accidental contact.

"A map?" he asked.

"The glove box contains multitudes." She withdrew a flask and waggled it at him. "Now it's a party."

"You carry open containers of liquor?"

She exaggeratedly scoped out their surroundings. "Sure hope the cops don't catch me."

"Ha ha." Inwardly, he flinched. The "protective big brother" routine he'd adopted with Delilah before her diagnosis showed up at the *worst* times. And he sure didn't feel brotherly toward the woman in the driver's seat.

Alex tipped up the flask, then offered it to him. "Want some?"

"What is it?"

"Fireball."

He grimaced. "Seriously?"

"No, because I'm not an eighteen-year-old sorority pledge. It's bourbon." She held the flask out to him. "Take a hit."

He wasn't much of a spirits guy, but he was staring down the barrel of an interminable night in a two-person hammock with a prickly woman whose smile he couldn't get out of his head. Anything that knocked him out faster was welcome.

"Thanks." He took a slug. Immediate regret washed over him. He coughed and spluttered as he handed the flask back.

"Not much of a drinker?" Alex asked.

He guzzled his water, then wheezed, "No."

"More for me, then." She sipped again, then capped the flask. "After we eat, we'll seal the trash in my cooler."

"Okay, but why?" He peeled the plastic from his jerky. Pungent, beefy scents filled the car. Not the complex flavors to which he'd become accustomed, but it was flavorful.

"Garbage attracts animals." She munched on crackers.

His gut twisted. "There are animals?"

She gestured toward the windshield. "It's a forest. Animals are a part of the deal."

"What kind of animals?" He peered outside. "Like, raccoons and squirrels? Or panthers and bears and other apex predators that might want to snack on me?"

Amusement danced on Alex's face.

"What?" he asked. "Fear of wild animals is reasonable."

"True, but as long as we lock up the food and leave a fire burning, we'll be fine. The macaws, howler monkeys, ocelots, tapirs, iguanas and poisonous frogs will leave us alone. If you want, you can sleep in here. But it kills my back, so I'm in the tent."

As the inky dark settled among the trees, he cracked his window. A symphony of insects was warming up for the night. Okay then. Sleeping among bugs *and* wild animals. Not what he had on his list of things to do in Belize, but he had to trust Alex.

Easier said than done.

Maybe she was telling him what he wanted to hear, like when he was a kid and his parents fought but promised they'd stay together. So he preferred to deep dive into topics with independent research and tried to predict future behavior. If he intellectualized the thing that spiked his anxiety, he staved off twisty, insidious, unhappy emotions.

But that wasn't an option in the middle of a forest.

Given Alex's reaction to his curiosity earlier today, she'd probably feed him to an ocelot if he asked more questions. Tonight, he'd have to sit with ignorant discomfort.

"Poisonous frogs aside, the hammock sounds like a better option than the Jeep. I've got back problems, too."

"That's the spirit. And don't worry about the frogs." She crunched into her apple. "They're bright red and easy to spot. They usually hop away because they like us less than we like them."

He rubbed his hands down his thighs. "That's not a consolation. Looks like it's down to a drizzle out there. Want me to start the campfire? I brought a kit."

"Of course you did." She playfully bumped his shoulder. "Yes to us starting a campfire. You dig the fire hole while I gather wood."

She opened her door and rooted under the driver's seat.

"You keep wood under there?" he asked.

"No. Here." She thrust a sheathed blade and a headlamp

toward him, then slipped another headlamp over her damp hair. "A machete makes the digging easier. You'll want it to be about four and a half meters—fifteen feet—from the tent."

"Thanks." Of course she had a machete. There was probably a bullwhip in here, too.

While Alex hunted for kindling and wood, he unearthed the rod-and-wick fire starter set from his box of supplies. With his cap pulled tight over his head, he paced off fifteen feet from the tent, then jabbed at the carpet of pine needles with the machete. The earth below the pine straw was spongy. Within minutes, he scooped a decent crater.

"S'cuse me." Alex dropped a pile of thick branches on the ground near him. "I need the big guy to split the wood."

He dusted his hands together. "I've never chopped wood, but I'll give it a shot."

She laughed. "Oh, sorry—the big guy is what I call my hatchet. It's in Betty. But if you want, I can start calling you big guy, too."

Thankfully, the dark hid the heat rising in his cheeks. The light from her headlamp bounced over the ground as she returned to the Jeep. That was definitely flirting. Wasn't it? He was so out of practice, he couldn't tell.

The Jeep's door shut again, and she was back with a hatchet. "Can you find rocks to border the edge of the pit while I chop?"

"Sure," he answered.

Decent-sized rocks studded the ground. As he dug them out with the machete, the satisfying *thunk* of splitting wood filled the air. They worked in companionable silence until Alex whittled down the pile.

"Okay, this should get us started." She laid kindling in the hollow. "The wood's pretty moist. If your thingamajig doesn't work, I'll get the gas can."

Bo *really* wanted this to work. He welcomed Alex's expertise but he'd like to bring something to the table.

Besides apples.

"Here goes nothing." He fed the wax-coated wick through the bore below the ferro rod, then frayed the edge like they did in the instructional video. Next, he scraped the ferro with the striker, firm and controlled, and produced a glob of sparks that caught the wick on fire. He held the flaming wick to the wood. The kindling smoked and sizzled, then caught.

"Nice. I might have to get one of those," Alex said.

He flushed with pride, then blew out the wick.

"Do you go camping a lot?" she asked.

"No, but I read the manuals."

"Wish I could learn like that. I'm more of a try-and-fail kind of girl. Once I get the hang of something, though, I'm an expert for life."

"And I wish *I* could learn like that. Leap without looking."

"Oh, I look. But I leap even if it's scary." She bumped his shoulder again.

The simple affectionate gesture made him happier than it should.

As full dark shrouded the forest, the fire's warm crackle lulled them into silence.

Alex stifled a yawn. "Today kicked my ass. There's not much to do now that the sun's gone down. Stay up if you want, but I'm settling in for the night."

Linger alone, like a tasty ocelot snack?

No thanks.

"I'll turn in, too."

As they unzipped their respective sides, he swallowed hard. This was not a big deal. They were two people, stuck in a situation together. Like a sleepover.

Yeah, good job lying to yourself, Ferguson.

"Keep your shoes on," Alex said. "If you take them off and leave them out here, you'll definitely wake up with an unwelcome guest."

She parked herself inside the tent, then zipped herself in. Shadows swallowed her as she switched off her headlamp and shoved it into the nylon pocket point near her head.

"In or out, Bo? You don't want to let bugs inside."

The hammock flexed and swayed under his ass. He much preferred the steady firmness of a mattress, but beggars couldn't be choosers.

"It's more comfortable if you lay diagonally," she said. "It spreads out the pressure."

He shifted, scooting his shoulders in the opposite direction of his feet, and... She was right. The material cradled him. Alex wiggled on her side, which bounced him a bit. Would the whole night be like that? Caught in the ripple of every move she made and measuring the distance to make sure he didn't accidentally cross any lines?

Sweet torture.

"This is surprisingly nice." He twisted toward her, and *whoa*, she was right there.

"Argh! That's in my eyes!" She squeezed her eyes shut as she laughed, then fumbled at his lamp.

She missed and ended up smoothing her palm down his cheek. Her touch scorched him, left an indelible mark that made him suck in his breath.

"Sorry." He wrenched the lamp from his head and flicked off the light. "Better?"

"Much." There was a smile in her voice.

"Didn't mean to blind you. Speaking of..." He plucked his glasses from his face. "Is there somewhere I can stash stuff?"

"Yeah, there are pockets in the stretched-out corners."

"Thanks." He tucked his glasses inside. Without them, the world took on a pleasantly obscured fuzz.

"I love sleeping outside," she sighed. "Don't you?"

"I've never done it before."

"Ooh, so I'm your first?"

Laughter sprang from this woman as easy as sunshine, and he enjoyed the hell out of her levity. More than he should.

"That was another joke, by the way."

"If you have to point that out, was it funny?"

She *hmphed*, and he folded his arms behind his head.

The darkness created a confessional feel. Rain pattered against the tarp, and strange forest sounds erupted around them. Neither drowned out the calm rise and fall of his tent-mate's breathing. When he woke this morning he never would've dreamed that he'd be horizontal next to Alex Stone, her lips within kissing distance.

More sweet torture.

Sleep was the only escape hatch.

"Well, good night," he said.

"Not so fast, Bo Ferguson."

Six

Her headache was gone, her belly was full, and a not-total-stranger in possession of excellent forearms and a good sense of humor was sharing her tent. During their arduous journey through the torrential downpour, Bo piqued her curiosity more than his sideways smile sent a thrill through her when they first met. Despite the bumpy roads and rivers of mud, he'd kept it together, which had helped *her* keep it together.

Then, when they set up camp, he'd been helpful, but clearly learning.

Which got her thinking...

Something about Bo didn't add up. Why did a man who'd never been camping, feared wild creatures and didn't know much about Belize want to drive cross-country to a specific, not-touristy part of her homeland? She *hated* not figuring things out. The last time she'd let low-level mysteries slide, it almost cost her everything.

The faint scent of laundry soap filled the tent. It was a miracle he smelled nice after the day they'd had. *She* probably smelled like a swamp. Alex widened her eyes. *Oh no.*

She tucked her nose toward her armpit. Phew. Powder-fresh scent holding strong.

Inches from her, Bo shifted, which bobbed the suspended

tent. Gentle movements that reminded her that a handsome stranger was within kissing distance. Jesus, she was more aware of him than she'd be if they were in an actual bed together. She blew out her lips. Nope. Nuh-uh. She shoved that thought away.

More shifting, more bobbing, all in silence. Peter would've been talking a mile a minute. Normally, she'd prefer the quiet so she could bathe in the forest atmosphere, but the not-speaking hung between her and Bo like an expanding balloon.

Could he feel that about-to-pop pressure, too?

Her options were to do nothing…and stay up all night, hyperaware of him. Or she could place a hand on his chest to still him, which… No. She licked her lips. That would open a sexy door she needed to keep closed. Or she could ask him what he was doing in Belize, which toed the line between professional and personal, but it was the least bad option in the bunch.

As his fidgeting rocked the tent yet again, Alex twisted toward the faint outline of his profile. His nose was as straight and perfect as the long center stairwell of a Mayan pyramid.

"Why are we driving to Ch'ooj Creek?" she asked.

His chest expanded with a deep breath. Interesting.

"It's a long story."

"Not sure if you've noticed, but I've got time."

His Adam's apple bobbed. "It's…ah…it's about a woman."

Oh. Her chest twinged with disappointment.

What the hell? She furrowed her brow in the dark. This was *good*. He was taken, and that helped bottle up her inconvenient attraction to him. The jungle was no place for fizzy feelings, not when they'd distract her from important things, like keeping them alive in a mudslide.

Theirs was a business arrangement. That's all.

Other parts of her body protested this decision.

She told them to shut up.

"And?" she prompted.

Bo sighed. "You want to hear this?"

"So, so much."

"I'm engaged. Or, I was?" He scrubbed his hair, causing it to stick up.

Alex curbed the urge to smooth it down. "That's a thing you should be certain about."

"I am. We're a 'was.' Past tense." His frown carved brackets around his mouth. "She came to Belize three months ago to work an archaeological dig. She was supposed to come home last week, but she sent me a text and broke up with me."

"She broke up with you via *text*?" Alex's heart squeezed. She met Bo all of thirty-six hours ago and already knew he'd prefer a scheduled summit about the end of a relationship. His ex was a prize-winning jerk to pull the plug like that.

"Yep." He sighed. "Text."

"That's so… I'm at a loss for words. Texts are fine if you're not feeling a connection or whatever after a couple dates, but you were *engaged*. To be *married*." She propped her head on her fist, which—whoops—tilted her toward Bo.

"Yeah." His voice was strained. "I'm aware."

"Brutal. So you're here to win her back?"

"Maybe? We were together for seven years—"

"Seven *years*?"

She felt awful for him. But selfishly, his sad tale made her feel better about her situation with Peter. At least she'd only been with him a mere three years before he'd humiliated her.

True, like Bo, she was as desperate to find her ex. Not for a reunion, though. Ew, no. She just wanted her money back.

Unlikely he'd still have it, but a person can dream.

Bo's motivations were more noble. Warmed her chilly heart, in a way. He was proof that there were people willing to have hard conversations rather than let their friends, romantic partners, or family go as easily as a losing lottery ticket.

Bo heaved a ragged sigh.

"Seven years," Bo confirmed. "And we've been friends since we were kids. I'm just… She's not thinking this through. If a breakup is what she wants, I'll make my peace with it, but I need to make sure she's okay."

Alex scrunched her nose. That was cringe-tastic nonsense. He hadn't flown from Baltimore to Belize *just* to check on a sudden ex. No one was that altruistic. There had to be *something* else. Maybe he wanted her to un-break up with him, or soothe his ego, or give back an awesome sweater she'd stolen.

Like it or not, now she was invested.

"I don't buy—"

Something snapped a twig in the brush. The hammock jerked as he sat up, and she fought physics not to land on top of him.

"What was that?" he asked.

"Probably a kinkajou. They're tiny. Nothing to worry about." She tucked an arm behind her head. "Before I can declare myself Team Bo, you seriously need to rethink that whole 'she's not thinking this through' attitude. It chafes like sand in my crack."

He grumbled, then threw his forearm over his eyes. "Yeah, when you say it back to me, I hear how it sounds. But we have *so* much history. I mean, ever since we met in middle school, I had a thing for her. To just throw it away…"

"You're a love-at-first-sight kind of guy?"

"I uh… I mean…" He glanced at her, then skyward. He blew out a breath as he tapped against his sternum. "Wow. I don't know why it's so hard to talk about this. But yeah, I guess I am. A love-at-first-sight kind of guy."

"Don't be embarrassed. I'm also a bartender, remember?" She nudged his shoulder, and tingles frizzled her fingertips. His uncertainty was endearing. "People tell me weird personal shit all the time. I can get the flask if that'll help."

"No thanks."

The bug concerto swelled in their conversational lull. Details. She needed details, pronto, of how this quietly vulnerable, attractive man was totally enamored with his ex. They'd help her squelch this weird bubbly feeling inside her.

"Back to love at first sight," she said. "And, go."

"It was a one-way street. And our timing wasn't right back then." His jaw muscles bulged. On a deep breath, he rested his hands on his chest, then returned his gaze to hers. "Still isn't, I guess."

The full-body flutter that ran through her was wildly inappropriate. Alex pursed her lips. She'd best remind herself that he was confiding in her about his ex, same as any lonely guy who bellied up to the Belize Dreams resort bar.

"Why wasn't the timing right? Were you both dating other people?"

"Mostly her. Me, I had family drama. My twin sister—"

"What's her name?" She trusted men who had sisters. It was like they had graduate-level emotional intelligence training. "And who's older?"

"Her name's Delilah, and I'm older by five minutes. Anyway, she was diagnosed with bipolar disorder when we were in eighth grade, and my parents split up soon after. I stepped up around the house while Mom helped her get treatment, straightened out her meds, fought with the school about her IEP and supports. Life was completely unpredictable, so I decided I wouldn't be. It was a lot."

Alex wanted to squeeze his hand. Her sister had anxiety attacks when they were kids. Julia was light-years better now, but watching a younger sibling—even one who's only five minutes younger—go through stuff like that was rough.

"By the time things steadied at home, Destiny had a high school sweetheart, and then we went to college. I dated too, so I thought I'd outgrown my crush on her. After graduation, I moved back home. Destiny stayed in New York until her boyfriend dumped her for his assistant. She came home to get back on her feet."

"And there you were."

"There I was." Another sigh from him, bigger this time, full of remorse. "To be honest, I was always there."

Okay, that nailed her in the heart. This poor, lovesick puppy. At least she had a clear-eyed view of her multiyear mistake with Peter. But Bo... He'd carried a torch for ages. It took forever to snuff flames like those, even when someone dumps a barrel of ice water on them.

"How long did you wait before asking her out?"

"A couple of weeks."

Alex groaned. "Oh, my dude. You didn't wait long enough. After a real and true heartbreak, you've gotta wait a few months, minimum. Anything faster than that and you're likely rebound material."

The rainfall picked up again, sizzling in the campfire.

Her advice was solid, but it didn't apply to her situation with Peter. He didn't *just* break up with her after three years. No, he ran away with her company's money, shattering her heart *and* wrecking her father's legacy in one maliciously efficient move.

Her stomach churned.

She'd been so stupid. *That* was the hardest part to forgive. She fancied herself this savvy, world-wise person, and she'd gotten fleeced by a slimeball with a bright smile. After that level of betrayal, she'd be ready to date again in about…

Never.

"You're expecting me to believe that adults who are attracted to each other wait for a prescribed amount of time before they have sex?"

The way he threw the word *sex* out there sent another flutter rippling through her.

"Absolutely not. I was talking about *relationships*. But sex? Go ahead and get it as soon as you can after a breakup. The best way to get over someone is to get under someone else, am I right? Just don't jump into a relationship. *Those* are what's complicated."

The wind blew campfire smoke in their direction, stealing her view of his profile.

"I was the rebound guy for seven years? I find that unlikely."

Alex's shoulder swished against the nylon tent as she shrugged. "You could be the unicorn. Right time, right place, different enough from whoever came before you that she sees you as a lifeboat."

"I don't like being compared to a lifeboat." His cheek stubble rasped under his scratching fingers. "And I didn't rescue her. We were good together because we had solid plans."

"I may die from the romance."

"Go ahead. Mock me."

"I shall. Nothing kills romance faster than words like—" she flourished her hands like a magician "—*plans* and *solid*. Romance needs a little mystery and excitement."

"Not for us. We talked for *ages* about what we wanted. Married this fall, three kids starting in two years. She'd teach archaeology in Baltimore or DC so we could stay close to our families. I'd work from home."

Alex's skin crawled. "You have the next ten years of your life planned?"

"More like twenty. I'd like to sock away enough in investments to retire early. But it's too soon to make that decision for sure. One of our kids could get into Harvard, or the economy could tank. Who knows? But it's best to be financially prepared."

Bo was fooling himself. Life didn't happen in neat logical leaps.

Look at her dad. He had lots of plans. If everything had unfolded the way he wanted, Dad would have handed the business over to her and Julia next year. When she first moved here, she'd laughed when he tried to teach her the financial side.

I'm not ready, Dad. You can show me the accounting software later.

In the distance, an animal snorted.

"What was that?" Bo bolted upright again, tipping her onto him.

"A tapir." She pushed against his—hmm, surprisingly firm—chest, and back to her side of the hammock. "They're adorable omnivores. No threat to us."

"It sounds like an angry toilet plunger."

She laughed. Bo's description was *exactly* what they sounded like.

As he settled, she asked, "Was your ex on the same page as you about your heart-stoppingly romantic calendars and mortgages and term life insurance?"

"She said she was. Now I don't even know what she wants to do with our cat."

"That's easy. If she didn't mention the cat, it's yours, and she's terrible." Because only terrible humans abandoned pets. "But wait—where does Belize fit with the twenty-year plan?"

"Field research. She needs it for professional bona fides. But it came up faster than I expected." He sighed. "She didn't tell me she'd applied."

Hmph. Alex didn't agree with his ex's methods, but she understood what it took to ditch the life everyone expected you to have. She did the same thing when she dropped out of college and moved here permanently.

"Personally," Alex said as she stretched. "I'm all about the carpe diem, so I get why she jumped on it. But it's kind of a chance for you to see her clearly before she does irreversible damage."

Whoops. Bitterness snuck into her voice.

Money wasn't the only thing Peter stole. He also swiped her confidence and the joy she found in her job. Before, each tour had been an opportunity for fun, awe and wonder. Now she saw people as dollar signs.

Like Bo over there.

"That sounds like you're speaking from experience," he said. "Want to talk about it?"

Clients were normally a no-fly zone when it came to personal details. They were there for a good time, and they wanted a charismatic, tough-as-mahogany adventure guide. Not a daddy's girl who could be felled by grief-soaked memories that popped up out of nowhere. But she ached to unburden herself, and Bo would be in her life for exactly three days.

He was safe.

With a surprisingly creaky voice, she said, "Remember how I told you my dad died?"

"Yes." Bo propped his head up.

"It kind of wrecked me. He was my best friend." She paused and took a ragged breath. "My mom and I don't get along, so as soon as I could, I came here. Dad preferred family-style tours to the cayes, beaches, ruins. I suggested we add adventure tours. Like, climbing ruins, camping in reserves. Things like that."

"That's why you're so comfortable in the forest."

She swallowed to clear the tightness from her throat. "Yeah. So, five years ago, we added my tours. Not many, but enough to test the waters, and they did really well. Dad brought in part-time financial help—that was how I met Peter. He was friendly and eager to do the accounting, which was fine by me because I've always hated that stuff. Then Dad got sick. Pancreatic cancer. It was quick, and my sister and I were devastated."

"Julia, right?"

She touched her mouth, surprised. "When did I tell you that?"

"This morning—before we got off the highway, you rattled off some facts about yourself. But I'm sorry, I didn't mean to interrupt."

"No need to apologize." She massaged her temples. "Where was I?"

"Devastation, and your sister," he said softly.

"Oh, right." Her eyes stung. "Jules and I decided that she'd stay in school and I'd run the business until she graduates. She gets her master's in hospitality next month. She'll get a job with an established resort to build up her experience, then quit and help with Stone Adventures."

"You're a liar."

A laugh popped out of her. "I beg your pardon? About what?"

"You said you don't make plans."

"Yeah, well, hold on to your butt, because here's where things go off the rails." She swallowed the bile that gathered in her throat. "During my dad's illness, I leaned heavily on Peter. Maybe it was the grief, but I fell for him. Like an idiot."

"Why an idiot?"

"Because certain things he'd do or say should have been red flags, but I let them slide because I thought I loved him. Right up until this past Christmas when he disappeared with the contents of the company's bank accounts."

"Ouch," Bo said.

"Yeah," she said. "Fucking ouch is right. I reported him to the police, but he's basically a ghost. I'm still disputing charges on our corporate cards, and I've got all of these vendors to pay. Good people, family friends. I refuse to stiff them and make Peter's theft their problem."

They'd been there for her in a way she could never repay. Their neighbor, Esperanza, coordinated everything when Dad was really bad: meals, housekeeping, rides to chemo, visits and, ultimately, his celebration of life.

Without them, Alex would have shouldered it all by herself.

Julia had been in college and grieving, too, so Alex hadn't expected anything from her younger sister. Mom should have done more, though. The divorce had been a decade before he got sick, but hadn't she cared about her daughters enough to help?

She'd never get over that abandonment.

Bo whistled. "That's harsh. But maybe you could apply for some kind of relief? I'd bet there's emergency small-business funds that you could tap into."

Irritation roiled Alex's gut. Like she hadn't already completed reams of paperwork that would go nowhere? He must think she was inept.

"And how many businesses do you run in Belize, Bo?"

"None, but—"

"So you don't know what you're talking about." She crossed her arms over her heart, then tucked her hands tight against her sides. "We were sharing sob stories, that's all. Did I tell you how to fix things with your ex?"

Nothing but the sound of a quadrillion bugs filled the night air.

After a minute, Bo said, "That's fair. Sorry. To make it even, offer me unsolicited advice on winning her back."

"That's impossible," she said. "Because, A, love is a fantasy, B, I'm in no place to care about anyone's happily-ever-after, and C, I don't know either of you, which is a vital part of any win-someone-back plan."

"Or, D, *because* you don't know us, you'll have a clear-eyed view of what went wrong."

Alex snorted. Bartender couples therapy? Blech. People either loved each other and wanted to make it work or they didn't, and nothing changed that. If she said much more, she'd snap at him, or worse, cry. There's no way she'd allow herself to do that in front of this guy.

"Not tonight I won't. Good night, Bo."

Seven

The bug net stopped Bo from tumbling out of the tent as he bolted upright. His lower back muscles protested as the hammock swayed with his jerky movements.

The scene was peaceful. Idyllic. Thin sunlight threaded through the dense tree canopy as various birds twittered and chirped above. Much different from the car horns and MTA bus's air brakes that filled his Cathedral Street home in Baltimore. He scrubbed his eyes with the heels of his hands. What had startled him awake? Was it—

"Rraaargh!" a monstrous growl erupted overhead.

Cold spiked through him, despite the steamy mist rising from the ferns. He jammed on his glasses. The impossible green surrounding him revealed nothing, and the rain thingamajig blocked most of his view. Hang on—there. Increasingly distant treetops bent under the weight of whatever was hustling away from their campsite.

"What the hell was that?" he asked.

No answer…because Alex wasn't there.

He breathed a deep, calming, pine-scented breath. Obviously she would sound the alarm if a dangerous Belizean creature was poised for attack.

A branch snapped overhead.

Unless the dangerous creature had *already* attacked and he was a prick hiding in a hammock while Predator was ripping off her face.

He yanked open the zipper. "Alex?"

Only jungle sounds replied. Not a good sign. He half fell from the hammock, then picked his way toward the Jeep. Not here, either. He stilled, listening to the sounds that filled the air. Bugs—cicadas, crickets, bunches of others he couldn't name—and birds chirping. The *raaargh* again, but farther away.

Wait—splashing.

Crocodiles were native to Belize…but he might be pulling that from a Bond movie. He should have read more about the country and less about his new mini camp stove. He veered off the muddy, rutted road and toward the sound of the splashing.

Carefully, he descended the steep, mucky slant of the rippling stream's bank. When he'd steadied himself against a tree, he looked up…

…and froze.

Alex Stone had stripped down to her shorts and deep pink bra, and was currently dragging a small wet towel along her arms and the tops of her breasts.

Electricity rocketed through his body.

Her toned midriff was the earthen color of tumbled river stones, while her limbs were a deep caramel. Tan lines showed she spent plenty of time outside. As she scrubbed, the gemstone tattoos flashed bright red, green and blue. With a languorous gesture, she swiped her nape. A rivulet of water twisted down the column of her straightened spine, dipping into her shorts.

His throat went dry, and something hot and liquid just behind his naval shifted. The rough bark of the tree scraped his palm as he wished his hands were gripping Alex instead. Bo widened his eyes. *Hell of a thought, Ferguson.* He was here for Destiny. She'd ended things, but his heart was tangled up in their history.

Alex, though.

His rapid pulse and hardening cock were hard to deny. He should leave. In a second. Before he could skulk away, though, a brilliant red bird perched directly above him emitted a jittery screech.

The birds of Belize were *not* on his side.

Alex caught him staring. "Hey there. Sleep well?"

"Fine." It took everything he had to maintain eye contact.

She held the towel out to him. "Want to rinse off?"

"No." The last thing he needed was for her to catch him with a hard-on. "Just wanted to make sure you were okay."

She flashed him a thumbs-up. "Mission accomplished. I'm awake, clean, and it stopped raining, so I'm golden. After breakfast, we'll hit the road."

"Roger that." He clambered back to the campsite like an ocelot was chasing him. *Roger that?* He'd never said that phrase in all of his thirty years.

He slapped at a fly trying to feast on his calf.

After dousing himself in bug spray, he brushed his teeth with water from the refillable pouches that Alex had packed. Alex, who wore pretty pink bras. What was *wrong* with him? He had *no* business fantasizing about her, not when he was here to find his ex-fiancée.

He lifted his Orioles cap to scrub his hair. This was just... biology. She was beautiful, he was horny, and his body absolutely did not care if fantasies about Alex were okay. Or if she liked him, for that matter, which he hadn't quite figured out.

His stomach growled, and he snapped his fingers.

Food, yes. That's why his thoughts were as muddy as last night's road. He thought better on a full stomach, and breakfast would keep his hands and brain busy. Fortunately, he'd come prepared. Best of all, the aging Quaker on the canister was a certified boner-killer.

The camping stove lit up with no trouble, and the kettle boiled quickly. He poured bubbling water onto small mounds of oatmeal in collapsible silicone bowls. As the grains steeped, he sliced in a banana, then sprinkled on brown sugar.

There. A delicious, healthy breakfast, and he hadn't fantasized about Alex's lithe body once.

Ah, hell.

With a sigh, he added walnuts to his bowl.

Snapping twigs and shuffling leaves heralded Alex's return. "Whew, that water was *chilly*."

Obviously. Her stiff nipples had peaked her bra while she stood midstream. But he kept that observation to himself.

"Hungry?" As he lifted his eyes to hand her a bowl, relief washed through him. She'd pulled on her chambray shirt. The rosy flush in her cheeks was new, though, and adorable.

"Whoa, a hot breakfast? Yes please." She smiled as she took it from him, then sat on a nearby log. "Thank you."

"Welcome." He shook instant coffee into two mugs, then added the rest of the boiling water. "Are you allergic to nuts?"

She raised an eyebrow. "Depends on the kind."

If that was supposed to be innuendo, it was terrible.

"Walnuts," he answered.

"Perfect. I can't stand almonds." She sat on the downed log next to him, then took the bowl he offered. "This is a nice start to the day."

He stirred his oatmeal. "Sorry about barging in on you earlier."

"Don't sweat it." She shook her head. "The first rule of the outdoors is there's no such thing as barging. Besides, I have bikini tops more revealing than this. I call it a working bra. Totally utilitarian and unsexy."

He begged to differ. And the idea of her in a skimpy bikini…

Bo buried his nose in his coffee mug.

"Should take us about ten minutes to pack up camp. Then we'll be on our way, and you'll be in Ch'ooj Creek by sunset." She sipped her coffee. "That thing you said last night, about winning back your ex… Is that still what you want?"

The oatmeal bricked up in his stomach. *No* came rushing to the surface. But that didn't make sense. Throwing away seven years, recalibrating his life, starting at zero… Destiny understood him on a bone-deep level, had known his family before they'd fractured. To give that up after a single text… He had to at least try to get her back out of respect for their history.

"Yeah," he said through a frown. "I think so."

"Good, because I have a plan to make that happen for you." She squeezed his knee, and electricity rocketed up his thigh.

Bo inched away from her.

"How comfortable are you with lying?" she asked. "Scale of one to ten, where one is George Washington and ten is Machiavelli."

"Maybe about a four?"

"Okay, I can work with that." She dusted her hands together, then drained her coffee. "If you wash the dishes, I'll do the tent."

"Wait. What's your plan?"

"I'll tell you once we're on the road. It'll give us something to talk about. Now go." She shooed him away. "Wash."

"Okay, okay." He gathered the dishes, then ambled toward the stream.

Alex's consistent confidence was infuriating…and intriguing. She was so *sure* about everything. No hesitation, no doubts. What an unshackled way to move through the world. His style was to tease out all the ways life could unfold.

And yet, he was wrong a good third of the time.

He dipped the bowls into the rushing water. The strong current in the stream knocked the remnants of breakfast away. He'd need to wipe them out with antibacterial soap later, but this got them clean enough for packing. When he crested the bank and spied the campsite, he found Alex, hands popped on her hips, staring at the back of the Jeep.

She turned to him. "We've got a problem."

Alex had lied. She had no practical advice for how Bo could win back his ex. Her philosophy was if someone doesn't want to be with you, let them go. But she wanted to help him figure it out because the hungry look in Bo's bright blue eyes when he caught her bathing matched the way she'd been feeling in the tent last night.

And that was bad news since she shouldn't act on her attraction.

It would be fun, though. The past five months had been an unending grind. She'd been too busy trying to save her financial ass to notice anything or anyone else. But she'd noticed Bo. Up until this morning, though, she hadn't thought he'd noticed her back. Not that way.

Until he'd gotten hard when he'd found her at the stream.

No-strings-attached horizontal fun—with the added bonus of washing away the memories of Peter—would be an undeniably excellent way to unwind. But this situation officially had more strings than a cargo net, because Bo was hung up on his ex. For both of their sakes, she had to shut this shit down, and if that entailed a long conversation about all of his ex's best qualities so she could help get them back together, so be it.

As of two minutes ago, though, they had much bigger problems to solve.

"What's wrong?" Bo had folded the hammock tent as crisply as one fresh off a sporting goods store's shelf.

"Flat tires." Alex thatched her unruly hair into a French braid, the easiest style to fit under a bike helmet.

"Oh. Need help changing them?" He shoved the tidy tent package into the back of Betty, then dusted his hands together. "I'm handy with a jack."

"Flat tire*sss*, Bo. Plural." She gestured toward the sad, deflated rubber in front of her. "I have *one* spare. The last time I checked, AAA doesn't serve this area."

"Fix-a-Flat?" he suggested.

If Bo's optimistic suggestions didn't annoy her, they'd make her laugh. He'd been in this preserve for twelve hours and now he was Bear Grylls?

"Bo." She pinched the bridge of her nose. "The tires are fucked. There's a branch sticking out of one of them."

"I *knew* we shouldn't have taken this route." He cupped his hands behind his head, glanced skyward, then back to her. "Should we use your sat phone to call for help? We can't hike through a jungle."

She'd reduced the satellite phone's plan to the bare minimum—ten minutes per month—to save money. No way was she wasting any of those precious minutes on a problem she could solve herself.

"We actually *could* hike, FYI." She rifled in Betty's back

seat, then returned with her socket wrench kit. "But we don't have to. We'll take the dirt bike."

"Both of us?" He raised an eyebrow.

She ground her teeth. She *loved* it when people who knew nothing about Belize and how to navigate its wild country-side doubted her solutions. True, she was younger than most of the grizzled salty dogs who served as tour guides, but she'd wiggled out of more scrapes than this dude could fathom.

"Your choice." She forced a nonchalant shrug. "Come with me, or I'll go solo, get help, and come back for you."

Bo jammed his hands into his pockets. "Hours alone in the forest with no cell reception and wild animals... Yeah, that's a hard pass."

"Glad you agree, but I was kidding. I wouldn't leave a jungle virgin alone for hours."

She fitted the socket wrench to the bolt that kept the bike rack elevated. The rhythmic click as she swiped the handle, followed by the loosening tug on the nut, soothed her. *Not* soothing, however, was the oppressive glare coming from Bo's direction.

"Will this tinker toy make it to Ch'ooj Creek?"

Click-click-click, swipe. "You insult my vehicles a lot. Betty and Veronica could get offended."

"Veronica?"

Alex patted the seat of the dirt bike. "At your service. And we're not riding her all the way north. A friend of mine has a place near the other side of the reserve. Should take about ninety minutes to get there."

"Can we get replacement tires there?" Bo paced around her as she worked.

His fidgetiness was contagious.

"Can you stop doing that? And what's this *we* stuff? If *I* can't get new tires, my friends will loan us a car, and we'll take *that* to Ch'ooj Creek." Alex removed the bolt, pocketed it, then used the bottle jack to lower the rack. Bo's prickly energy twitched her nerves, and the best thing for that was work. "This'll go faster if you help. Loosen the straps around the handlebars."

A rose-bellied lizard scampered from under Betty and toward the safety of the rocks edging the road. If she pointed the small creature out to Bo, it would probably make him yelp.

The Velcro grouchily rasped as he peeled the strap apart. "I can't believe you don't carry multiple spares."

"Who carries multiple spares?" She squatted to spin the nut off the bolt spiked through the bike's foot peg. "This is your fault, anyway. If you hadn't insisted I stop to make camp, we'd probably be there by now."

"Or we'd be dead in a ditch. Flat tires are better than ditch death."

"You're so dramatic."

Sweat beaded on her nape. The dense tree coverage filtered out the direct sunshine, but the day still promised to be hotter than balls. They'd best get moving.

"I'm not dramatic. I have a good imagination."

"Well, stop imagining things. Hold the bike?"

He held Veronica steady as Alex plucked the bolt from the other foot peg. Squatting down here, she had an unfettered view of his calves. Strong, with a dusting of hair. None of which she should notice since she was trying to keep her distance from him. He was an annoying client, with whom she had a *professional*, uncomplicated relationship.

She rose, then shoved the wrench and bolts into her back pocket.

"Thanks," she said, and began to lift the bike off the rack.

"Stop," he said. "Let me."

She let go of Veronica. "Who do you think put her up there?"

"You." He grunted as he hefted the bike and set it on the ground. "But I'd rather you not pull a muscle if you have to drive us out of here. I'm assuming you won't let me drive?"

"You are correct, sir." She flicked out the kickstand, then tucked the bike's bolts into a canvas bag strapped to Betty's inside back wall.

"Where are the helmets?" he asked.

She couldn't resist needling him. "In Azul Caye."

"Seriously?" He raised an eyebrow. "You know what they call bikers who don't wear helmets? Organ donors."

"Calm down, Mr. Gullible. They're in the back." She opened the passenger door, then emerged with her wallet, flask, water pouches and his backpack. "Can I throw this in your bag?"

Without waiting for an answer, she unzipped the top.

Interesting. She'd expected the passports and papers carefully sealed in ziplock bags, the neatly folded clothes, but not…

"Why do you have a big velvet box in here?" She hugged the bag as she bounced on the balls of her feet, irritation mostly forgotten. "Are you trying to woo her with precious baubles? I have to see this."

"It's not what you think."

She withdrew the jewelry box and dropped his bag. Hmm. The flat rectangular box was too big to be an engagement ring. The hinges creaked as she opened it.

Oh, pretty. Tucked against the pillowed satin insert lay a necklace. A sturdy gold chain threaded through a beautiful round locket. She didn't normally yearn for girly stuff, but this was both strong and delicate. The locket's base was silver, and a decorative layer of gold petals formed a rose on its surface. From its center, a starburst of rubies winked at her.

"This is lovely." She traced her finger over its surface.

Stupid jealousy trickled through her. Her past boyfriends had tended to give her practical gifts. Multi-tools, emergency road kits, flashlights that would survive an apocalypse. She appreciated them, but it would be nice if someone occasionally gave her a girlie gift and acknowledged she could be delicate, too.

"It's a family heirloom." He gentled it from her grasp. "It's a tradition for the eldest son to give to his bride."

"Ah, so your mom's in on this swoop-into-Belize plan, too? She must like Density."

"Destiny," he corrected as he shoved the box into his backpack. "And my mom's not thrilled, but she trusts me."

Alex did her best to hide an irrepressible smirk. Good for his mom. How could you like someone who broke your son's heart? Unless your son is a complete tool who deserved to be dumped harshly, a proper mom would come out swinging. After the way he'd empathized with her last night, Bo didn't strike her as a tool.

"We should secure the Jeep," Bo said. The straps of his backpack were narrow against his rounded shoulders.

Alex toed one of the pancaked tires. "Um, she's not going anywhere."

"Not what I meant." He collected the limbs that they hadn't hacked down for firewood last night. "I don't want the tires to sink farther into the mud."

"Overkill much? We'll only be gone for four hours."

Bo dragged more limbs behind the tires. "Our track record isn't great. Better safe than sorry."

She didn't agree, but if complying got them out of here faster, then so be it. After she reversed onto the platform of tree limbs he'd made, she exited the Jeep and handed him his helmet.

"Ready to ride?" She swung her leg over the dirt bike's seat, then patted the vacant back half. "All for you, big boy."

He eased his helmet on. "Not sure I like that nickname."

The bike sank a few centimeters as he settled behind her. Whoa. He might not like the nickname, but he was a big boy *indeed*. The wall of muscle behind her sent a sizzle up her spine, which was *not* a welcome sensation. To fight her urge to melt against him, she splashed metaphorical water all over that sizzle.

"Does what's-her-face know about the necklace?"

"Des? She knows it exists, yeah."

Alex jammed the key into the ignition. "But you didn't propose to her with it."

"It's the wrong jewelry. After I asked her to marry me, we picked out an engagement ring that's worth way more than the necklace."

Oh, this sweet, clueless soul. "Didn't you even *mention* the necklace? I mean, if I were dating someone who had a family heirloom that he can *only* give to the person he wants to spend the rest of his life with, I might be…deflated if it didn't come up."

"It's more of a wedding-day gift."

She flipped the kickstand up with the heel of her boot. "Maybe. But you could have done both. An engagement ring *and* the necklace?"

He let loose a breath that tickled her neck. "I— Damn. I *could* have done that."

But he didn't, which was an interesting fact she hoped he'd ponder while they wended through the mountains. The dirt bike's engine would drown out conversation, which was good, because she'd be tempted to point out this might mean he never thought of his ex as forever family. And that was really something he should figure out for himself.

"One other thing, Bo? Grab my waist." She sealed her back to his chest, then firmly belted his arms around her midsection. She wouldn't admit anything *she* was feeling, but this moment called for honesty about another subject that had been fairly obvious this morning at the stream. "And if you get hard again, don't let go. I don't want you to die, and I promise I won't read anything into it."

As the engine rumbled to life between her legs, muffling his response, she couldn't ignore how much she enjoyed his thick, steady arms around her.

Eight

This was *terrifying*. Bo closed his eyes. Nope, that was worse. His stomach dropped as they flew over a hill, then landed with a thump.

He had no clue how long they'd been on this death mobile. Ten minutes? Two hours? Eternity? Engine noise and the whipping wind obliterated conversation. The only thing that had kept him from plunging into a panic attack the second he sat on the dirt bike was his warm armful of Alex.

This close, his lips nearly brushed her nape, which smelled of vanilla. She'd slept in a forest, bathed in a stream, and still carried a scent like his favorite cupcake.

Didn't make her less of a maniac, though.

She barely decelerated for a switchback. A wake of pebbles screamed through the air behind them. One wrong bump and they'd be thrown. Sure, the helmets would protect their skulls, but the dirt road would flay the flesh from their bodies and break their bones to powder.

This was how he'd die.

A familiar gripping sensation in his chest choked him. No, no, no. He would *not* have a panic attack, not in front of this ballbuster. But it was *so* hot outside. Was this normal? And his helmet was tight, squeezing him at the temples.

Breathe in one, two, three, four, five, and out, one, two, three, four, five.

As sweat beaded on his upper lip, he forced himself to notice the azure skies, the shadows the fluffy white clouds cast on the lush green pines that carpeted the wrinkled mountains.

Abruptly, Alex pulled onto the shoulder.

"What the hell, man?" She flicked out the kickstand, then hopped off the bike. "Why are you breathing all over me?"

"I'm…having…a…panic…attack." The air wouldn't come. His rib cage rattled like his heart was trying to escape.

"Oh, fuck." Alex tossed her helmet to the ground. "I've got you. Tell me five things you see. Now, Bo. What do you see?"

"You," he wheezed as he shut his eyes. This was it. This was how he ended, on a Belizean mountain with a beautiful almost stranger.

"Uh, uh, Organ Donor." She jerked his helmet free, knocking his glasses askew. "Keep 'em open. That's one. Four more things."

He blinked against the bright Belizean sunshine. "Guardrail. Trees. The road."

"Gimme one more." Alex rested her hands on his knees, which made it pretty fucking tough to focus. Jesus, was he so horny that it cut through a panic attack?

She squeezed his knee. "Bo."

In the distance, a river burst through the pines and cascaded down the mountainside. "The waterfall."

"Good." Alex slipped her hand into his. "Four things you can touch."

"You." He gripped her wrist. "This seat is scorching my ass. My backpack. You."

"You used me twice, but I'll allow it," she said. "Three things you can hear?"

His overactive heart was showing signs of calming.

"The waterfall." He strained his ears and heard a familiar clicky squawk. "A toucan. Your voice."

"Good. Now tell me two things you can smell."

Breathe in, one, two, three, four, five… An intoxicating mix of rich, spicy scents laced the air. The most prevalent ones, though, were…

"Pine. And vanilla."

Probably should've said something else.

She raised an eyebrow. "One thing you can taste."

He licked his lips. "Salt."

A thick cloud passed overhead, giving them a break from the sun's heat. His pulse was a dull thud in his throat, and his head was more…attached, and less like a balloon.

"Good." She squeezed his knees again, then let go.

His backpack jerked slightly as she freed a water pouch, then handed it to him.

"Cheers." She tapped her flask against the tepid pouch, and they both sipped.

The liquid stung his raw throat.

"Does that happen to you a lot?" she asked.

"No." He tipped his head backward to let the sun wash over his face. He hated his panic attacks, preferred not to discuss them, tried to hide when they happened. He hated his vulnerability during an attack. The only people who'd witnessed him have one were his mom, Delilah, Destiny and the ER doctor who'd diagnosed him when he'd had his first one after his father fucked off to Vegas. And now Alex. But it wouldn't be fair to shut down the conversation since she'd helped him.

"They happened a lot after my dad left. Therapy helped. Takes a lot to trigger them now."

"Careful, or I might feel insulted."

He was grateful she didn't ask about his dad. That history might trigger her since it was too close to her own financial situation.

"I kept imagining you'd lose control and we'd skid over the edge."

"Okay, now I *am* insulted. But you must have a powerful imagination."

"It's a blessing and a curse." He eased from the bike. His clenched lower back protested, but not to the point of pain. After a deep backbend, he parked his ass against the railing that led to a scenic overlook.

Alex joined him.

"Couldn't you retrain your imagination? Like maybe…" She flipped her palms toward the sky and shrugged. "Instead of dwelling on potential doom, be optimistic about how things could go great?"

As she smiled, the freckle he'd noticed that first day at the bar—the one above the left corner of her mouth—seemed to bounce.

What would it be like to kiss that spot?

He knocked back more water. "I'm a realist. The past is the best predictor of the future."

She scrunched her face. "Jesus, I hope not. Because if you're telling me my past is my future, I might fling myself off this cliff."

"Yeah, me too, I guess."

Lots of things in his life had gone sideways. His dad leaving, Delilah's unpredictability before her diagnosis, kicking the asses of the playground bullies who teased her, his mother's focus on everything *but* him... Yeah, he'd be quite happy if all of that stayed firmly in the past and never darkened his door again.

That was part of the reason he'd gotten into working with algorithms. Life was much more manageable if you could predict what was likely to happen. No pitfalls, accidents, set-backs—just smooth sailing.

No pleasant surprises, either.

Like that gorgeous waterfall. When he'd awoken this morning, he couldn't have predicted he'd witness a natural wonder. Or see Alex peeled down to her underwear.

Talk about a natural wonder.

"Hello? Bo?" She bumped shoulders with him. "Didn't you hear me?"

"Sorry, no. I was in my head."

"That happens to you a lot, I bet." When he didn't answer, she continued. "How'd you correctly identify the toucan?"

"One attacked me at the resort yesterday morning."

"Oh, shit. You mean Rocko?" Her giggles morphed into face-scrunching chortles. "Sorry, sorry, sorry. That bird is such an asshole, but it's hilarious that he swooped at you."

Despite himself, he laughed. The remaining tension in his body melted like sugar.

"It wasn't a great start to the day."

He would, however, like to start his days with unpredictable, belly-busting laughter like this. Destiny didn't get jokes. She found things amusing, but she'd never lost control and doubled over. No, she was even-keeled and preferred the rest of the world behave that way, too. In the past, he'd gravitated toward that calm like a moth to a flame, like it was the most rational, reasonable way to move through life.

Now he wasn't so sure. Without flat tires, a death trap dirt bike, or a panic attack, he wouldn't have gotten his arms around Alex, a glimpse of her nurturing side, or witnessed joy lighting her up brighter than the Domino Sugars sign in Baltimore's Inner Harbor.

The valleys and the peaks seemed to be where the fun happened.

"I bet Rocko was a surprise." She thumbed tears from her eyes. "He gets mad at tourists who don't feed him."

"I'll pick up some birdseed for the return trip."

"Don't encourage his bad behavior." She stretched her arms overhead, causing her tank top to ride up and expose the smooth skin of her midriff.

Nope. Not looking there.

He snapped his gaze to the pebbles underfoot, then kicked a rock over the edge. "I'll cede the resort to him when we get back."

"*If* we both go back. Depends on how things go in Ch'ooj Creek, doesn't it?" She winked. "You good? Ready to get back on the bike?"

"Yeah. Just go easy on the sharp turns." He took a final glug of water, then slipped it into his backpack. He held the open maw of the bag out to her. "Flask?"

Wordlessly, she tossed it inside.

He bent to collect his dusty helmet from where Alex had tossed it.

"You have pretty eyes," Alex said as she snugged her helmet on her head. "They match the sky."

His pulse picked up speed. He liked that she'd noticed something besides his loss of control. For her to express admiration like that, quick and easy… This felt like flirting. Instead of dissecting the way that made his insides vibrate—and whether or not that was a bad thing—he'd go with it. Their not-actually-near-death experience inspired him to stick his neck out and return the compliment

"Thanks. My mom says they're striking." *His mom?* Fuck, he was bad at this. "Your eyes are pretty, too. They match…"

The rich mud that kept them mired in the jungle last night, but that was a terrible, insufficient comparison. Her irises were lively, soulful and flecked with gold, and saw him the way he wanted to be seen. She'd treated him like a playful partner instead of the noble good guy everyone needed him to be back home. None of that was lighthearted, though, so he stood there, tongue-tied and vibrating with tension.

"Bo Ferguson, your charisma knows no bounds." She jerked her thumb over her shoulder. "Can you jump on the back, please? I'd like to get to my friend's place by lunch."

"On it." After pulling on his helmet, he climbed onto the seat behind Alex.

"Do I need to force you to hold on to me *every* time we ride?"

Before he could ask her how often she expected to ride with him, she twisted the ignition, and they shot onto the road.

Alex gently throttled the bike to crest the hill. *Easy does it.* She didn't want to trigger another anxiety attack for Bo. Thank God the ability to talk someone through one had come back to her in a snap.

Her sister suffered from them in high school. That had been a rough time for Jules. Mom's third marriage had meant they'd moved again and transferred to a new school. Alex was a senior and ignored everyone, but Jules was younger and tried to fit in. Her eager and open personality didn't blend with SoCal coolness, though, and the poor kid had been low-key bullied. Therapy helped her get them under control in LA, and she'd never had them here in Belize, not even during Dad's funeral.

Alex glanced at the emerald on her forearm. She owed Jules a phone call. They hadn't properly caught up in ages. Between the shit with Peter and Julia's final semester in grad school, they hadn't talked much since the holidays.

Hadn't talked much *during* the holidays, either. Alex was consumed with saving Stone Adventures from bankruptcy. At the same time, she didn't want to burden Julia. The easiest tactic was to avoid her younger sister altogether.

"Is that it?" Bo shouted.

The picturesque village of Benque Viejo del San Julian emerged in the distance. The brightly colored houses and buildings made Alex's heart smile.

Alex nodded. "That's it."

She reduced her speed as they wound toward Mariele's resort, which lay tucked between the mountains and the village. Hmm. Things were busy today. San Julian was on the cusp of growing into a small city, so it always bustled—but in a quaint way, with fresh markets, errands, neighbors greeting each other. Today, there were banners, streamers and…

Fuck.

The road to the resort was closed off.

She paused, idling.

"Is this your friend's place?" Bo gestured to the small green house where she'd stopped.

"No." She pointed toward the mountain. "That is. The road's blocked."

"Does that mean we walk?"

"No. There's a back road."

At least, there should be one. She sifted through the network of paths she'd explored in the five years since Mariele and Hernesto had bought this place. A route lit up in Alex's brain. Messy, maybe, but doable.

"Hang on," she said as she turned down an alley.

A few minutes later, they motored onto a mud-soaked dirt path. Even at reduced speeds, the bike kicked clumps of sodden earth back at them.

"This is not a road," Bo shouted.

"It'll get us there."

A broad, shallow puddle lay ahead of them. At least, she hoped the puddle was shallow. It must be. The grade of the trail on either side was essentially flat.

Bo gripped her waist. "We should test that out first. It could be deep, or a sinkhole, or…"

"We'll be fine." She gunned it through the puddle, and they *were* fine, except for the sheets of backsplash that rained down on them.

Bo hugged her tight. His firmness against her back was… whew. It took all of her discipline to keep the bike upright.

His voice tickled her ear. "That was so dangerous."

The word *dangerous* in Bo's mouth licked an inconvenient sizzle up her spine. The vibration of the engine between her legs wasn't helping matters.

"We're fine!" She revved the dirt bike and zoomed up the hillside before arriving under the portico of Sweet Winds Resort. As she cut the engine, Mariele rushed toward them.

"Excuse me?" Her friend waved her hands. "You can't park that here."

Alex removed her helmet. "Then it's a good thing we aren't staying."

"Alex!" Mariele wrapped her arms around her. "What the hell are you doing here? Why are you filthy? And who's this?"

"I'm Bo." He tugged off his helmet, and his hair adorably stuck up at odd angles.

Mariele raised an eyebrow, then shook Bo's outstretched hand. "And who is Bo?"

"He's a client," Alex cut in. "And he's what the hell I'm doing here. We're on our way north and blew out Betty's two rear tires. Can you or Hernesto help me out?"

Mariele's face crumpled. "Oh honi, we would, but not today. It's the last day of the Chocolate Festival. It's a big week for us—we make twenty-five percent of our annual revenue during the festival, so I can't spare anybody."

Alex pursed her lips. "It's not an emergency, but we're already delayed and…" Alex snapped her fingers. "We can strap two tires to the dirt bike, and I'll go change them. Easy."

"Alex," Bo and Mariele said at the same time.

Their shared warning tone annoyed her. "What?"

"You can't take tires *and* me," Bo said.

"I don't need to take you. After I change the tires I'll come back for you."

"That's even worse," he said. "Trying to do all that alone is foolish. We can wait."

Anger flared in her gut. "*I'm* foolish? *You're* the one who wanted to go on a cross-country adventure without any outdoors experience. I know what I'm doing."

He shook his head. "*Risky's* a better word. I don't want you to get hurt."

Which was sweet, but infuriating. Mariele stood silent, her

gaze darting between them like she was watching a tennis match. Whoops. Right, they had an audience.

"Can we borrow a car and bring it back in a few days, Mariele? Anything with four-wheel drive would be great."

Her best friend shook her head. "No, sorry. The roads are closed for everything but emergencies on festival nights. We don't want to run over drunken tourists. Honestly, I'm shocked you got through to us."

Alex toed the cobblestones. "We drove the dirt bike on the walking trail."

Mariele raked her gaze over the two of them. "Ah, that explains the mud."

"Are you sure there's no way out?" Alex asked.

She had five days to get the payment to Belisle. Plenty of time, but she hadn't handled stillness well since Dad died. If she stayed in motion, she couldn't sit with grief, or worry about debt, or her future, or her messy relationships with her sister and mother.

"I'm sure." Mariele beamed. "But this is fate! We had a guest check out of the honeymoon cottage early. You can have it. I'll get you fresh clothes so you two can clean up and join the festivities. Ooh, and I can take you on a tour of our expansion."

Expansion? Alex's insides twisted. The last time she'd been here, the project was a dream. She and Mariele had grown up in each other's pockets, so she was happy for her success... But it highlighted how her own goals had gone horribly off track. She'd drowned in reams of paperwork after Dad's death. Then Peter had taken whatever focus she'd had left. The fallout from that debacle had put her solidly in the red emotionally. None of that was Mariele's fault, and her bestie deserved a friend who would celebrate with her. So, as much as she wanted to push through to Ch'ooj Creek, she'd stay and gush about the improvements at Sweet Winds without being a burden.

Alex flicked some drying mud from her wrist. "Thanks, Mariele. We'll stay, but I can't ask you to do all that. Just stick us in a broom closet."

"You didn't ask. I offered. And I can't have you running around the resort looking like you got caught in a mudslide. Not exactly the vibe we're aiming for in our little slice of heaven." She gestured for them to follow her. "Come with me."

Inside, she approached the front desk clerk. "Zelma, could you please prep keys for the Forest's Edge Bungalow for my special friends?"

"Yes ma'am." The clerk efficiently clacked at her keyboard, swiped the plastic resort key cards, then tucked them into a paper envelope. She snagged a trifold map from the plastic standee next to her terminal. "Señora, will you be showing them to the suite? Or…"

The walkie-talkie at Mariele's hip crackled to life.

"Mi lov, where are you?"

"At the front desk," Mariele said as she held the button. "You'll never believe who's checking in—Alex and… I'm sorry, what was your name again?"

"Bo Ferguson."

Mariele winked, which she did *not* love. That was a friendly "my bestie clearly likes you so *I* like you" wink. Yes, she was attracted to Bo, but she didn't want someone who knew her as well as she knew herself making coy assumptions.

"Alex and her friend Bo Ferguson," Mariele said.

"He's not my—"

"That's wonderful," Hernesto said through the walkie-

talkie. "But we're having a minor crisis at the chocolate fountain. The chocolatiers claim the temperature is suboptimal."

Mariele winced. "I'll be right there."

"Who knew chocolate was so stressful?" Bo said.

"Tell me about it. If this festival weren't so lucrative I'd say
to hell with all of it." Mariele flapped open the trifold pam-
phlet, circled a house on the map, then handed it to Alex.
"Your bungalow is here. Make yourself at home, and I'll send
clothing to you."

Welp, they were definitely staying.

"What should I do with my bike?" Alex asked.

"The valet will tuck it out of sight. Keys?" Mariele opened
her hand, and Alex dropped them on her palm. "Thanks. Have
fun. I'm off to solve chocolate problems."

As her friend disappeared, Alex tugged on Bo's sleeve. "Let's
go. It's this way."

She started up a stone path.

"You're sure?" he asked.

"Seriously?" She flapped the map at him. "Didn't we es-
tablish that I'm the empress of navigation?"

"Not sure we settled on empress."

She batted a fern out of the way. "My point is, I know
where I'm headed."

Physically, anyway. If she had to be stuck somewhere, the
Sweet Winds Resort was ideal. Her sore neck muscles hinted
that a hot shower and a night in a luxurious bed with three-
hundred-thread-count linens would be welcome after last
night's impromptu campout.

Not to mention all the Belizean chocolate they could in-
dulge in at the festival.

"How long have you known Mariele?"

Alex veered left. "Always. Our dads were best friends."

Mariele was as much a sister to her as Jules, which, of course, she would never say out loud. Her relationship with Mariele was easier, too, because Alex never measured up to her little sister's expectations. But it's not like being three years older meant she'd cracked some life code that gave her access to all the wisdom of the universe. She was a typical twenty-eight-year-old who was still figuring shit out.

"She's clearly doing well for herself."

"Yes, she is," Alex said. Mariele's background was more humble than hers, but she'd turned scholarships and winnings from her pageant years into a business school education. That, and years of hard work, led to them buying and renovating the Sweet Winds Resort. "I'm proud of her. She's kind of who I want to be when I grow up."

At the top of the steep path, they found a small house surrounded by leafy green plants.

Bo whistled. "This is beautiful."

"Isn't it?" Someday, she and Jules would have places like this dotting their beachfront property. Alex gulped. As long as she could hold on to it, they would.

They climbed the stairs toward the wide front porch, and she pressed the key card to the reader. After the lock's tumblers clunked, she and Bo entered the one-room bungalow. The tastefully decorated suite featured a sitting area, a wet bar and a king-sized four-poster bed. French doors led out to a huge balcony.

"C'mon, let's enjoy the view." As Alex flung open the French doors, three crimson birds arrowed through the valley below. "Wow, I haven't seen scarlet macaws in *forever*."

"Are they endangered?"

"Yes, due to deforestation. Conservationists are building up the population in captivity, which are usually released into the wild to thrive. Since we're close to the preserve we're bound to see more."

"Sounds like you." He leaned against the railing. "Thriving in the wild."

Happy bubbles pinged through her. She shook her head to clear away the compliment. Casual nice comments from Bo shouldn't thrill her like that, even if they were accurate.

"Man, that's the corniest line I've ever heard."

"It's an observation, not a line. You were cranky at the resort when we met, but since we set foot in the forest, you've been invigorated. Like a light's been turned on inside you."

She might actually pass out from him being able to read her so clearly. Alex gripped the railing and inhaled the sweet scent of the forest.

"Being on the road, or in nature…" She twisted her grip on the railing. "It takes me out of my head. I'm not stressed about bills or growth strategies."

Or how much she missed her father, wished her mother had risen to the challenge of guiding her daughters through their grief after he'd died. Or how disappointing she must be to Jules. "I'm an in-the-moment kind of person."

"I need to be more like that," he said. "Most of the time I'm focused on next week, next month, next year. I should learn to focus on the now."

Alex hiked her lips up in a smile. "Now who's lying? You didn't hesitate to hop on a plane. That's pretty in-the-moment."

"I didn't, but…" He rubbed at his stubble, which, for the record, looked great on him.

"But what?" she prodded.

"Sometimes I wonder if I'm here because I invested so much in a specific future that letting it go feels like letting go of who I thought I was, which is a little scary."

"Romantic." She snorted. "Dear Density, please don't dump me because I've sunk a bunch of time into our relationship."

For the first time, he didn't correct her misuse of his ex's name. Instead, he turned toward her, and she sucked in a breath. The heat in his eyes caught her off guard.

"Other times, I wonder if there's another reason I ended up right here, right now."

The knock at the door jerked her attention away from him.

Nine

Bo peeled himself from the railing to answer the door. He both appreciated and was annoyed by the fresh distance between him and Alex.

Her ability to cheer on swooping red birds, even though the last two days had gone off the rails... He was hypnotized. What would it be like to be *that* in your body and not focused on some future version of perfect? He was so worried about looking back on his life in regret, like his dad, that he never stopped to appreciate now.

As he opened the door, a uniformed staff member held a garment bag and a canvas tote, while another proffered a tray covered with a silver dome.

"Greetings," the one with the bags said. "A delivery from the Castillos."

"Thanks." He opened the door wide, then stepped aside. "You can put it wherever."

As the two young men made short work of hanging the garment bag and arranging the tray on the coffee table, Bo fished two crisp five-dollar bills from his wallet.

"Gracias," they said.

Alex entered the room as the taller of the two staff members informed them, "The Castillos invite you to dine with them at 7:00 p.m."

"Thank you." Alex lifted the lid from the tray and clapped.

Bo smiled at her delight, then closed the door behind the bellhops.

"What's that?" he asked.

"All my favorites," she said. "Conch fritters, dukunus, garnaches and panades. And fruit, if that's your thing. Come eat while it's hot."

"That looks like calamari, tamales, tostadas and empanadas."

"I mean, they kind of are? But they're Belize's take and use local spices. Speaking of which…" She uncapped the bottle. "Marie Sharp's hot sauce."

Alex broke open a…what'd she call it? A panade? And liberally doused half with the bright red sauce. She gobbled it up without hesitation, and a drop of sauce lingered near the freckle at the corner of her mouth.

"You've got a little…" He touched his face to mirror the spot.

"Can't take me anywhere." She swiped her thumb over the sauce, then sucked it clean. "Mmm. That is so good."

She flopped back onto the love seat, moaning. All he could do was stare. Her indulgence was possibly the hottest thing he'd ever seen.

"Must be, for you to make a noise like that."

"I make all kinds of noises." She sat forward, tapped the seat next to her, then held out the remaining morsel. "Sit down and try it. You'll moan too."

"No hot sauce?" he asked.

"We might bicker, but I don't want to kill you."

Hmph. That spiked his competitive nature. He picked up

the bottle she'd used. The label claimed it was 'comatose heat level,' which couldn't be much worse than Taco Bell fire sauce.

"I can take the heat."

Her freckle bounced as she laughed.

"If you insist." She sprinkled the sauce on the panade. "But don't say I didn't warn you."

"I promise."

He *could* take the panade from her, but the urge to eat directly from her hand won out. Unable to stop himself, he kissed the tips of her fingers for a fraction of a second. Moves like that weren't him. He usually second-guessed the hell out of his options, but today something else was driving him.

"Um…" Alex gulped. "Do you like it?"

The panade itself was delicious, all rich hashed fish and refried beans, but the sweet sting of the hot sauce lit up his tongue.

"Tasty." He'd never admit his mouth was on fire. He was desperate to be in the driver's seat with Alex about *something*, come hell or high water. Both of which they'd been through on this trip already.

Alex raised an eyebrow. "Color me surprised. Again. About the hot sauce, and that you're so relaxed. I thought you'd be steamed about another unexpected overnight."

"I'd be an asshole if staying at a luxury resort made me mad." He peeled cling film from the top of a glass of lemonade. "We're making the best of bad luck, that's all."

He crunched into a conch fritter to stop himself from admitting the main upside in these delays. He didn't want to say goodbye to Alex. Not yet. Belize was great, but it didn't hold a candle to her. She intrigued him.

If things had gone according to plan, they'd be at Ch'ooj

Creek right now. The sinkhole, the rain, the flat tires and now the chocolate festival blocking their exit... The universe was telling him to slow down.

To enjoy himself.

There was more to this than plain indulgence. Something he couldn't put his finger on. But he felt it in his bones, in his heart, that he shouldn't rush to his final destination. He was meant to linger, to stop and smell the bright orange blossoms in the arrangement on the coffee table. To enjoy the unexpectedly good company of Alex Stone...

...who had gobbled up a full third of the tray while he'd been distracted.

"Have you attended this festival before?" He bit into another panade.

Alex flicked open her pen knife and sliced a star fruit. "No. Mariele's invited me every year since she and Hernesto bought this place, but I was so busy with tours, I couldn't get away."

"Except for this year."

She sighed and nibbled at the citrus. Her lips shone with the fruit's juice. He swiped a slice to learn what her lips must taste like.

"Not really a getaway since I'm working. But I'm glad we're here. It makes Mariele happy, and who doesn't love chocolate?"

He lifted a shoulder. "Me."

She laid her hand to her heart. "Active dislike? Or you can take it or leave it?"

Neither. When he was a kid, he'd taken a Hershey bar to school in the third grade and it had melted all over the inside of his backpack during recess. From that point on, he was done with chocolate. Too unpredictably messy.

"It's fine. But it isn't any better than, say, Jell-O."

"I pity you." She poked him in the chest. "You've clearly never had amazing chocolate."

He wanted her hand back on him.

"I have. It's okay."

"Sir, you will eat your words—and a fistful of the best chocolate in the world. It was *invented* here." She gestured outside. "The ancient Maya were the first to discover its amazingness and cultivate it into the wonder that it is today."

"I'll eat whatever you want me to, but don't be surprised when I'm underwhelmed."

"You won't be, stubborn ass." She threw a grape at him. "But we should look presentable at dinner. Do you mind showering first? I want to luxuriate in that swimming pool of a tub."

He blinked to clear away the image of her in a tub. "Uh, yeah, sure."

"Well, go on, then." She swept her fingers toward the bathroom. "Shoo."

He popped a grape into his mouth, then entered the bathroom. Blissful heat rained down from the showerhead after he turned its valve. To keep the mirrors from steaming, he opened the French doors that led to the balcony that ran the length of the house. A bamboo privacy screen divided this area from the space outside the bedroom. Better to shuck his clothes out here and avoid flicking dried mud all over the tub that Alex wanted to enjoy.

"Everything's *fine*, Jules. Seriously, I just wanted to say hello."

Ah, hell, Alex was out here, too. He turned quietly, careful not to alert her to his presence as he ducked back inside to give her privacy. But Alex's voice chased him, like the bathroom was specifically built to catch and amplify anything said on the balcony. The shower did nothing to muffle her words.

"In fact, I'm playing tour guide to a hot American in the middle of the western forest preserve." Alex laughed into the phone. "Nah, that's not in the cards. I really like him but he's here because his fiancée broke up with him and he wants to win her back."

He clenched his neatly folded shorts.

She was just repeating what he'd told her. But the certainty in her voice…it didn't match how he felt. Not anymore. Since he met Alex, he'd experienced amazing and terrifying moments, most of them unpredictable, all of them breathtaking. Now that he'd allowed himself that taste, he couldn't go back to the version of himself who mapped out every hour of the day.

"That's what I said," Alex sighed. "But I don't think he believes me. It doesn't matter, though. You know my rule. No more mixing business with pleasure. Now tell me about school."

He caught his breath. Alex had called him a hot American.

Alex, who was easy to talk to, even when she was biting off his head. Alex, who was undeterred by the challenges they'd faced on this trip. Alex, who glistened in the morning sun, making him wonder what her curves would feel like. He'd gotten a chaste taste of her body during their ride here, and he'd bet everything he had that sex with her would blow his mind.

His hard, restlessly throbbing cock agreed.

He rotated the shower valve to cold.

As Alex finished securing her damp post-bath hair into crisscrossing French braids, a knock sounded at the bathroom door.

"You okay in there?" Bo asked.

"No. Three ninjas attacked me as I was shaving my legs."

Mariele had packed a bundle of toiletries, cosmetics and hair products for her. Light lip gloss and eye shadow were all the makeup she'd chance in this heat. Anything else would melt faster than sandcastles at high tide.

"Ha ha. Dinner's at seven, so we should head out."

Her watch on the sink's vanity showed six forty-five, but she wouldn't bother pushing back. Bo was devoted to punctuality. They'd be unfashionably early by Belize standards, but she could always stall at a festival vendor.

"Almost ready," she called.

She slipped into the dress Mariele had sent—a simple ivory midi with a neckline that dove past her breastbone. *Jesus, Mariele.* Since puberty, her pageant queen bestie had cajoled her to dress in daring, barely there clothes whenever they hit the town. Alex was more comfortable in practical gear since she liked to be prepared for impromptu hikes, zip-lining, cliff-diving, or kayaking.

Tonight would be an adventure of a different sort.

She twisted and shimmied to test out the dress's coverage. The deep dip of the front meant her bra was a no-go, but miraculously, everything stayed put.

"Hey, Bo, what'd they give you to wear?" She grabbed her phone, knife and wallet, then wrenched open the door. "'Cause Mariele basically gave me a tight doily, and...oh."

Bottom to top, Bo looked *good*, the perfect blend of casual and fancy. Pristine white canvas shoes, white pants, a blue denim shirt that hugged the swell of his broad chest, and a lighter blue seersucker sport coat.

"*Oh* good? Or *oh* bad?" he asked. "The fit is slimmer than I prefer. Not sure anything's getting in these pants pockets, and this shirt is missing the top buttons."

She raked her gaze over him. What would the soft skin right above his collarbone taste like? Her pulse quickened. Man, this outfit was *doing* things to her. Hot nerds were apparently her catnip.

"Good." She gulped. "Definitely good."

"Because they also sent a T-shirt with pajama bottoms, and I could wear that instead."

"Don't you dare."

His lopsided smile made her stomach flip. "You clean up nice, by the way."

"True." She smoothed the bodice of her dress. "But I dirty up better."

Joke, joke, she'd meant it as a joke, but whoa, his molten gaze could loosen her dress's fastenings from across the room. Alex clamped her mouth shut. She didn't trust herself to keep her chitchat in the appropriate lane. Eventually, he blinked.

"I like you both ways." He scratched at his jaw. "What I mean is, you don't need to clean up to look gorgeous."

Her heart fluttered…but she couldn't resist poking at his awkward discomfort.

She popped her hand on her hip. "Does that mean you like me dirty?"

"I like you, period."

Ah, hell, the sincerity dripping from those words was her kryptonite. Now it was her turn to go full awkward.

"Oh," was all she could manage.

Bo approached her. "I make you say 'oh' a lot."

"Because you surprise me." She scooched past him, and

the light brush of her arm against his sent a shiver thrumming through her. Which was dumb, because this was Bo. He was her *client*, and he was chasing after his ex, and he lived in the States.

On the other hand...

Those last two facts made him *more* appealing, because a fling with someone who was both emotionally and geographically unavailable cemented the whole flingy aspect to anything that might happen between them.

One, maybe two nights were all she could offer anyone these days. Even if she had time for more, she couldn't trust him with anything more, heart-wise. Ego-wise, either. No, the shallows were the only place she could swim romantically right now.

And that client bit was nonnegotiable.

After setting her stuff on the bedside table, she dug through the canvas tote. "Why didn't Mariele pack a purse? Where am I supposed to put all this?"

Bo laughed. "You really need your knife this evening?"

"Nobody has a *specific* need for a pocketknife." She scooped up her belongings. "That's the point. There are dozens of situations where they're handy. And it's my good luck charm."

Also, it was her father's and she never went anywhere without it.

"I can carry your stuff for you," Bo offered.

She raised an eyebrow. "In those pants?"

He opened his suit jacket. "This has pockets. I can carry your phone and knife. You don't need a wallet. Chances are good your friends will cover dinner. Anything else is on me."

"Bo, I can't ask you to pay for me."

"You didn't. I'm offering." He held out his hands to her.

Alex's heart hammered in her chest. This was like giving him her security blanket. Over the past two days, he'd been nothing but careful.

"Thank you." Alex thrust the knife and the phone at him.

He slipped them into his pocket, then opened the front door of the bungalow. "After you."

As she passed him, she caught a hint of spicy cologne. Her knees weakened. The laundry soap scent was classic, but this was a sexy grace note. Either way, she was an absolute sucker for a man who smelled good. After Bo secured the door, he met her on the path, and they made their way toward the main part of the resort.

Alex chose her steps carefully along the flagstone-and-gravel walkway. Ugh, these were dumb, impractical shoes. She spent her life in hiking boots, slides, or barefoot. Not ten-centimeter wedge heels. Shit, one of her traitorous ankles wobbled. She caught herself on the slim trunk of one of the silver pimento trees lining the path. Embarrassing, but at least she salvaged her balance.

"Here." Bo offered the crook of his elbow to her.

"I'm fine." Alex brushed the thin fronds of the tree from her face.

"Obviously, but my offer is selfish. If you twist an ankle, it'll slow us down tomorrow." He nudged his elbow toward her again. "I promise I'll keep you steady."

Refuse his tempting elbow, and she'd keep the bright and shiny boundary between them. Take it, and she'd signal she needed him. Plus all the touching and she'd be caught in his cloud of seductive cologne goodness. She couldn't trust herself not to—

"Alex, come on." He waggled his elbow. "I don't bite unless asked."

"What's that supposed to mean?"

"You tell me." In the sport coat, his shrug took on a decidedly relaxed Belizean resort attitude. "It's your joke from last night, when we set up camp."

Last night she'd used it as a goofy icebreaker, but coming from Bo's lips... The tantalizing threat carried a heated undertone that lit up her skin.

"Fine, I will accept your selfish offer." She slipped her arm through his, and *oh*.

There was that flutter again. His biceps were firm under her hand. No surprise there. His polo shirts didn't exactly cling, but she'd spent the morning with him pressed to her back, a shield between her and the world.

"Why would your friend give you shoes you can barely walk in?"

"Revenge." Alex paused as a gecko skittered across the path. "Mariele's begged me to let her do a makeover on me since we were kids."

"You don't need a makeover."

"That's what I keep telling her."

They walked around the lagoon-like pool. Several women in barely there bikinis gave them not-so-casual glances that lingered on Bo. As a bartender, she clocked the look as an attempt to figure out how "together" they were. Brazen, since she had her arm wrapped around him and everything. Alex shot a gimlet gaze back at each of them.

Bo kicked a rock from the path. "While you were taking your marathon bath..."

"It was an hour."

"Sure, we'll call it an hour. Anyway, I read up on the Chocolate Festival."

"The whole time? There can't be that much info on it."

"I also read the instruction manual for the entertainment system and caught up on work messages. The street fair goes through the evening, but after dark, the entertainment shifts from a family focus to a more adult-oriented atmosphere."

"What does that mean? I can't imagine Mariele's planned an orgy."

"Um, no." He cleared his throat. "The thing about chocolate being an aphrodisiac… Tonight's Sweet Winds wine and chocolate party has a reputation for matchmaking. People go to the party expecting to meet their soulmates."

She recoiled. She hated the idea that there was only one true person for her out there. There was too much risk, too much potential devastation in that concept. She might never find them, or worse, find them and a dumb logistical reason would keep them apart.

"That's ridiculous."

"I'm just telling you what I read. Apparently, for the past five years, the resort has hosted two dozen weddings for couples who met at this party."

Her mouth dried. "That's not us. We've already met."

Hell, that came out bitchier than she'd intended.

"And I don't like chocolate."

She lowered her shoulders, grateful he'd ignored her tone and played along.

"You'll eat your words after tonight. Why are you warning me about this, Bo?"

"To prepare for the speed-date atmosphere for single people. I can play your…whatever you want to keep guys at bay.

Unless you're convinced your one soulmate's in there guzzling wine and chocolate?"

Ugh, she was not. Bo was the only person here who caught her eye. But he was off-limits for good reasons...reasons that were getting harder by the minute to remember.

"I'll be fine," she said.

"Whatever you want." Bo cinched her closer as the crowd thickened.

Across the plaza lay the resort's expansive dining deck. Strings of yellow bulb lights cast a muted glow on the resort's guests. Beyond the deck, the mostly set sun's last flares of tangerine and gold mingled with the inky purples and pale blues of the sky.

As they cut their way through the festival-goers, more women swiveled their heads in Bo's direction. Would she have to deal with this all night? He was a catch and anyone would be delighted to bring him back to their room.

Jealousy spiked through Alex.

She was being ridiculous. He didn't *belong* to her. She just...

Alex's breathing shallowed as the realization hit her. She'd been her old self these past few days. Confident, unflappable, lighthearted. If Bo's company was the magic ingredient, she wasn't ready to give him up. And why should she? His ex had cut him loose, and—

A man in a straw fedora bumped into her.

"Sorry." He let his oily gaze linger. "But maybe we'll catch each other later, angel?"

"She's spoken for," Bo cut in.

His lie sent a complicated thrill through her. She didn't *need* a rescue, but she liked that he offered her one.

"My bad." Mr. Fedora held up his hands as he melted into the crowd. "Didn't realize."

"Sorry, I know you could handle that, but…you stiffened up."

"That was because…" Because she wanted him and realized there was no good reason not to take this man to her bed. Mr. Fedora was just an unfortunate coincidence.

Bo searched her eyes. "My offer stands. I'll be your one-night boyfriend to keep soulmate seekers at bay. Like that guy."

He jerked his head toward a dude in a tank top and backwards baseball cap whose gaze was locked on her breasts. She sighed. Bo's earnestness was adorable, but he'd need to keep his arm around her all night, signaling to people she was his girlfriend.

Girlfriend. What a weird word for people their age.

A vendor's stall across the plaza caught her eye. There *was* another universal symbol they could use to thin down attention from lovestruck people at the party. Best of all, she'd ratchet up Bo's idea in a sincerely ridiculous way. That was her style, after all.

Jump in with both feet and hope for the best.

"Come with me." She tugged him away from the party and toward the street fair vendors.

"We'll be late to dinner," he said.

"Mariele will forgive me." Aha, *there* was the vendor she wanted.

"May I help you?" the man asked.

"Yes," she said. "We'd like wedding rings, please."

The old man's face lit up. "The Chocolate Festival strikes again!"

Bo murmured, "We want wedding rings?"

The proximity of his low voice to her ear sent a delicious shiver through her body.

"Yes, we do." She surveyed the variety of options, then pointed to a matching set of hammered silver rings. "I like these. What about you?"

She turned to Bo. He obviously had *so* many questions.

"If we're wearing these," she whispered, "fewer people will hit on us. Neither of us is here for that, right?"

Understanding dawned on his face. "And those are the ones you like?"

"Yes. I like simple."

"What the lady wants, the lady gets." Bo handed over enough bills to cover the purchase.

The old man slipped the rings into a velvet bag. "Congratulations and best wishes for health, wealth and prosperity."

Fantastic. She needed all those things.

"Thank you!" She took the bag and dragged Bo toward the fountain at the town's square. There, she shook the rings into her palm. "Here you go, Mr. Ferguson. I promise to love, honor and cherish Belizean chocolate."

"You won't let the chocolate thing go, will you?" He slid the ring onto his finger.

A foolish bolt of lightning shot through her heart.

Her mom's turnstile approach to marriage had made her cynical about vows. Something about Bo wearing a wedding ring, though… The thick band of silver broadcast that she'd claimed him, and that he was happy to put that claim on display.

She found the whole thing unspeakably hot.

He rolled his knuckles. "Fits like it was meant for me. How's yours?"

She slipped it on, then flapped her hand. The ring didn't fly off.

"Perfect." With a smile, she jerked her thumb over her shoulder. "Let's go."

Ten

Bo's offer of an elbow hadn't been *completely* for Alex's benefit. One glimpse of her in the sexy ivory dress, and he'd mapped all the ways he could touch her…respectfully. But the urge to signal that everyone should back the hell off her was uncontrollable.

When she'd pitched this ring idea he was all in. As she'd selected the bands, he'd waited for guilt or grief about his broken engagement to show up, but none had come. Instead, the slide of the simple silver ring over his knuckle had caused wild, tingling heat to radiate through him.

Happiness, that's what it was.

Probably because he'd found a way to do Alex a favor. With everything hanging over her head, and after so much of this trip went wrong, they deserved a good time. Their problems would still be there in the morning, but for one night, he could be like Alex and set his worries aside. He could choose fun.

He fiddled with his ring.

This lightness was a new sensation. One that he liked.

"Mariele's over there." Alex squeezed his biceps, and electricity jolted through him.

What he would give for her not to stop there. He wanted her hands on his hips, his chest, his cock. Her mouth, too.

She'd taste amazing, he knew it, salty and sweet swirled together. All of which he should stop thinking about while he was wearing these tight pants.

As they entered the fray of the crowded al fresco dining area, Mariele wrapped them both in a hug.

"You two look *much* better," she said.

"What the hell is with this dress, Mare?" Alex swept her hand down her bodice. "It's all wrong for me."

Bo couldn't disagree more.

"You're not leading a Mayan pyramid hike, Al. You look great." Over Alex's shoulder, Mariele locked gazes with Bo. "Doesn't she?"

"Yeah," he said. "Really great."

Inwardly, he groaned. That was an insufficient compliment. Since she'd opened the bathroom door, he hadn't been able to keep his eyes off her. Her intricately braided hair, tanned skin and white dress with the daring neckline gave wild warrior princess. One who might take him to her palace bedroom for an untamed night of passion.

Stop that, he warned himself.

"Told you." Mariele bumped hips with Alex. "Our table's this way."

They delved through the crowded patio. Toward the back, they found Mariele's husband holding a conversation with several well-dressed people.

"Ah, there's my better half," Hernesto said.

"James, Ana, Vilma, Sharon—this is my great friend Alexandra Stone, and Bo…"

"Ferguson," he supplied.

He pulled out the empty chair next to Mariele for Alex,

but she promptly sat in the one he hadn't touched. Okay then, he'd sit next to Mariele.

"Hi, nice to meet you," Bo said. "Do you all live around here?"

"No." James's mop of curls bounced as he shook his head. "Ana and I are from Los Angeles."

Vilma laid a crimson-manicured hand on her partner's shoulder. "And Sharon and I are from Toronto."

"We each own boutique resorts," Mariele explained. "We met at a convention, get along famously, and are flirting with the idea of formalizing our relationship."

Vilma swirled her wineglass. "And we've pledged to visit each other's locations to check out the goods, so to speak. Last month, James and Ana's, this month, Sweet Winds, and next month, they'll brave the cooler Canadian climate."

Ana flicked her shimmering blond hair over her shoulder. "Are you hoteliers, too?"

"No." Alex shook her head. "I run an adventure tour company."

Waitstaff deposited plates of garden greens in front of them. Alex dove into hers, while he subtly sniffed at the dressing. Just oil and vinaigrette.

"What's an adventure tour?" Ana asked. "Like, Indiana Jones cave-diving?"

"More like Marion Ravenwood," Bo said.

"Yes to cave-diving," Alex said. "Or exploring ruins. Or hiking through the jungle. It depends on what the clients want. I can accommodate any adventure."

"She's too modest." Bo reached for his water. Alex was amazing, and he wanted everyone to know it. "We've done things I never would have dreamed of doing."

"How do you mean?" Vilma raised her wineglass to lips that matched her nails.

Alex nudged him with her foot under the table. Was she urging him not to speak? Why? He had nothing but good things to say.

"We camped in the jungle, doubled up on a dirt bike to ride here, then spent the afternoon recuperating in a beautiful resort, and now we're here at dinner with all of you. None of this was on our original itinerary, but it's been a blast." Bo sipped at his water. "I'd never have guessed that I'd be into spontaneous exploration."

"Alex is great at surprise adventures." Mariele batted her eyes. "How did you find her?"

"At the Belize Dreams resort. I was staying there, and I needed a guide to an archaeological dig site that isn't well mapped."

Mariele snapped her gaze to Alex. "Why were you at the Belize Dreams resort?"

Ouch. Alex was fully digging her heel into his toes. Message received. She didn't want him to say she worked there. Her best friend should already know that, but hey, that was Alex's choice. He scooped up a generous forkful of salad.

"Socializing." Tension radiated from Alex, from the stiff way she held her glass to her forced smile. "Cozying up to a resort is a good way to find clients."

"Unusual to be a woman tour guide," James said. "It can get rough out there."

Alex raised her glass. "Agreed, but I can handle myself."

"She's the *best* guide," Mariele said. "I offered her a job, but she heartlessly rejected me."

"Because I have my own company to run." Her flat voice held none of the bounce or warmth from earlier in the day.

"You could be a subcontractor."

Alex shook her head. "Not to a resort. They tend to offer only boring family fare."

"But those are the kinds of tours your Dad ran," Mariele said. "Day trips to the caves, the barrier reef, or the Lubaantun and Nim Li Punit ruins. They could be your base income, and the wilder stuff could be extra."

Mariele's advice made sense to Bo, but then again, what did he know? Best to stay out of a debate between old friends. He and Delilah got like this, too. Their words were the tips of icebergs with loads of hidden meaning and shared history lurking under the surface.

"That's not where my heart is." Alex's eyes sparked in the low amber light. "I want people to experience things they can't get to in a minivan."

"Is there money in that?" James asked. "Most of our guests want drinks, luxury and uncomplicated fun."

Alex sipped her wine through her clenched jaw. He recognized her expression. She'd been like that behind the wheel of her Jeep when they slouched through the jungle in the rain. She was treading this conversation as carefully as a rutted, mud-drenched road at twilight.

After a few beats, she said, "People pay to summit Mount Everest, don't they? Some tourists are up for an adventure."

"Some, but not most," Ana said. "Belize has such nice beaches. Why not encourage vacationers to visit them?"

"Because Belize is more than beaches."

Uh-oh. There was the frosty smile she'd given him that first day at the Belize Dreams resort, when he'd assumed Alex Stone, guide extraordinaire, was a man. She must think Mariele's business colleague was underestimating Belize, or Alex, or both.

"Apropos of nothing," Mariele said, then deftly led the conversation away from Alex and her company, and asked the others about their promotion plans for the coming quarter.

"You okay?" he murmured.

"Fine." Alex drained her wine.

The three other couples continued their hotel conversations, and Bo picked up on themes that were consistent in his own workplace—differentiators, marketplace presence, the unbeatable power of word-of-mouth advertising. But Alex would perceive his chiming in as an act of treason, so he focused on his meal.

And damn, what a tasty adventure dinner turned out to be.

A mahi-mahi fillet, seasoned with local spices, served over cilantro rice and topped with a chunky tomato concoction that Mariele said was creole sauce, with fried plantains on the side. Bo was risking the integrity of Hernesto's pants, but he couldn't help himself. After two days of protein bars, beef jerky and oatmeal, his senses were overwhelmed with all things Belize.

"Any chance I can get the recipe for this meal?" Bo asked.

"We don't share trade secrets." Hernesto grinned. "But you're welcome back any time."

Bo's chest hollowed. A return trip here was unlikely.

What if this *wasn't* the last night he was here? The people surrounding him, his borrowed clothes, the foreign scents of the resort's body wash and shampoo… They made him feel like a different person, one that he hadn't realized he could be, in a place he'd never pictured himself.

And yet he was enjoying himself like he was born to it.

The waitstaff quietly cleared their empty dinner dishes, then delivered a decadent chocolate mousse. As Alex picked up her spoon, the dramatic flourish of an old pop standard played from the dance floor.

"Oh. James, it's our song." Ana grinned at her husband. "We have to dance."

"Yes, we do." He rose then held a hand out for his wife.

"We love this song too. If you'll excuse us?" Vilma and Sharon followed Ana and James to the dance floor.

"What do you say, mi lov?" Hernesto asked.

"I'm staying here." Mariele leaned back in her chair. "I've been on my feet all day."

Her husband kissed her knuckles. "Praise God. I feel the same way."

Bo was out of practice, but he was sure his moves would come back to him. Dancing would give him an excuse to have his hand on Alex's back, her arm around his shoulder, and it would give him a perfect reason to tug her close, like he had during the bike ride here.

He turned toward Alex. "Did you want to—"

"Nope." She shook her head.

Okay, that was a supersonic shutdown.

"Bo," Hernesto said. "Come with me to the bar. Let's refresh the drinks."

"You'll be okay?" he asked Alex.

"Yeah, I can manage ten minutes alone with my best friend."

The bright-eyed girl from the jewelry shop was gone, replaced by a prickly woman who looked like she needed a hug. Her mood had soured as soon as those other couples talked about their dreams becoming a reality in concrete, rebar and reservations.

But he'd take her at her word. Not the easiest thing for him. His default move was to stabilize rocky moments for people he cared about. This trip was showing him, though, that not every situation needed a fix, and not every fix needed him.

He'd do better to save his energy for the ones that did.

"Be right back." He followed Hernesto to the bar, but hung out on the customer side as Mariele's husband drifted behind it to craft their next round of cocktails.

"Thank you for the loaner clothes," Bo said.

"Eh, no problem." Hernesto shoveled ice into four glasses, then splashed in cranberry juice and amber rum. "Consider them a gift from me to you since you wear them better anyway. At least, Alex thinks so."

"What makes you say that?"

"Come on, man." Hernesto skewered three cranberries, then rested them against the ice in the glass. "The leaning toward you, glancing at you, asking you to pass her the salt."

"She didn't want the salt?"

This was a revelation. Alex was direct with him. Bossy when their safety was at risk. It hadn't occurred to him that she wouldn't be that way about her feelings.

"What she wanted was your attention. There's more to you two than you're letting on, isn't there?" Hernesto scanned him. "No offense, man, but you don't look the type to wake up one morning and decide he needs an adventure."

"True." Clearly, he was easy to read. "It's about a woman."

"I can tell." Hernesto grinned.

"No, another woman." Bo scratched the back of his neck. "She's up north, and—"

"Nah, man. It's gotta be about Alex. I've known her as long as Mariele has, and I'd bet this place—" he looped his finger in a circle "—that she's into you. Whoever you *think* is out there, I'm telling you, there's someone special here."

Bo couldn't deny the truth of what Hernesto said. He also couldn't deny the twitch below his belt whenever Alex came near. He wanted to peel the barely there dress from Alex more than he wanted to breathe. She enjoyed life to the fullest and he was dying to know if that was true in bed, too. His name on her ecstatic lips would be *everything*.

The problem, though, was the reality of why he was here.

"But this other woman…tomorrow…"

"No one's guaranteed a tomorrow. And if this other woman's so special, why's she somewhere else? I say this next part as a friend—"

"We met an hour ago."

"As someone who will be your friend, because our ladies are best friends." Hernesto pointed directly at him. "Stop bav."

"I…what?"

"It's Kriol for stop being afraid. Alex likes straight shooters. She has no time for hints and innuendo." Hernesto handed the tray to Bo. "Take these to the women."

Mariele slid into Bo's empty seat and clutched Alex's wrist. "Now that everyone's gone, *tell me* who the hot nerd is."

Alex raised an eyebrow. "Bo Ferguson, from Baltimore, Maryland. He's a client."

"That is *not* what I mean. He salivates over you like you're a bar of IxCacao chocolate."

"He doesn't like chocolate."

"Well, he clearly hasn't tried the right kind."

"That's *exactly* what I said." Alex drained her glass of water. She didn't want to talk about Bo or the frisson of heat that ricocheted inside her every time he brushed against her. If they started that conversation, her best friend would drop truth bombs she wasn't ready to hear.

"You're dodging." Mariele let go of her wrist. "Spill. Did he really hire you as a guide?"

"He did." Alex sighed. "His fiancée broke up with him. She's an archaeologist and is working a dig in Ch'ooj Creek. I'm taking him there."

"Oh." Mariele sat back. "That complicates things."

"No, it doesn't, because there are no *things*." She dug into the chocolate mousse, which melted in her mouth. "That's delicious."

"Of course it is. So, the archaeologist—she dumped him, yes? They are finito?"

Dammit. She couldn't keep Mariele off this topic. She was like a retired American hunting Spanish shipwreck treasure off the Barrier Reef.

"And this trip is to…what? Win her back?"

"Sort of?" She clutched her spoon. "They were together for seven years, and she broke up with him via text, and didn't mention anything about their cat, which makes her an objectively terrible person. Also stupid, because he's funny, and sensitive, and reads instruction manuals like they are bestselling novels. I have no idea why someone as good-hearted as him would be with someone awful, much less go to all this trouble to find her."

"I see." Mariele leaned back. "Interesting."

Alex's skin prickled under her best friend's appraisal. "What?"

"You've got it bad for him, and you don't know what to do with your crush because you're not a morally bankrupt person who steals other people's lovers."

Alex froze like she'd been caught naked.

Actually, scratch that. She was comfortable in her skin.

This was worse.

"Nuh-uh." She shoveled more chocolate mousse into her mouth.

"Excellent denial." Mariele nudged her knee. "Allie, come on. You are entitled to some fun. It's wonderful to see you happy again."

"I'm not happy, I'm buzzed." She gestured to her empty wineglass.

"Psht. You've got the tolerance of someone twice your size. When I came to console you in December, you weren't in a good place. Now you seem better. Why do you have trouble admitting you're happy?"

"Because, Mare. The last time I was truly happy, my dad was diagnosed with cancer. The next time I *thought* I was happy, my boyfriend stole my life's savings. So I don't trust happy, because it's a signal that the universe plans to sucker punch me."

Alex exhaled. The things she bottled up around other people were okay to firehose at Mariele. She didn't have to treat her best friend like delicate china, unlike her mother, her sister… They wanted emotional support from her that she didn't always have the energy to give, and she ended up sticking her foot in her mouth and hurting their feelings. That never happened with Mariele, though.

"Oh, honi, happiness doesn't always come with a sting." Mariele draped an arm across Alex's shoulders. "You say Bo is here to find his ex. Have you considered she's an ex for good reasons? Take a chance. You're the one who's all about taking risks, aren't you?"

"Oh, what do you know?" Alex threw her hands in the air. "You met Hernesto when you were sixteen."

"That doesn't mean I don't know about risk." Mariele gestured toward the main building of the resort. "Building this place up was a struggle. We're *finally* turning enough profit to expand again."

Alex's heart pounded. She adored Mariele and Hernesto, wanted the best for them. Always. Spending an entire meal listening to them talk, however, about their brisk business and potentially partnering with those other couples to form a network of boutique resorts… It had triggered a powerful wave of jealousy.

"You can't compare the two, Mare. Risking money is different from risking your heart."

She should know. She'd done both and failed.

"Who's talking about hearts?" Mariele flipped her palms skyward. "I'm talking about a fun night, or two, or three. Go for it. The way you two are looking at each other, you're halfway in bed already. Dah no so, dah naily so."

Alex shook her head at the Kriol saying—*if it's not so, it's nearly so.*

"It doesn't matter how hot he is, or how much I like him. I can't. It's too scary."

Behind her, someone cleared a throat.

Heat blazed up her spine, then swirled across her cheeks. She stared into Mariele's delighted brown eyes. *Fuck. Me.* There was only one situation that would make her best friend this happy. She'd said all that to prompt her best friend to give her more reasons to stop worrying and take what she wanted.

Sweat beaded on her hairline. "He's behind me, isn't he?"

"Yes, he is." Bo set the tray of drinks on the table, then sat next to her. He dug his spoon into the chocolate mousse that had been set at his place. "Is this the infamous Belizean chocolate I've heard so much about?"

"It *is*," Mariele said. "Beware, though. It's an aphrodisiac. Seventeen village children owe their existence to the Sweet Winds chocolate mousse. We'll bump that number up to at least twenty after tonight."

Alex's shoulders tensed. "Mariele, I am begging you to stop talking about aphrodisiacs."

She didn't dare look at Bo. Her attraction to him was undeniable, like he was the North Pole and her compass persistently pointed toward him. Now that he knew, what would he do with this information? Be a gentleman and pretend he'd heard nothing? Go cold because she'd misread him? Or satisfy her curiosity about what his naked chest felt like?

"Why?" Her best friend casually lolled her spoon in the air. "It's all true."

"I take back what I said about chocolate. That's delicious." Bo had eaten half of it. "Sure you don't want to dance?"

Dancing was high on her list of things she did not do, but she was desperate to get away from Mariele and closer to Bo.

"Yes." She pushed back from the table.

Bo took her hand. His big grip inspired the heat in her cheeks to redirect itself to a decidedly more intimate place. Thank God her arousal wasn't as obvious as his had been, but this contact… She didn't have an exact roadmap for where this adventure was headed. All she knew for sure was his warmth, his strength—and that he'd slipped into the driver's seat in this situation.

For that, she was grateful.

On the floor, a smooth melody layered itself on top of the

M.C. Vaughan

syncopated drumbeats. Bo twisted toward her, then held her close. There the heat went again, this time flaring from the sensitive spot where he pressed his palm to the small of her back.

"I'm not a good dancer," she said.

He murmured, "That's okay. I am. All you have to do is let me lead."

His cologne wafted from his pulse point. She resisted the urge to lick him.

"That's hard for me," she said.

He spun her away, then reeled her back until they gently collided.

"I know."

His hips swiveled to the beat of the music. *Oh my*. If he could work his hips like this on the dance floor, imagine what they could do…

Stop it, she told herself.

"How do you know how to dance?" she asked.

"All hot guys know how to dance. They teach it in hot guy school."

"Shut up," she said through a laugh.

He twisted her so her back was glued to his front, and after a few swinging beats, returned her to facing forward.

"Come on, Bo. Tell me."

"I took lessons. I'm rusty, though. I haven't danced for a while."

"This is rusty?"

He was as sure-footed on the dance floor as she was clambering through the jungle. Another spin, and the world whirled. Another return. Strength radiated from him, and the shifting shoulder and chest muscles under her grip sent a thrill through her. Bo Ferguson was fit, limber and in control of her body. A shiver rippled over her.

She'd give him more, if he'd let her.

"What were the lessons for?" she asked.

"You are tenacious."

"Always. So?"

"I took lessons before senior prom. I felt awkward at dances, so I decided to rectify that."

"Your prom date must have been thrilled."

The music downshifted to a slower rhythm, and Bo clasped her to him, bringing her focus to his delicious full bottom lip and the scruff on his jaw.

"I didn't go."

With their hands woven together, he steered her around the dance floor. She picked up on his silent signals, allowing herself to follow.

"After you went to all that trouble? Why not?"

"She asked someone else."

"Tell me the name of this person so I can add her to my mortal enemies list."

He laughed. "Destiny Richards."

Alex puckered her face. "Your ex-fiancée? Ew. Well, that's efficient, at least. She was already on my mortal enemies list. But why didn't you ask anyone else?"

He lifted the shoulder on which her hand was resting. "It wouldn't have been fair to ask someone and then spend the night pining for someone else."

"Counterargument. A friend would've been happy to make Density seethe with jealousy. Sometimes people stick you into a box, and they need a swift kick in the heart to make them see you in a different light."

He leaned close and murmured in her ear, "You think that would've worked?"

Fire skated down her spine. His lips were right there, next to her cheek. All she'd have to do is turn her head three millimeters to the left and they'd be locked in a kiss...

"Yeah." She gulped. "But her loss."

"Yeah. Her loss." His chest rose with a sigh.

She searched his face and didn't like the shadows she found in his eyes. "Bo, you know that, right? I've only known you for a minute, but it's *absolutely* her loss. What you lack in forest knowledge and comfort with ambiguity, you make up for in fierce dedication to instruction manuals and sweet dance moves."

"They are pretty sweet." He deeply dipped her in the middle of the dance floor.

A photographer popped a few snaps. "Kohn gi ahn wahn kis!"

With her still bent backward in his arms, Bo asked, "Did he ask us to kiss?"

"You understand Kriol?"

Bo lifted her upright. "No, but he's making a kissy face at us."

"Pleez." The photographer folded his hands together. "Wan kis. Fi di nyoozpaypa."

"That okay with you?" Bo asked Alex.

She should say no, but selfishly... She could get the taste of Bo that she'd been wanting since meeting him at the Belize Dreams resort, and it would be an uncomplicated freebie because she could say she'd merely satisfied the photographer's request.

"Yes," she said.

"You asked for it." Heat consumed the levity in his eyes.

Oh boy. She was in more trouble than if she were cave-diving without a headlamp.

Even in her heels, he was at least ten centimeters taller. She rose on her toes to close the distance between their mouths.

He tilted his face at a perfect angle to hers.

Time stretched and slackened, like a drunk, happy thing. The melodic thump of the live band, the scrape of the festival-goers' shoes on the dance floor, the beep and pop of the pho-tographer's camera shutter and flash—all those sounds hushed and faded until her heart beating in rhythm with Bo's was all she knew.

The anticipation had her jumping from her skin.

But, oh, the reality was better.

Bo's lips were firm and sweet and smooth, like a mango in peak season. The sensation contrasted with the stubble shad-ing his jaw. She liked the rough parts of him, couldn't resist sliding her hand against his cheek. As his tongue swept hers, she thrilled at the low moan that escaped him.

"Tenk yu fi di picha." The photographer's gratitude burst the bubble around them.

"Welcome," Bo said.

Alex wasn't capable of words. There in the middle of the dance floor, Bo Ferguson had kissed her stupid. Gently, he released her, and her body protested. That single kiss was *not* enough. She would never forgive herself if she didn't explore the rest of him.

Tomorrow, he might belong to someone else.

But tonight? He was hers.

"Come on." She tugged him away from the crowd. "That was just the start."

Eleven

Bo's gaze lingered on the ropy twist of Alex's braid against her back as she led him from the dance floor. It bisected the strap at the top of her dress, as well as the pale tan line from a bikini top. What he'd give to explore those patches of skin, to peel this dress from her...

He'd fought to keep his gaze respectful all night. Dinner was especially difficult, what with the swell of her breasts peeping between the deep vee of her dress. Harder still was while they were pressed close and dancing. It had taken all his willpower to recall the steps and command her around the parquet floor.

Not that he'd ever describe it like that to Alex. He wouldn't put it past her to tie him up to show him who was in command of whom.

The dance floor, though... Alex in his arms was everything he wanted it to be. She was a mix of sharp and soft, and then that kiss...

"Where are we going?" he asked hopefully.

"To the cottage." Alex wove through clusters of bodies. "Too many people out here."

Away from the mass of revelers, the refreshingly cool air chilled the dewy sheen on his skin. Glowing lights illuminated the dark walkway. With their hands linked, they fell into a side-by-side stride.

Next to him, Alex shivered.

He let go of her hand, then shrugged out of his jacket. As he draped it over her shoulders, she murmured a thank-you.

When he clasped her hand, she squeezed his back. His insides vibrated in response, and he let out a long breath. He wasn't sure what his heart shifting to another person so easily said about him, but that's what had happened.

It was time he owned it.

"Have you ever stayed here before?" he asked.

They crossed through the pool area. Low beats played through strategically placed speakers, and shadows drifted under the water's surface as people swam, then popped up to splash each other and laugh.

"Ages ago, but it was different then." Alex avoided the pool's splash zone. "Mariele and Hernesto took advantage of the downtime during the lockdowns to renovate. The upgrades were brilliant, especially since people were desperate to travel once restrictions were lifted. They're raking in money hand over fist."

"I can see why. You will, too."

She squeezed his hand. "I appreciate your optimism."

His pulse quickened, and he briefly closed his eyes. *Please* let his palms stay dry. He hadn't been this nervous around a woman since he'd lost his virginity.

They rounded the corner to the bungalow. Heat radiated through his chest. The future held two distinct options. For once in his life, he was bound and determined to go with what he wanted to do instead of what he *should* do.

Only if Alex wanted that too, of course.

He glanced at the amazing woman next to him.

Please let her want that, too.

They climbed the steps to the cottage.

Bo opened the door. "After you."

Alex crossed the threshold, then groaned.

Hmph. Not the mood he was hoping for. "What's wr—
Oh."

A candlelit room greeted them. LED candles, which made
good sense since they'd been left unattended. Rose petals blanketed the bed, and an iced bucket of champagne rested in a
stand next to the love seat.

"I didn't do this, I *swear*." Alex waved her hands at the romantic touches. "This must be part of the honeymoon package."

Alex tossed his suit jacket to him.

"This is *so* over-the-top. Mariele's treating us like puppets.
I'll get someone to clear it out—let me change first. We've
got an early morning. You take the bed and I'll bunk on the
couch."

No, no, no. He could salvage her soured mood. Just a couple of well-timed sweet words and they'd be back to where
they were on the dance floor.

With a grin, he said, "Don't be—"

She closed the door to the bathroom.

"—silly," he finished.

Dammit.

If she'd lost interest, he'd force himself there, too. He was
a tower of willpower. A gorgeous woman was stripping down
on the other side of that door, but he was mature enough to
keep his cock in check.

He viciously dug through the bag for the pajamas he'd spied
earlier. He should be thankful she'd thrown walls up between

them. It would save him from making irresponsible choices, like his father.

But as he stared holes into the closed door, he was anything but thankful.

Alex's one-eighty stung like hot razors in his heart. Destiny dumping him had knocked the wind out of him, but this… this was worse. He didn't know how he knew it, but he and Alex were exactly where they were supposed to be in the universe, and they were screwing it up.

He unbuttoned Hernesto's shirt, then hung it in the garment bag. Before he could unlatch the belt from his pants, the door to the bathroom flew open.

With color high in her cheeks, Alex said, "Oh."

That was the third time he'd made her say "oh" tonight. Wouldn't be the last, if he could help it. He chose not to cover up so she saw what she was missing. An egomaniacal thought that he'd unpack later. But she licked her lips, and he loved it.

"Need something?" he asked.

"I can't get out of my dress. The clasp is stuck. I need my knife."

Ah, right. The blade was tucked inside his jacket pocket.

He crossed the room to her. "Turn around."

"You don't have to—"

"Ruin a dress? I agree." He lifted her braid and shifted it over her shoulder. Jesus, that simple act caused his cock to rage against his fly. Her sweet vanilla scent filled his senses, and her body heat warmed his chest.

Goose bumps fanned across her bare back as his fingers skimmed her nape. He nearly groaned as she shivered. Her body's reaction to him couldn't lie.

She was feeling this, too.

But he respected her choices.

"Stop wiggling," he said.

Her shoulders rounded as she crossed her arms. "I'm not."

"You are. I can't believe cutting your way out of the dress was your plan. Why do you always jump to the most extreme solution?"

She lifted a shoulder. "It was the first idea I had, and first ideas save time."

"Disagree. First ideas are the easiest solutions, not necessarily the best." He kinked his knees to inspect the fussy clasp. Ah, there. The hook had snagged through several threads. "I let the problem percolate until a better solution pops up."

As he worked, his breath shifted the baby hairs on her nape. He twisted the hook, then shimmied it back and forth until...

"There. You're free, and the dress is still in once piece."

As he straightened, he eased the gold zipper down, revealing the white thong beneath her dress. His already-hard cock thickened, tenting Hernesto's tight pants. If last night in the hammock tent was torture, this was hell.

She turned, clutching her slackened dress against her body. With her eyes flashing like gems, she placed her index finger in the divot of his chest.

"Bo Ferguson, I'll make you a deal."

Alex couldn't miss the telltale bulge in his slim-fitting pants. Ten minutes ago she had a mini-flip-out about the candles and the roses and the *blech*, romance. She didn't want *romance*. Promises, hope and trust were the building blocks of romance. She couldn't afford those. Not right now, and maybe never again. Tonight, though, she could have laughs, heat and a chance to distance herself from the memory of her last lover.

"Why do you use both my names?" he asked.

"To get your attention."

"You always have my attention." He raked his hungry gaze over her. "What deal?"

She could drop the dress and make it obvious, but crossing this line required words. An agreement. Clear terms.

"We are both technically single and the sexual tension between us is ridiculous. It's distracting. So here's the deal—one night of no-strings-attached, shallow, get-it-out-of-our-system sex. But promise me it won't be awkward in the morning?"

She almost believed what she was saying.

He cupped her cheek.

The contact sent her heart skittering. Holy cacao, if that itty-bitty baby of a caress knocked her sideways, she might lose her bones if he dipped a hand into her—

"Is this one of your knee-jerk, haven't-thought-it-through, brilliant ideas?"

Unable to speak, she nodded.

"Okay then. As long as we're clear that neither of us are thinking things through."

His mouth collided with hers, and oh, his kiss was even better this time around. She twined her arms around his shirt-less torso, eager to smash her naked flesh against his. She let the dress fall to the floor, and her mouth vibrated with Bo's moan, all heat and—

Her lips cooled as he withdrew.

"What's wrong?" she demanded. Her skin was tight and she would burst if he stopped touching her. All their two steps forward, one step back moments made her desperate for forward, forward, *forward*.

With a pained expression on his face, he said, "I don't have any condoms. There's not thinking things through, but then there's *really* not thinking things through."

"Wait." Alex snapped her fingers. "Mariele slipped an optimistic amount of them in the bag she gave me."

The tension melted from his shapely shoulders. "I like your friends."

"Yeah, they're keepers. Back in a second."

She dipped into the bathroom to find the strip of condoms. In the light drifting in from the bedroom, she caught her reflection. Eyes bright, lipstick smudged, wearing nothing but a smile, her thong and the ring they bought earlier.

She was ready for this.

As soft love songs played in the main part of the cottage, she peeked around the door frame. Bo stood at a console in the corner, hand in pocket, fiddling with the remote.

"Bored?" Alex joked.

He turned toward her, and *oof.* The shifting candlelight licked up his torso and along the breadth of his shoulders, like it was giving her a map of the places she should explore on his body. She might regret this in the morning, but that was Tomorrow Alex's problem.

Tonight, she wanted this man desperately.

"You like music, so I read the instruction manual earlier. Is this too schmaltzy?"

"It's perfect." She tossed the condoms onto the bedside table, then closed the distance between them. "Are you blind without your glasses?"

"Nah. Everything's just a little fuzzy."

"Good. I don't want to break them." She removed his glasses. "Can we dance again?"

"Whatever you want."

He smoothed his palm down her naked back, then cupped her ass. His chest against hers was warm, his light chest hair causing a friction-filled delight as they swayed to the low, thick beat of the music. His smooth guidance steered them toward the bed.

"I have a very important question," he asked.

She didn't like Very Important Questions. She liked jokes, levity.

"If it's about solving the climate crisis, I have ideas."

He undulated his fingers against her skin. "It's less complicated than that. More of a survey. What turned you on most tonight? The chocolate or the tight pants?"

"Definitely the pants. Speaking of…" She undid the button, then peeled them from his hips. Whoa. Nothing but bare skin and glorious hardness greeted her.

She raised an eyebrow. "No underwear?"

"There wasn't any in the bag." He hooked his thumbs in his waistband and shoved down. "Figured this was how men dress around here."

Alex licked her lips. God, he was beautiful. Bo's gaze was like a decadent drag of a match up her spine.

"So, here's the thing," she said.

"More conversation?" He kissed her, held her close, and *oh*. His warm muscled goodness melted her brain. As he nibbled a trail from her ear to her shoulder, she fluttered her eyes closed.

"You might be tempted—" she gasped as he ran his thumb over her stiff nipple "—to be sweet and romantic and take your time, but I haven't had sex in three forevers, and what we did on the dance floor was amazing foreplay. I'm good to go."

"Duly noted. But I'd like to collect more information about

you." He then guided her hips, coaxing her to turn around. "Hold on to the post."

She obeyed, no questions asked. Desire pooled between her legs. This was a decisive Bo, the man she'd encountered on the dance floor. His body heated her back.

Alex shivered with anticipation.

He traced her skin from her shoulders to the curve of her waist. "Do you prefer gentle?"

"Sometimes." She arched her back as he skimmed his hands back up to cup her breasts. Her nipples perked under his attentive thumbs.

"How about a little rough?" He tweaked the delicate flesh, nudging her the edge of pain, and she groaned in response. "See? That's useful information."

"Happy to help."

"I can put it to use in other places, too."

She gasped as bent to nip at the sensitive spot where her neck and shoulder met. He released her breast, then tiptoed his fingers south.

"And here." He whispered into her ear as he cupped her between her legs. "Do you like over-the-cloth action?"

Tension coiled within her, a delicious itch that required a very specific scratch.

"Or is this better?" He slid his fingers under the triangle of cloth and between her slick folds.

"Better," she gasped.

"You're so wet." He wheeled her clit, nice and easy and gentle. "But maybe you'd like me to go faster."

Alex clutched the post. If she let go, she'd collapse from the pleasure he was giving her. With his chest against her back, one of his hands between her legs, and the other alternating attention between her ripe breasts, unbearable delight was building in her core.

"You want to come, don't you?"

A simple "yes" was all she could manage. Had she spoken aloud? Words, thoughts, were impossible. The pace of her panting matched the rapid magic he was working on her. The pleasure inside her tightened, tauter still, until—

"Not yet." He withdrew his grip, leaving her dazed and ready to scream. "I want you on the bed. Now."

She slipped into the midst of the sheets he'd peeled back. With their gazes locked, he tore the packet open with his teeth.

Whoa, Bo was a grower.

Lucky her.

"You won't need this." He eased her thong from her, then prowled onto the bed. The languid grace he'd shown on the dance floor was again on display. As he made a roof over her, he nudged her legs apart with his knee. She opened for him without hesitation.

Bo searched her face. "You still okay with this?"

"Yes. So much yes."

He bent to catch a nipple between his teeth, and her back bowed against the bed.

"Are you sure?"

"Bo, *please*," she begged. Begging wasn't her style, but she couldn't help it.

"Since you said please." He lodged himself at her opening, and slowly, torturously slowly and in control, he moved forward until their hips were joined.

She moaned, but she wasn't alone.

Bo clasped his hands with hers, and his unrelenting ring bit into her finger as he rolled his hips. Fuck, she'd been right about him. His moves were magic, and she was stretched, and full, and oh, the friction was everything, building up, and up, and up until…

He shifted into a kneeling position, breaking the rhythm, dammit.

"What are you—"

"Lift your hips."

As he tugged, she did as he asked, and *oh*. He wedged his thighs under hers, and he picked up speed, landing his cock deeper this time. Faster, then faster, until all she knew was Bo holding her, thrusting in her, his gaze all over her.

"I can hold out as long as—"

A sound she'd never made before tore from her throat as her inner dam broke. Her core squeezed around Bo, over and over and over again until she lay there, boneless and satisfied and barely knowing her own name.

"—you need me to." Bo massaged his thumbs along her quivering hips. "But something tells me that won't be a problem."

"Excellent deduction." A breath shuddered from her. *This* was the height of hedonism. Bo's thickness lodged within her, as waves of satisfaction lapped at her.

She wanted more.

As she bucked her hips against him, he answered with a gentle thrust.

"Greedy." The slick slide of him was glorious in her post-orgasmic state. "Fast or slow?"

"Fast, and hard." She gasped as he thrust according to her specifications. "I'm not—" she sucked in her breath "—greedy. This is mutually beneficial."

"Agreed." He draped her leg over his shoulder, kissing her inner knee.

Electricity bolted from that spot to the bundle of nerves between her legs. And *oh*, those nerves were getting attention from Bo. He circled his thumb around the swollen nub as he pumped into her.

No, she couldn't possibly be coming again. She'd never—

As her orgasm swept over her, Bo shouted and collapsed with her, pulsing. After a few moments of gasping, he brushed her loosened curls from her face.

"That," he said, then kissed her. "Was amazing."

Outside, the happy trill of a nightjar filled the air.

Same, little bird.

"It was." She traced the bridge of his nose.

With a grin, he dropped another kiss on her lips, then withdrew to tidy up. She shimmied under the covers, already cold without him in the mountain's chilly night air.

Bo slipped into the sheets with her. "Okay if we bunk together again tonight?"

"On the condition that you tell me one thing. *Where* did you learn all…" she swirled her hand to encompass the bed "…of that?"

Please don't let him say from his ex.

"I read the *Kama Sutra*." He shifted to his side, then propped his head on his hand. "And my sister gets tons of magazines with helpful articles on how women's bodies work."

"You read instruction manuals. That's so on-brand for you."

Her cheeks ached with her smile. Despite her best intentions, tenderness bloomed in her heart. He was so goddamned *earnest*. His lack of guile was refreshing. He said what he meant. No layers of subterfuge, no secret she was supposed to unpack based on his tone.

He trailed his fingers over her shoulder. "Did it work for you?"

"Uh, *yeah* it did. I've never come twice in one..."

"Night?"

She shifted to her side to face him. "No, I've done that, but never that close together in one, ah, session."

He twisted his lips.

"What?" she asked.

"If this is a one-night-only, get-it-out-of-our-systems situation, then I want to try out other heavily researched positions. And selfishly, I'm determined to give you more orgasms in one night than anyone else ever has or will."

"Is that so?" His heart thumped against the palm she'd laid on his chest.

"Yes." He brought it to his lips to kiss her fingertips.

Alex ignored the warning lights flashing in her head. Try as she might to run away from the truth, she couldn't claim this was just sex. Not anymore. He'd been honest and vulnerable with her in the past few days. She didn't have enough of that in her life.

But that was also Tomorrow Alex's problem.

"I'm up for the challenge."

Twelve

The high-thread-count bed linens caressed Bo's body as he stretched. He turned to wrap Alex in a good-morning hug and ask how she felt about morning sex.

But he came up empty.

Her side of the bed was a rumpled twist of sheets. He blinked, then fumbled for his glasses. A note was tented over them.

B—Left early with Hernesto to swap out tires. Be back as soon as we can.—A

She'd left without him? His chest tightened. She should've woken him. Not ditched him and left him wondering where she was.

Especially after last night.

He dropped his head onto the pillow. Wow, last night. Hot, hard, soft, wet. Confident. And so much fun. He'd believed her when she said sex would satisfy the tension between them.

How incredibly, stupidly wrong they'd both been.

He could never forget the way she'd quivered in his arms, or the orgasm that rocketed through him when she'd moaned and clung to him. Last night hadn't cleared Alex from his system at all. Instead, he'd discovered his body was a perfect match for hers.

But then she'd left him behind.

Bo tossed the note on the nightstand. He hated when people made decisions for him. Like when his parents split up, and they'd decided he and Delilah were better off with Mom. Given Dad's downward spiral into gambling addiction, Bo would've agreed.

The point was, they'd never asked.

The same thing happened with Destiny. She'd had every right to break up with him since she was unhappy in the relationship. No argument there, and she'd clearly made the right call based on how quickly his feelings for Alex had launched. The thing that made his brain itch, though, was he hadn't had a clue that his ex was feeling that way, had no idea how long he'd been missing her signals.

To figure that out, he still needed to talk to Destiny.

Someone knocked at the door.

"Hang on." He snagged a robe from the bathroom.

On the other side of the front door, a hotel staffer waited with another garment bag.

"Your clothes, sir."

Bo took them. "Thanks. Hang on a second."

He fished in his suit jacket for his money clip. Alex, he noted, had reclaimed her pocketknife. Bo handed a five-dollar bill to the bellhop.

"Thank you. Oh, and sir? Señora Castillo invites you to brunch in a half an hour, but if you are otherwise engaged, she understands. What shall I tell her?"

Bo riffled his hair. He was grumpy about Alex's disappearing act, but it would be churlish to refuse Mariele's invitation.

"I'll be there, thanks."

"¡Muy bien! I'll inform her."

After a brief shower, Bo dressed in his freshly laundered

clothes. The trip to the main building of the resort was much faster without a high-heeled Alex. Families were already splashing in the pool, and a chubby-cheeked toddler's delighted squeal sanded the edges from his bad mood.

Mariele sat at a table tucked near the bar, scrolling through a newspaper on her tablet.

"Hi," Bo said. "Thanks for the invitation."

She set down her device. "I'm glad you joined me. I'm intrigued by you."

"That's the first time anyone's said that about me." He draped a napkin across his lap. "I'm an open book."

"An open book who makes Alex happy, judging by the mood she was in this morning."

"Is that so?" A sly smile spread across Bo's lips. Indiscreet, but he couldn't help it.

"She practically floated out of here with Hernesto."

Nice to know she'd been in a good mood, though he would have liked to have confirmed that detail for himself.

"I took the liberty of ordering for you," Mariele said as waitstaff delivered several breakfast dishes. "It's the house specialty—eggs over easy, fried tomatoes, beans and fryjack. Based on the itinerary Alex shared, you need hearty food."

"I thought we were making it up as we go."

"Alex is a bit of both. Mostly has a plan, but is willing to let herself be surprised." Mariele drained her delicate espresso cup. "You're headed to Carmelita. It's the last proper town before the dig site. You might actually make it to the site today."

He spluttered his water. He might reach Destiny today?

He dabbed at his chin with his napkin. "If we don't, does Carmelita have any hotels? When I've left it up to Alex we've either slept in the jungle or begged for a room."

"No one begged last night, but I take your point." Mariele tapped on her device.

Within seconds, his phone buzzed. "Where'd you get my number?"

"Alex, obviously." She gestured toward his phone. "Those are my friends. I'll make the arrangements. Shall I ask them to reserve one room or two?"

"Two." Alex had been clear about their one-night-only situation. However… "Adjoining, if that's possible?"

"I don't see why not. It's slightly off-season. You'll have the place mostly to yourselves."

Alone with Alex sounded like paradise. Even if she didn't do relationships, he'd enjoy their time together and let tomorrow worry about tomorrow.

Which would be the first time he approached anything in his life that way.

"Thank you." He shook a few drops of Marie Sharp's hot sauce onto his eggs, then layered a morsel of everything on his plate into a blissful, savory mix. He'd have to investigate the delicious spice combinations used in Belizean dishes.

As he chewed, Mariele twisted the tablet toward him. "You and Alex made the paper."

He choked on his eggs.

There, in full color, was a shot of him devouring Alex like he'd just returned home from war. The passion practically sizzled on the screen.

"Good publicity for the resort and the festival. This will help feed the rumors that Belizean chocolate is an aphrodisiac. Is that what got into you two last night?"

He sipped his coffee. "I don't know what you're talking about."

"I see." Mariele folded her hands and rested her chin on the roof they made. "Let me be direct, Bo. Life has broken my best friend's heart more times than is fair. Will you, too?"

"That's not…"

He wanted to say that wasn't their deal. Hearts were not in the mix, per Alex's orders. Unless…she said something to Mariele.

"Not to be rude," he said, "but this isn't any of your business."

"Agree to disagree." Mariele sliced off a bite of tomato. "Alex likes you, but won't admit it to herself because the people she likes leave. Her mom and sister are in the States, her father died, and the ex-asshole—well, I'm sure you know all about him. I am the quasi-exception to the rule, but even I live three hours away."

His heart twinged.

His flight back home was in three days, so he'd be leaving, too.

Although… He could always change it and stay— Wait, what the hell? Absolutely not. No. They'd just met. It would be nuts to upend his life. His mom, his sister, his job were all in Baltimore.

Dammit.

Bo shoved a bite into his mouth to give himself a minute to process everything. This whole impulsive trip was the result of not sifting through his feelings about Destiny. If he'd pumped the brakes and strapped his ass to his couch, he would've accepted the breakup, seen it for the good thing it was. But then he wouldn't have met Alex, who'd probably run screaming from him if she knew he'd considered moving here for a split second.

He rubbed his forehead as dozens of conflicting ideas flicked through his brain. He hated muddled thinking. This only happened when what he wanted didn't make sense. And what he wanted was Alex.

"I assume she told you why I'm in Belize?"

"She did." Mariele poured fresh coffee from the silver pot. "Forgive me for interfering, but from what I can tell, you both lie to yourselves."

Bo furrowed his brow. "You've known me for like, six minutes. I don't lie to myself."

"Not intentionally." Mariele lifted a shoulder. "Alex tells me you're here to find your ex, whom you were with for many years. She took a job here, in another country, right after you got engaged. Then, just before she was supposed to return home, she broke up with you in a text, and you came running. Correct?"

Jesus, when had Alex had time to convey *all* of that? When Mariele ran the list back to him, he sounded at best impetuous—at worst, like someone who couldn't take a fucking hint. He'd been so preoccupied with Destiny's choices and how he hadn't predicted them that he hadn't taken a hard look at his own.

"I assume your silence is confirmation." Mariele twisted the delicate coffee cup on its saucer. "Did you ask your ex to marry you because you wanted to spend your life with *her*? Or because it was time to settle down, and she was the obvious choice?"

"I…" His breakfast sat like a brick in his stomach. "That's none of your business."

Mariele raised an eyebrow. "You could have answered that you asked because you love her, that you need her in your life."

This interrogation stung like Old Bay in a cut. "It was implied."

"Was it?" Mariele eyed the silver gleaming on his left hand. "Because last night, you only had eyes for the daredevil woman who wore a ring that matches yours. For the record, I've never seen her happier. It would be a shame to ruin two people's potential happiness because of fear."

"I'm not afraid." He gripped his cutlery tight.

"Ooh," said the person who had screamed his name as she came for the fourth time last night. "Can we order more fry-jacks for the table?"

Alex plunked into the chair next to him.

Alex carefully avoided Bo's gaze. Was she proud that she'd shimmied out of the warm rumple of their bed so she didn't wake him? Or that she'd fought the urge to kiss his sleeping cheek?

Nope, not proud.

But acts of self-preservation weren't always noble. She'd never regret their night, but the tender affection that glowed between them needed to be nipped in the bud. To snuff out her growing attachment to him, and hopefully, weed out any feels he'd caught for her, she'd avoid discussing last night. Her squishy romantic heart left her vulnerable to being swindled. She couldn't repeat that mistake.

Not now.

Not ever.

"Thanks for lending me your husband," Alex said to Mariele as she reached for the coffeepot. "What's this about fear? Something to do with ocelots?"

"I could've helped with the tires," he said.

Well, *that* was out of left field.

"I didn't want to wake you, and Hernesto's done this kind of thing with me before."

"Still." Bo set down his knife and fork. "I wouldn't have left you behind."

Bo and Mariele exchanged a look. Fantastic. Her friend had a busybody streak bigger than the Belize Barrier Reef, so she'd probably asked Bo a bunch of deeply personal questions.

"I'll tell the staff we need a plate of fryjacks with honey." Mariele pushed back from the table. "That's still your favorite way to eat them?"

She shot her a thumbs-up. "Yes, please."

After Mariele left, Alex bumped shoulders with Bo. "Thanks for making us back the Jeep onto those branches. The front tires sank into the mud a few inches. If the back ones had sunk too, it would've taken way longer to change everything out."

"Welcome." Bo sipped his water.

"It's so hot, and it's only eleven." Alex plucked her shirt from her abdomen to encourage a breeze against her sticky skin. She picked up Bo's glass of ice water. "Mind if I have some?"

As the water's refreshing chill coursed down her throat, Bo thinned his lips.

"Not in the mood to share?" she asked.

"You took your ring off."

She set his glass down. "Rings and manual labor don't mix, and I'd like to keep all my fingers. Is that what's bothering you? The ring? We didn't *actually* make a vow to each other, you know."

That came out snarkier than she'd intended, but the best defense was a good offense, right? She didn't like his grim frown. They had a *deal*.

"Yes, I know there were no vows." He laid his napkin on

the table. "You stay and eat, and I'll go back to the room and pack."

A lump formed in her throat. "Okay."

Alex couldn't risk another word, or she'd say something she'd regret, like *come back* or *I'm sorry*. Much better—and more responsible—to hold the line against a man who'd be out of her life as suddenly as he'd entered it.

She wiped her hands down her face.

Holding the line sucked.

"Fryjacks with a side of fruit." Mariele slid the plate in front of her as she sat in the chair that Bo vacated. "Sustenance after a sex marathon."

"Hush." Alex shoved the tiny dipper into the mini honey jar and drizzled sweet golden goodness over the fryjacks. The crunch of the dough was perfection.

Mariele cleared her throat. "As your best friend, I would be remiss if I—"

Alex held up her hand. "Don't."

"You don't know what I'm about to say."

"It's one of three things."

"Please." Mariele huffed. "Anything could be on the tip of my tongue."

"Unless it's about me. Then, it's either A, I should talk to my mother more; B, I should talk to my sister more; or C, you like Bo and I should keep him around."

"I…resent the fact that you are correct." Mariele poured her a cup of coffee.

"It's sweet that you're watching out for me." Alex chugged the delightfully strong brew. "But I'm a big girl. Eyes wide open and all that. Bo's here to chase a woman who is not me. I'd be silly to think last night was anything but a good time."

"Why would you be silly? You can't have a—" Mariele hooked her fingers into air quotes "—'good time' unless you make a connection with someone."

"You are *adorable*. I've been single for much longer than you, so take it from me—I can have fun with someone and have it mean absolutely nothing."

"I'm sure you can." Mariele bumped her shoulder against Alex's. "That doesn't mean that's the case here."

"What do you want me to say, Mare? It doesn't matter if last night was *not* nothing, because fiancée."

"*Ex*-fiancée. And who says he's chasing *her*, anyway? Maybe he's chasing closure."

Ah, hell. Closure would be *exactly* what Bo wanted. He was incapable of being satisfied with ambiguity. Alex gripped her fork until the metal bit into her fingers. She'd allowed herself a night with Bo because he was taken, and that made him temporary, and *that* made him safe.

But what if he wasn't?

"Don't be ridiculous," she said. "Most guys do not spend a fortune on closure. He wants her back."

"What if Bo isn't like most guys?"

He isn't.

Alex popped a sea grape into her mouth and furiously chewed the sweet orb to avoid talking. The cracks that had been forming in the walls around her heart since that first night in the jungle threatened to topple everything.

"It's ironic." Mariele leaned back in her chair. "For an adventurer, you sure need a strong shove when it comes to romance."

Alex dropped her napkin on the table. "There *is* no romance. Thanks for breakfast, but I've gotta go pack. I'll stop by the front desk to say goodbye, okay?"

"Okay. In case you change your mind about romance, I'll throw helpful items in Betty."

"Not necessary," she called over her shoulder.

"You've got time for a nooner!" Mariele shouted.

Alex flipped her the bird.

What did Mariele know? True, she'd sniffed out Peter, warned Alex to be careful because he was isolating her from her friends. Mariele also urged her to accept her mom as she was instead of who she wanted her to be, because that was the only way for her to find calm in that relationship, and to embrace that Julia would be a solid shoulder to cry on once she graduated.

Hmph. Turned out Mariele actually knew a lot.

Alex smacked droopy green leaves out of her face on her way to the bungalow. She sighed as it came into view. Inside those four walls, she and Bo had created a beautiful night.

Laughter, and heat, and peace.

She rested her hand against the door. What would it be like to have that every day? But that was a pipe dream. The world eventually tainted romance with things like bills and taxes and drudgery. Although…it might not be drudgery if she was doing it all with someone she loved.

The door opened under her palm, and she found herself facing Bo.

"I thought I heard someone lurking."

"I wasn't lurking."

The room had been set to rights. Bed made, clothes packed, dishes cleared. The evidence of their torrid tryst was gone. Her stomach heavied with disappointment. Which was dumb, because last night was *supposed* to be ephemeral.

"Are you all packed?" she asked.

"Yeah. Wasn't much, so I caught up on work emails."

"What about the rings?"

"I put them in the box with the necklace for safekeeping."

A lump rose in her throat. Her ring was cozied up to the necklace meant for Density? Gross, gross, gross. She pivoted toward the bathroom, desperate not to let Bo see the obvious horror on her face. What she *should* be feeling right now was nonchalance, not seething jealousy.

After flushing, she returned to the room.

"That's it, then. Let's hit it." She left without looking back.

At the front desk, they hugged Mariele and Hernesto with promises to come back soon. Bo tipped the valet, and they climbed into Betty. Silence filled the cab. She started the engine, then eased around the resort's loop and onto the road leading to the village.

This was fine. Definitely not awkward.

Alex tapped her fingers on the steering wheel, aching to upshift to a faster gear. But that was ill-advised until they left the pedestrian-heavy village streets and merged onto the highway. She fiddled with the radio, but all they got was static.

The quiet pulsed in the air, thickening until she felt like she was drowning in it.

She sighed. "Oh my God, Bo, *say* something."

"Like what?"

"Anything. Comment on how blue the sky is, or the gorgeous green of the pines, or how amazing the resort's fryjacks are."

He peered at the sky. "Definitely blue."

"Seriously, what's wrong? Why aren't you talking?" She braced herself for the onslaught. He could be pissed about her sneaking out, leaving him behind... Or that their two- or three-day trip would easily be four or five.

"Nothing, okay? Nothing's wrong. And *that's* what's wrong."

She wrinkled her brow. "I need you to break that down for me."

"Last night..." He blew out his lips. "Look, I'll be honest with you. Last night was the best night of my life. I should feel guilty, but I don't. I am happy and irritated."

Alex hid her smile.

"Irritated?" she asked.

"Yes, because you left without waking me up. But that's only like, five percent of how I feel. I'm ninety-five percent happy."

"That's...precise."

"That's me." He folded his arms over his chest. "Why don't I feel guilty, though?"

"Don't waste time questioning a good mood." She held her breath. If he said one word about getting back with his ex or hinted that last night was anything less than passionately magical, she'd burst.

"But I don't want to be an asshole."

"You absolutely are not. You are free and clear, Bo Ferguson. She dumped you."

Was that harsh? Probably. Julia accused her of blurting things without sugarcoating them. She wouldn't blurt everything, though. Last night, when she said that Bo was Density's loss, she'd meant it. The follow-up was that he was Alex's strong, dependable, kind, funny and devastatingly handsome gain.

She cut her gaze to Bo, who remained silent.

Shit, maybe that last bit *had* been too harsh.

Alex upshifted as she merged onto the highway. The new

tires she and Hernesto had bolted onto Betty this morning gripped the road like a long-lost relative. Sigh. At least she'd gained back control somewhere.

"Honestly," Alex continued. "You should be at least twelve percent glad that she dumped you now instead of fifteen years down the road, like my mom did to my dad. At least what's-her-name saved a whole potential family from heartbreak."

He flicked his gaze toward her. "Twelve percent?"

"You like precision. Here's what I'm wondering. And please understand, I have zero ulterior motives with this question." She was such a liar. "If your ex says she made a mistake and she wants you back...would you take her back?"

Nothing. He said nothing. Holy hell, *whyyy* was it taking him so long to answer a very simple question? Bo's protracted silence stabbed her in the heart.

The truth was, no matter what his answer, he'd be out of her life in two days.

The air whooshed from her lungs.

"You know what? Forget I asked."

The radio finally picked up a signal. She cranked it and let the music drown out her thoughts and any possible room for conversation.

Thirteen

Shadows from fluffy clouds swam along the shaggy green mountains, making it seem like the earth breathed, but none of the gorgeous scenery made an impression on Bo. Lost in thought, he held tight to the Jeep's grab bar. Alex's question poked at the tender parts of his chest and…

There was no pain.

The bruising he'd sustained from the broken engagement had healed. He'd come all this way, and spent a chunk of their wedding savings, to fix their relationship. But something fundamental had shifted inside him. He didn't want that anymore.

Maybe the change had started with his sister's brutal honesty. Or possibly before that, when Destiny said she wasn't sure about marrying him. Her uncertainty had churned his stomach, but he'd met her with an ocean of understanding, worried that she'd leave him if he pushed too hard.

Which she'd done anyway, and he'd survived, just like he had when his dad left.

But to answer Alex's question—no, he wouldn't take Destiny back. They were done. He couldn't build a life with a person who had one eye on the door, someone who wasn't happy with who were together. Hell, he hadn't known how wrong things were with Destiny until he felt how right they could be with Alex.

But he still needed to know *why* she'd broken their engagement.

He had his suspicions. Mainly that he was fixated on the idea of them together, was oblivious to the reality. But if there were other things, he wanted to know so he could deal with them head-on. He couldn't change and do better in another relationship, give that person a better version of himself, unless he knew what he'd done wrong.

He chanced a glance at Alex, who was driving the car with her elbows so she could open her stubborn water bottle.

"Can I help you with that?" he asked.

"Nah, I've got it." The metal cap spun free, and she guzzled the water. A trickle escaped the side of her mouth and trailed the curve of her breast. What he'd give to be able to lap at that rivulet.

He returned his gaze to the mountains.

Alex had insisted on one night only, and he'd accepted her terms, but maybe she could be persuaded to reconsider. He was a work in progress and might not be deserving of her, but he couldn't give up without trying.

"We're getting close." Alex plugged the bottle into the cupholder between them. "Carmelita's the next exit. We shouldn't push on to the dig site today. By the time we catch a ferry across the river, then hike into the jungle, and you have your showdown, we'd likely be there past dark. I am guessing you don't want to spend the night at your ex's dig site."

His lower back muscles clenched. It was one thing to have an uncomfortable conversation with Destiny. It would be another to be forced to stay in her company, on her turf, for an overnighter. Especially with Alex in tow.

"That's correct."

"Good, then we'll check into the hotel, get dinner, and a good night's sleep for once."

Bo grinned. A good night's sleep was the last thing he wanted. Staying in town tonight felt like a reprieve, and another shot at getting Alex back in bed. Nothing was guaranteed, but the odds had increased. All he needed to do was roll the dice.

She signaled, then cut across two lanes of traffic. "We'll head to the dig site first thing."

"We can take our time," he said.

She gracefully eased them through narrow, mazelike streets clogged with people and cyclists. It was better that she was behind the wheel. Even if he could drive stick, this situation would probably trigger a panic attack.

"There's not much time to take," she said. "I need to be back in Azul Caye by Saturday."

"For work?"

They stopped to allow an adult leading small schoolchildren holding a rope across the street in front of them.

"No, to pay my loan shark."

The clench in his back returned, vicious and tight. A memory wormed its way to the surface. *Bo's a smart kid*, his dad had quietly pleaded with his mother. *He'll get scholarships. I need the money we put aside for college. You've got to help me. These guys'll break my legs.*

"Are you in trouble?" he asked. "Do you need protection?"

If anyone laid a hand on her he'd rip them to shreds.

She flicked her gaze to him. "Jesus, Bo. No, not like that.

It's the shit with Peter. I owe money, that's all. But thank you for wanting to be my muscle."

He'd be whatever she needed him to be.

Hang on, what? Bo clutched the grab bar in front of him. He was shocked he'd thought that. Even more shocked that he meant it. This was not how he did things. He was slow, methodical, weighed all the consequences of his choices.

Until he met Alex.

"That's home tonight." She pointed toward a bright orange hotel at the end of the busy road. "They've got decent rates and a good location."

She parked in a nearby lot. He checked his phone. Two bars. Not worth the frustration of googling to check that they were in the correct place.

"Is that the Victoria Hotel?" he asked.

Alex shut off the engine. "Yep, the colonizer herself. Why?"

"Mariele made reservations for us. She said the owners are friends of hers."

Alex twisted toward him. "When did this happen?"

"This morning." He unbuckled his seat belt. "I wanted to have a backup plan. I liked the jungle, but I'm definitely more of a hotel kind of guy."

Especially if it led to another night with Alex in his arms.

"But *I'm* the tour guide." She wrinkled her forehead. "You don't need to make backup plans, especially if it means conspiring with friends of mine."

He laughed, but she did not.

"There's no conspiracy." He slipped out of the Jeep, then folded down the passenger seat. "She did us a favor, that's all."

"I don't need favors."

"I do, because I learned something about myself on this trip."

A lot of things, actually. Like brunette spitfires were his type. That having an idea of what he wanted from his future was good, but only if he balanced it by living in the moment. That his preconceived notions of the right way to do things could—should—evolve. And that the place where he was born wasn't necessarily the place where he belonged.

"What's that?" Alex huffed.

He grabbed his duffel. Though they were freshly laundered, he'd like to burn the clothes he'd been wearing for three days.

"I'm a little vain, and I don't want to look like I slept in the rough when I see Destiny. So I wanted to make sure we had reservations at a hotel. Why are you mad about this? I booked two rooms, if you're worried that I'll crowd you."

"I'm not worried." Her unbuckled seat belt slithered upward. "And I'm not mad. But if I don't like the room, I might hammock it up in the parking lot."

Ouch. She'd rather sleep in a parking lot than near him? Oh, hell, maybe she'd done some pondering of her own and regretted last night.

"Suit yourself," he said casually.

"I usually do."

Check-in was brief and uneventful. As the clerk slid their keys into paper envelopes, she said, "There you are, Mr. Ferguson and Miss Stone—adjoining rooms on our top floor. The view is amazing from up there."

"Thanks," they said in unison.

As they waited for the elevator in the Creamsicle-colored lobby, warm currents of air drifted from the lazily spinning ceiling fans.

"Adjoining rooms?" she asked.

"Yeah." He'd leave it at that. "I like Mariele's place better."

Alex shifted the straps of her pack. "Why? The decor?"

"No, because we had a nice time there."

Understatement, obviously. His world had tilted on its axis last night. But he wouldn't push Alex when she so clearly preferred not to talk about what happened.

The elevator doors opened. Inside the car, he poked the button for the third floor.

The short, silent ride ended with a ding.

"We're this way." She jerked her head to the left. Her room came first. "This is me. Want to meet up for dinner at seven?"

What he *actually* wanted was to follow her into her room and kiss her until her lips were the same deep pink as the skin of the dragon fruit he had with his breakfast.

"Sounds good," he said.

Inside his room, he flopped onto the bed. The closed adjoining door was like a pulsing, living thing. Was Alex on the other side, twisted up in these same confused feelings? Last night was supposed to be get-it-out-of-his-system sex. Instead of putting out the flames of attraction that had flickered since they met, last night had blown them into an inferno.

Alex under him, on him, wrapped up in his arms, screaming his name.

He threw his forearm over his eyes. He couldn't stay here. Staring at the silent door would drive him crazy.

A walk would clear his head.

He stuffed his phone and key into his pocket, then slipped from his room. The hot press of the afternoon sun soothed him. Should he check his work emails? Nah. No one had texted. It was gratifying that the team was rising to the occasion.

But he still needed a distraction.

Before he could talk himself out of it, he dialed his sister. She picked up on the first ring.

"Your cat's a dick. Since you've been gone, she's peed in my shoes, unraveled all the toilet paper and swatted my phone off the counter. You owe me a screen."

He laughed. "She has abandonment issues."

"Same same." Delilah sighed. "Did you find what's-her-face?"

"Del, you haven't forgotten her name."

"I prefer not to say it. I'm afraid she'll appear like Beetlejuice. So, what's the deal? You found her, obtained closure and are coming home to save me from this she-beast, right?"

He strolled along a dirt path. "Almost. We're at a hotel near the site. Apparently, it's across the river, then at the end of a long hike, so we'll go there tomorrow."

"Who's we?"

"I hired a guide." A colorful collection of small houses lined the street. Most of them featured solar panels and freshly planted gardens.

"What're they like?"

"Alex is…" He riffled his hair. "Infuriating. She never sticks to a plan. Leaps without looking. But she's smart and competent, so everything works out. And she's told me to relax at least a dozen times."

"Is she pretty?"

"Gorgeous." He avoided the path of tourists riding rented bikes.

"Oh boy," Delilah said. "You like her, don't you? Like, *like* her like her."

His stomach squeezed. He'd dialed his twin for distraction, but maybe he'd actually called to ask her to gut-check him on this. She was no fan of Destiny's, but she'd also tell him if he was a jackass for falling for someone else.

"What if I do?"

Delilah laughed. "You poor dope. Let me guess—you've tied yourself in knots because you're *supposed* to be devoted to what's-her-face, and if you were wrong about her, you're wondering what else you might be wrong about in this tidy life you've built for yourself."

He pursed his lips. He *was* predictable.

"Maybe."

"I've said it before, but you could really benefit from therapy."

He pictured Del pinching the bridge of her nose like she always did when she was exasperated with him.

"So, what's your plan now, big brother?"

"What do you mean? Ch'ooj Creek is the plan."

"Still? Your ex did you a favor by breaking things off. Take the W, Bo. Ask this Alex lady to dinner, enjoy paradise, then come home and save me from your cat."

Delilah's advice sounded easy to follow, but he had to prove to himself that his wounds were closed, fully healed, not prone to infection. Anything less wouldn't be fair to Alex. If, of course, she was interested in him for more than a night.

"I'll be home soon, I promise. But I have to talk to Destiny first."

"No, you don't, actually, but I hope you find what you're looking for," Delilah said. "Tell Alex I said she sounds cool. Oh, I've gotta run. Dinner's here."

He checked his watch.

Six o'clock in Baltimore, which made it five here. He'd best return to the hotel, hit the shower and clean himself up for dinner.

★ ★ ★

Alex pursed her lips as she checked her reflection in the hotel's full-length mirror. The fluttery cerulean sundress's bias cut skirt was wild. Demure on the right, sexy as hell on the left. The bag Mariele dropped in Betty had contained this dress, strappy sandals and a G-string, all with the tags still on. Mixed among the clothes was a bottle of pinot noir, chocolate bars and condoms.

So. Many. Condoms.

She should change back into her T-shirt and shorts or she'd give Bo the wrong idea.

Before she could kick off her sandals, someone knocked on the front door. Bo? Maybe, but then why hadn't he knocked on the adjoining door, the more intimate door?

Jesus, who called doors intimate?

"Coming," she called.

Maybe he wanted a reset on their client/guide relationship. Which was *fine*. Perfect, actually. Even if he didn't fall back in love with his childhood sweetheart, he'd be leaving for the States by the weekend.

Message received, buddy boy.

She'd keep *all* the distance, starting now.

"Alex?" Bo knocked again.

"Coming." She flung open the door, and her traitorous knees wobbled.

His whole ensemble was casual sexy. The rolled sleeves of his white button-down, his three days of scruff, damp hair to which he hadn't applied any product so his slight curls ran free…all of it *worked* for her.

Which was bad, because she was supposed be building walls higher than Machu Picchu with him.

"Hi." She entered the hall and closed the door behind her. "What are you in the mood for?" Quickly, she added, "Dinner-wise, I mean."

Her cheeks flamed.

"There's a place down the street that smelled fantastic when I went for a walk earlier."

"Lovely day for it."

Lovely day for it? She didn't use words like *lovely*. *Bastard, jack-ass, grumpy*, sure. But never *lovely*. The elevator doors opened, and she shifted her weight as it glided toward the first floor. She was searching, searching, searching for a conversation starter that involved neither the weather nor her messy feelings about last night, but came up empty.

Great.

The elevator doors opened, and they crossed the lobby in silence. Ugh. *This* was why she shouldn't mix business with glorious, mind-blowing pleasure. These next twenty-four hours would be pure torture if they couldn't talk.

Bo held the door of the hotel open for her. The warm air, heavy with precipitation, clung to them. Her lack of a migraine indicated the humidity wouldn't change into heavy rain. Nothing would delay their trip to Ch'ooj Creek in the morning.

"Thanks," she murmured.

The lowering sun's tangerine beams kissed the varied greens of the trees covering the hills below them. A wispy cloud danced across the otherwise clear sky. The moon and stars would be out in full force later. Ordinarily, she'd scope out a spot to enjoy the celestial show in a town mostly free of light pollution.

But inviting Bo to go for a starlit stroll *might* send the wrong signal...

"Pretty sunset," he said.

"Yep." She widened her eyes. It was like her throat was corked.

Belizean life teemed around them. Tables dotted the street outside cafés, and delectable aromas emanated from within. Her stomach rumbled.

Maybe dinner would inspire conversation?

Probably not, but it was a decent theory.

"Here we are." Bo stopped at an eatery with a thatched roof overhanging its porch.

Alex paused. This was one of those grab-and-go places with picnic tables scattered nearby. No intimate nooks, inhibition-lowering bottles of wine, or seductive candlelight. Just laminated menus and a shared table they'd park at for fifteen minutes while they ate.

"Looks fantastic," she said.

When it was their turn, Bo told the cashier, "One fryjack stuffed with eggs, chicken and cheese, one with honey, two sides of watermelon and two waters, please."

Alex twisted toward him. Did he order for her? No, no, no, that was not happening. That was how things started with Peter. Little helpful no-big-deals that led to her opening the door to the company's accounts.

I'll take care of dinner, take your time with the tour… Don't worry about the bills, I'll handle them so you can focus… I'll make the deposit run to the bank, you stay here while the next group arrives…

"Uh, hang on." Alex stepped forward. "Cancel the fryjack with honey, please. I'd like the…" She scanned the posted specials. "Conch soup and a Belikin, please."

The cashier wrote the ticket. "Anything else?"

"No, that's it for me." Alex reached into her purse.

"I've got this." Bo slipped a few bills from his money clip.

She wouldn't argue. The more he paid, the more of her own cash she'd be able to fork over to Belisle. Frankly, it was a nice change of pace from Peter, who'd advised her to pay for everything so they could write it off as company expenses.

She shifted to the section of the porch where people waited for their orders.

"That was super 1950s of you," she said as Bo joined her. "Do you always order for people? Or is that a special treat just for women?"

"No." He palmed his neck. "Sorry. That was dumb. But you liked them so much this morning, and you came back to the cottage so fast... I wasn't sure you'd finished your breakfast. I figured they were a slam dunk."

"I don't like to eat the same thing for every meal, Bo. I prefer to mix things up."

She peered up at him. The soles of these silly sandals were thin as cardboard. She didn't like how much taller than her he was this evening.

"I should've realized that." He folded his arms, causing the muscles in his forearms to bulge, basically at her eye level. "Is conch soup good?"

Not as good as his forearms...

She lifted a shoulder. "Never had it."

"Why order something you might not like?"

"Because if I stick to the things I know I like, I'll never discover if anything suits me better. It's not exactly a huge risk." She flipped her palms to the sky. "I like conch fritters. I like soup. But if I hate conch soup, the worst that'll happen is I'll go back and order a fryjack. Food's the lowest threshold for adventure out there, Bo. Live a little. Eat the weird stuff."

"We lived a little last night," he murmured.

Something sizzled through her. Delight or fear, she couldn't tell. It might be both.

She held up a finger. "We're not talking about that, remember?"

Alex twisted away from him.

They'd eat, they'd go back to the hotel, they'd sleep, they'd go to Ch'ooj Creek and then they'd say goodbye. That was always the plan.

"Alex…"

"Shh. I like this song."

Total lie. The thick beat of the Caribbean music playing over the loudspeakers was unfamiliar. Swear to God, if her mother called at this moment, she'd answer. *That's* how desperate she was to avoid a conversation about last night.

"Bof?" a kitchen staff member called from the pickup window. "Order for Bof?"

She wasn't proud of the laughter that pealed from her.

"That's you," she said. "Bo F."

"I'm here." He collected their tray of food while she claimed an empty half of a picnic table. A small family—mom, dad, and a toddler—occupied the other half. She made a silly face at the happy kid, who giggled and made the face back.

Bo eased his legs over the bench, then took his plate from the tray. As he pushed it toward her, the robust soup—more of a stew—slopped over the paper bowl's edge.

"Sorry," he said.

"No harm no foul." She dipped her spoon into the dish.

This was *so* good. The tomato-based broth, diced vegetables and morsels of tenderized conch made for rich flavoring. Some kind of spicy pepper dazzled the back of her throat.

"You have to try this." She held the spoon out to him. Ah, hell. She'd forgotten their awkwardness. But what was she supposed to do now? The spoon was mid-dangle.

He rucked up his forehead. "You sure?"

"It's soup, not my virginity," she said.

Heat circled her cheeks. What was *wrong* with her? Better question—what was wrong with him? He was letting her wave her proffered spoon for an embarrassing amount of time.

"I wasn't confusing the two. What's that chunk in the middle?"

"Pumpkin, I think."

"Pumpkin? Really?"

"Don't be afraid of something different."

He leaned forward. "I'm not afraid."

She regretted her offer. The simple skim of his lips against her spoon made her catch her breath. His mouth was responsible for half her orgasms last night.

He leaned back. "It's good. I bet there's Old Bay in there."

She stirred the contents of the bowl. "Old what?"

"Old Bay. It's a seafood seasoning from Baltimore." He chugged water. "Conch soup tastes like Maryland crab soup, but spicier. And with a hundred percent more pumpkin."

"You can take the boy out of Baltimore, but you can't take Baltimore out of the boy." The crisp bubbles of the Belikin lightly scrubbed her throat as she washed down the spices.

"The boy has rarely left Baltimore. Well, Maryland, anyway."

She tilted her head. "But you've got the whole East Coast there for the exploring. Mountains, caves, oceans, lakes, rivers, everglades…"

"I didn't have many reasons to leave."

"Curiosity is reason enough."

"I'm learning that." He locked gazes with her for an eternal second, then took an enormous bite of his meal.

She wished she'd gotten the conch soup *and* a honey fry-jack. No, no regrets. This was delicious. Trying something new was always the way to go.

"Want some?" he offered.

"No thanks," she said.

Lighthearted people ambled past. Chatty, giggly and sun-kissed. Like they'd materialized from a tourism brochure. She and Bo were like that yesterday, which led to last night…

"So." He cleared his throat. "We should talk."

She raised her eyebrows. Bo was breaking the rules. This was a first.

"Can we meet up at seven tomorrow to get a jump on the last leg?"

The soup curdled in her stomach.

"Logistics is what you want to talk about?" Alex dropped her spoon. "Seven a.m. is perfect, but that means an early night. See you in the morning."

Fourteen

"Alex," he called after her. "Alex, come on. Wait."

She did not wait.

Bo tossed the remains of their meal in the trash, stacked the tray, then chased after Alex. She wove through the crowd with ease, almost as though she were trying to lose him. The bright blue of her dress was a teasing beacon in the fading light.

Man, she was fast.

As he burst into the hotel lobby, the elevator doors dinged shut. He took the stairs, but she must have beaten him to their floor. She was nowhere to be seen.

He let himself into his room and roughly shut the door behind him.

Bo couldn't win.

He tried to play by her rules, respect her decrees. All day, he wanted to tell her that he was desperate for her. It was too soon for him to feel that way, but damn if that wasn't where his heart was. She'd declared that conversation off-limits, though, which meant he couldn't share ninety-eight percent of what was running through his head. It had taken him ages to land on a neutral topic, and even *that* had pissed her off.

He tore off his watch and tossed it onto the nightstand.

Despite the ceiling fan and the temperate night, his room

was too warm. As he paced, he unbuttoned his shirt. Back and forth, back and forth, passing the adjoining door to her room. She was on the other side of it. Getting ready for bed, avoiding him, and unilaterally deciding when they could talk to each other and which topics were acceptable.

Well, fuck that.

He knocked on the adjoining door, three decisive raps that stung his knuckles. The door opened fast, like she'd been waiting there with her hand on the knob.

"What?" she demanded.

The fire in her eyes was impossible to miss, and her scent made his mouth water. Rationality was leaving him, fast. He held on to the sides of the door frame to stop himself from barreling into her room.

"Today's been awkward as hell because I'm trying to respect your wishes." He tightened his grip on the door frame. "But I am absolutely *not* sorry, and never will be, about last night. Even though you don't want to talk about it, it's impossible to shut up about the best night of my life."

The fact that she hadn't slammed the door in his face was encouraging.

With his heart hammering in his chest, he continued. "I've been thinking about it all day."

She licked her lips. "Perv."

"Please, Alex." He held up his hand. "Stop. Don't undercut this with jokes. Give me a minute to say my piece, okay?"

"I…" Alex dipped her chin. "Sorry, go ahead."

He took a deep breath. The last time he'd gone to confession, he was fourteen. Admitting to Father Cronin that he resented his parents and all the expectations they'd dumped on him was *nothing* compared to what he was about to say aloud.

"Here's the thing that knocks me sideways." He shifted his grip to the top of the door frame, knuckles aching as he resisted the urge to touch her. "After four days, you see me clearer than someone I was with for *years*, a person who knew me since I was a kid. The way I am with you—the bickering, the laughing, the dancing—I'm not like this with anyone else. Hell, I didn't know I *could* be like this. And this guy? I like him. I like who I am when I'm with you. So I need you to know that our onetime thing has changed me forever."

She blinked a few quick blinks, then one slow one.

He could drown in her dark brown eyes.

"Are you done?" she asked.

His heart dropped out of his chest, through the floor and deep into the roots of Belize. This was worse than Destiny's text. At least he hadn't been facing her during an epic rejection.

"I…" He dropped his arms to his sides. "Yeah, I'm done."

"Good." She walked to her front door.

His insides shriveled. "I'll just… Good night."

"Stop." She slipped the do-not-disturb door hanger on the outside knob, then closed it and flipped the security bar.

Tendrils of hope threaded through him.

"Why?" Asking was a gamble, but he had to take a chance.

"Because that is the nicest, sexiest thing anyone has ever said to me. If we have tonight, that's a gift. And I would like to unwrap that gift."

His legs wobbled. "What about you, though? Do you like who you are with me?"

"Very much so. I'm still me, but…calmer? Definitely more punctual." She placed her palm in the center of his chest. "Are you nervous? Your heart's racing."

"I'm not nervous. I'm happy."

The gentle collision of their lips set off fireworks in his chest.

Alex slipped her fingers into his waistband and tugged him into her room. "There's something I want to come clean about, too."

"What's that?" he asked.

She shut and locked the inner door. "We're not hitting the road at seven."

She looped her arms around his neck. The incredible mix of citrus and vanilla scents that he'd been drunk on for days washed over him. He brushed errant curls from her face. The mischievous spark was gone from her eyes, replaced with molten desire.

For him.

"You've got that right."

As he covered her mouth with his, her welcoming lips opened for him, drinking him in. All that mattered was the luscious, infuriating woman here in his arms.

"What changed your mind?" he murmured.

"Last night wasn't enough," she said simply.

It would never be enough.

The thought nearly knocked him from his feet. He wanted to know everything about this woman. What did she look like first thing in the morning? Was she grumpy before coffee? What was the meaning of the ruby, emerald and sapphire tattoos inside her wrist? Did she come while she was on top?

That last question gave him an idea.

He waltzed her toward the balcony. With a flick of the latch, they were outside.

"You wanted to check out the view?" she asked.

Yes, but not the way she meant it.

"We're on the top floor. No one can see us." He kissed her, then eased onto the chaise longue. "Straddle me."

"Sir, yes sir," she said.

The weight of her against his hips, pinning him, massaged him through his shorts. He gripped her thighs. The moon had risen high in the lavender sky. Bright winking stars surrounded Alex, like she was the center of a constellation.

"Ever done it outside?" she asked.

"Never."

"You'll like it." She flipped the panels of his shirt to the side, then ran her hands up his torso. She trailed kisses down his neck, to his chest, then lightly bit his nipple.

As he hissed, he tunneled his hands into her hair.

She ground against him. "Why, Mr. Ferguson, you seem a little excited."

"More than a little," he growled.

"*Hugely* excited." She nibbled his jaw. "Enormously excited."

"And overdressed."

"I can take a hint." She helped him wriggle out of his shorts, then slid her hand along his cock while cupping his balls. "Do you like blow jobs?"

"Do I—" *Hell*. Her mouth was all hot, wet, heat.

And *pressure*. Oh man, the intense pressure had his eyes rolling back in his head. But no—*no*. Eyes open, because if he fully immersed in the glorious feel of her tongue on him, he'd come in forty-seven seconds.

She let him slip from her lips, and he was equal parts relieved and devastated.

"Don't leave," she said.

No problem. He couldn't trust his legs.

She returned with a condom. "Let me dress you for the occasion."

"Be my guest."

Alex slid the latex down his shaft, slowly, carefully, torturously. Next, she reached under her dress and shimmied. Off came her flimsy excuse for underwear. She swung her leg up and over him, torturously close.

"I'd ask if you're ready," she said. "But it's pretty obvious that—"

"Get down here," he begged as he fisted the folds of her dress.

With a gleam in her eye, she sank onto him. They both moaned, and he couldn't believe he'd ever agreed to one night with Alex. Her dress rucked up, revealing the tanned, athletic expanse of her thighs.

Heaven.

He squeezed her hips. "Ride me."

The bright moon limned her skin in silver as she rose and fell against him. He flattened his palm to her chest, felt her heart beating as she moved with him. Her core squeezed him, slick and tight, like she couldn't bear to let him go. Emotion thickened his throat. This was how sex was supposed to feel, this marriage of joy and fun and lust.

"Alex," he gasped. "I—"

"Shhh." She touched her finger to his lips. "Just enjoy the ride."

Alex clutched his shoulders to brace herself as she rocked her hips. God, *yes*. Bo filled her, stretched her, massaged her from the inside. Best of all, the sensation she'd had last night, the one that delighted her and scared her, was back.

In his arms, she felt safe.

His hooded gaze was worshipful, and she basked in it. In the moonlight, his blue eyes were dark, shaded with his desire for her. He slid his hands from her hips, the traveled up her back, to her...

"What are you doing?" she gasped.

"Letting your hair loose." He tugged the elastic from the end of her braid. "I want you wild."

While she rode him, he unbraided the simple style. She groaned as he tunneled his fingers through the thick waves, massaging her scalp.

"Beautiful," he said. "You're so damned beautiful."

Closer. She needed to be closer to him.

"Take off my dress," she said.

He obliged without hesitation, and the blue cotton landed on the balcony floor.

"Oh, this pink bra." He cupped her breasts through the material. "I've been fantasizing about taking this off you since the creek."

"What's—" *Oh*, that thrust hit the fabled spot inside her. "Stopping you?"

He popped the closure that lay against her sternum, and her breasts spilled out.

"Touch me," she gasped. In this desperate state, she had no time for hints and hopes. "Like last night."

He buried his face against her, licking, sucking and gently biting, a perfect repeat and *exactly* what she craved. This time, he did it with a fistful of her hair, tugging her head backward. The night was thick with stars. He belted an arm around her back and scooted them forward on the lounger.

"Lean back," he said. "Arms behind you. Hold on to the edges."

After last night's mind-blowing pleasure, she took his instructions without debate. At this slight angle, she was completely open to him. He worked her clit while his other hand skimmed her body.

"Pull your legs up onto the chair," he said, voice hoarse. "I want to try something."

"Like this?" she asked, her ankles hooked behind his thighs.

"Yes," he said, and began to thrust.

Oh, sweet Jesus. His cock hit her magic spot, over, and over, and over.

"I love watching your face," he moaned. "I love everything about this night."

Warning bells sounded in her head.

She reached for him, wrapped her arms around his shoulders so she could kiss him quiet before he said something they'd both regret. They were sealed together, chest to chest. His hands threaded in her hair as he thrust into her, again, and again, groaning.

The tension building within her was unstoppable, a train barreling toward its destination. A bit more, a bit further, and…

There. The stars above were nothing compared to the ones on the backs of her eyelids.

Bo's moan followed hers, and his cock quivered within her. They were a tangled mess of arms and legs and sweat.

"What was that position?" she breathed.

"Cowgirl at first, then lotus. With some of my own special tweaks."

She ran her fingers through his hair, then whispered, "Good. Now I can ask for it again."

As the morning sun beat through the balcony's glass door, sweat slicked Alex's aching head, her neck, her back, and between her breasts. She tried to flip the covers back, but couldn't, because the reason she was so hot anchored the linens to her midsection.

Bo had slept in her room with her.

A fluttery thrill rumbled through her, at odds with the nugget of pain thumping her temples. He'd offered to go back to his room last night, but she couldn't bear to let him go, wanting to savor him all night.

But could you blame her? Look at him.

In sleep, he was the picture of peace.

Hot peace.

With his scruff, his firm jaw, his broad shoulders and taut midsection—but not *too* taught, because she liked her lovers to feel like men and not marble. She'd clocked all those features that first day back at the resort, but then she got to know him and somehow his personality made him hotter.

That and the way he interacted with the world. His curiosity was unquenchable, and thoroughly endearing. And she had no idea how, but he understood her. He took her less-than-stellar moments, the grumpy ones where she said things she wished she could reel back, and he didn't take them personally.

She'd made him sleep in a jungle, ride for hours on a dirt bike close enough to a cliff that he'd had a panic attack, then forced him into an intimate dinner with her best friends. He'd done it all with no complaint.

Last night, when he said the past three days had been the best of his life? She had to shut him up before he made her cry. Alex knew she was a lot. But unlike everyone else, Bo didn't demand that she be less.

And that scared the hell out of her.

At Mariele's, she thought she could hook up with him

feelings-free because he was *taken*. But he'd said things last night that sounded like he wanted more from her, something she couldn't give to someone who was leaving her. Something she couldn't give to anyone, because the last time had almost cost her livelihood, home, and father's legacy.

The air in the room thinned.

She needed to get out of here, now, before he woke up and hauled her in tight. She wouldn't be able to resist, and that would shove her into deeper emotional shit. Later today, his ex would have a light bulb moment about *precisely* how stupid she'd been to let him go. Bo would take her back, because they had history.

And there *she'd* be, the sad, pathetic woman who hadn't learned her lesson and once again handed her heart to someone who'd pummel it to rubble.

Hell to the no.

She refused to be that person. Alex gingerly picked up Bo's hand, like she was trying to relocate a sleeping pit viper. She set it down in the valley between their bodies, then slid from between the blankets, down to the floor.

Shit. Where were her clothes?

After the lounge chair, they'd come inside, split a protein bar since neither of them had finished their dinner, and ended up back in bed. Bo had remembered to collect the clothes they'd shed before locking the balcony door.

She peeked at the chair in the corner.

Yes. Victory. She quietly flailed until she caught her bra and the hem of the dress, then slithered into both. Now her sandals…

"Alex?" Bo's morning voice was rough. "What are you doing on the floor?"

She stiffened. "Nothing."

Excellent response.

"Do you plan to stay there?"

She trailed her finger against the floorboards. "It *is* super-comfy, but no. I have some stuff to take care of before we head north."

He riffled his fingers through his hair. "Give me a minute and I'll come with."

"Oh, you don't have to." Unsexy though it might be, she wiggled into her underwear and tugged them up. "Stay. Ease into the morning. Order room service."

He sat up in bed. "I'd rather come with you."

"I hear you, and I receive that." She placed her hand against her chest. What in the name of pop psychology hell did she just say? "But it'll be faster if I go it alone. I'll be back in a half hour, forty-five minutes tops. And then we can deliver you to your ex. Go team!"

She fist-pumped the air.

Clearly, she'd lost her mind.

"Alex, wait." Bo sat up.

Space. She needed space. She'd be fine later today when he ran toward his ex like she was gold at the end of the rainbow. She wouldn't barf with envy.

"No thank you."

She snatched her hiking boots and her bag, then ran from the room. She sprinted toward the stairwell and down to the lobby before Bo could find his glasses and come after her.

Why had she devolved into such a weenie?

Because you're afraid.

Her phone buzzed in her hand. She flipped it over to answer and tell Bo she was fine. Except the name on her phone wasn't Bo's. It was a call she wouldn't take in a million years, except this morning was already fucked, so she might as well.

"Mom?" she asked.

"*Hello*, honey. How *are* you?"

"Fine." Alex bumped open the front entrance's doors with her shoulder. "What's up?"

"We haven't spoken in three months, and *that's* the best greeting you can offer?"

Yes, because at the end of their last conversation—during which Alex had been bitterly complaining about the deluge of bills and paperwork caused by Peter's embezzlement, that she was stressed and drowning in the effort of trying to make things right—her mother's sage, helpful advice had been for her to "get a grip."

She pinched the bridge of her nose. "Was there something you needed?"

"A mother can call her daughter to check in."

"She sure can. You usually don't, is all."

"I'd like to call more."

"Nothing stopping you." Alex's shoulders bunched. "Although this is way too early."

For years, she'd been wanting her mother to show an interest in her day-to-day. Why did it have to happen on the worst possible morning?

"I wanted to be sure to catch you. We'd like to visit. It's been too long."

She creaked open Betty's door, then tossed her bag on the passenger seat. "But you said you'd never step foot in Belize again."

"Sweetheart, you know I speak in hyperbole. I miss Azul Caye, and I miss you."

Fifteen years ago, her mother divorced her father. From that point on, Alex and Julia had flown back and forth by themselves because they'd been, in her mother's words, *old enough for the adventure*. In Alex's opinion, it had been so her mother could avoid Dad's bewildered hurt.

"How does October sound to you?" Mom asked.

"I'll be here." Alex slipped on socks and shimmied into more functional, less sexy underpants that would prevent chafing. "The borders are open. And who is we? You and Julia?"

"No, actually. My beau, Jim."

"You're still dating? You were with him before the holidays, weren't you?"

"That's right. And on that note… You'll be thrilled to know the flechazo has found me again. Are there any elegant venues that would be suitable for a reception in town? We'd love a destination wedding."

The flechazo, the unexpected strike of love. Or, as Alex liked to call it, bullshit. This would be her mother's third marriage since she'd moved back to Southern California. Alex had not been shocked when the others ended in divorce inside of three years.

No one fell in love at first sight.

Alex tipped her face skyward. "Aw, Mom, really?"

"Yes indeed, Alexandra." A smile suffused her mother's voice. "We're not officially engaged, but we're headed that way."

"And let me guess." She jammed her foot into a boot. "This guy has a fortune."

"He's comfortable, yes. But more importantly, he's kind and has a sharp intellect. Your father was the only person I married for love alone, but after we went our separate ways, I needed to be more…career-minded."

Gross, gross, gross.

"Mom, I need to let you go. I have errands to run."

"Understood, and I'll be in touch more frequently. But don't tell your sister about this. She's in finals and I'm trying not to distract her."

As always, Mom treated three-years-younger Julia like a daughter, someone whose emotions should be protected, handled with care.

Whereas she treated Alex like a bestie.

"Love you," her mother cooed.

After ending the call, Alex wiped her hand down her face. This would be her mother's fourth marriage, and she wanted to do it *here*. On her father's turf.

God, love made people assholes.

Alex twisted the keys in the ignition. She would *not* wallow. Not today, not ever.

She had shit to get done.

Fifteen

Well, hell. Bo rested his elbows on his tented knees. He wasn't a genius, but Alex's pattern was obvious.

At night, she was real with him. Vulnerable. Let down her guard and let him take control, and let herself be someone other than an adventurous Amazon capable of handling whatever life tossed at her. Once the sun came up, she turned back into someone who was embarrassed by the fact that she had a heart.

A passionate one, at that.

One that matched his own.

Alex's dash from the room was hard not to take personally, but he understood it. She needed solitude to process her feelings. Seemed a little unhealthy to him, but he couldn't do much about it. Their story had an ending before it had even begun.

All through his shower, he debated trying to keep…whatever this was…going with Alex. Once upon a time, he'd thought long-distance could work if a couple had history to lean on, but obviously not, or else he wouldn't be here.

Could he and Alex date while living a couple of thousand miles apart? No, ridiculous. One of them would need to move. Alex didn't have much family here, but her livelihood was more deeply rooted to Belize than the mangroves. He, on the other hand, could work from anywhere. His family was in Baltimore, but they were fine. Mom had hit her stride as an office manager, and Delilah was wrapping up her PhD. They didn't need him like they used to.

He wiped the steam from the bathroom mirror.

The fact that he was thinking about the logistics of a long-distance relationship with a woman he'd met days ago and who had, in fact, just run out the door was completely out of character for him.

Then again, the nearly bearded man staring back at him was different from the one who'd left his house on Cathedral Street nearly a week ago. The change wasn't just about the facial hair, the tan, or the handful of weirdly shaped bug bites he'd google as soon as he had a decent signal. No, he was calmer, more confident, less convinced he needed to plan out everything.

Like today, for example.

He still had no idea what to say to Destiny.

Hey there. Fancy meeting you here. Why'd you dump me? What'd I do wrong?

His opening line didn't matter. All he needed to do was find out when and why her feelings had turned, then say goodbye.

He reached for his toiletry kit, then patted shaving cream on his cheeks. The razor ran smoothly over his jaw. Minutes later, and for the first time since he'd arrived in Belize, the clean-shaven face he was accustomed to seeing stared back at him. *Ouch.* The aftershave stung. Must've nicked himself.

He tossed the hand towel on the side of the sink.

What to wear? Not many options in his duffel.

His short-sleeve button-down had seen better days, but it would do. Destiny said it brought out his eyes. After dressing, he shimmied the velvet box from his backpack. The hinges creaked as he opened it. The hammered metal rings cuddled in the corner.

When he'd boarded the plane, he intended to use this heirloom as proof that he wanted Destiny—and the life they'd planned—back. But he'd changed. Not just while he was here. No, it started when Destiny left. Nothing outrageous. He'd started cooking, jogging around the neighborhood instead of on the treadmill, grown his hair, and tried on clothes that fit his frame better... The goal had been to fill the extra time, but the small evolutions suited him.

Over dinner one night, he wondered why he hadn't experimented with change before.

Because. Delilah had flicked a morsel of bacon-wrapped pesto pork tenderloin at him, which Lorelai had gobbled up happily. *You default to what's familiar to avoid disappointment. It's invigorating to try new things.*

He'd never admit it, but his sister had been right.

Since he'd arrived in this paradise, a more important, profound shift had occurred. He wasn't constantly worried about what *might* happen, or how to game the result to get what he wanted. Nope. He was present, focused on *now*.

Was that Belize, or was it Alex?

Through the adjoining door, he heard her enter her room. Bo clapped the velvet box shut and wedged it into the plastic bag containing his chargers, passport and emergency pair of clean socks.

"Hello?" he called.

The adjoining door framed her. His heart twisted. In her rumpled state, she was gorgeous. The tension that vibrated from her, though, and the wariness in her eyes... He wanted to fold her in his arms, but she looked like she'd spring apart at the slightest touch.

"Get everything handled?" he asked.

"Yeah, and..." She widened her eyes. "You shaved."

"I did. Today was the first day I had running water and my razor." He tossed the kit into his duffel bag, then zipped it shut. "Am I bleeding? You're staring."

"I haven't seen you without stubble. It's different."

"Is it bad?"

"No, just different." A delightful pink blush washed over her cheeks.

Wow, he loved it when her gaze lingered on him.

She retwisted the bun of her hair, tightening it. "Are you ready? We're all gassed up, bananas and apples acquired. We can hit the road."

"Did you want to shower first?"

She popped her hand on her hip. "Why? Do I look like I need to shower?"

"No, you're beautiful." He'd love it if she stayed like this, with his scent all over her.

Primal, obviously. But he couldn't deny it. He leaned in the frame of the open door, unable to resist invading her space.

She knitted her eyebrows. "Don't."

"Don't what?"

"Call me beautiful." She clamped her hands around the back of her neck. "Because after we complete our contract, you will leave Belize, and it will be much, *much* easier if we stay away from all the squishy nice things you might be tempted to say to me."

It killed him to keep his hands to himself.

"So I'm your client again? That's all? Like you said that first day."

"You have to be, Bo."

"What does that mean?" he asked.

She wiped the air clear between them. "Nothing, because we aren't a thing."

That stung worse than the aftershave.

"Alex—"

"Actually, I *will* take a shower." She nudged him backward into his room. "I'll meet you downstairs in fifteen. There's a breakfast stand outside the hotel if you want to grab something."

Before he could object, she shut the door and twisted the lock.

Damn, that hadn't gone as expected. But everything Alex had said was true. He'd leave, and it would be easiest if they didn't complicate things further.

But oh, he wanted to.

Complicated was apparently where all the good stuff was.

He slipped his backpack on. The stand outside smelled delicious. Fryjacks, naturally. He'd gain ten pounds before he left this country. When he reached the front of the line, he ordered two stuffed with ham, eggs, potatoes and cheese, and one plain with honey.

By the time the order was up, Alex appeared.

"I ordered extra if you're hungry," he said. "Plain with honey."

"I..." Her eyes glistened. "I already ate. Ready?"

So that was how it would be today. Back to the invulnerable Amazon.

"Ready," he answered.

For what, he couldn't say. Because for the first time in his adult life, he truly had no idea what he was doing.

Alex swallowed past the lump in her throat. She knew how to deal with dicks like Belisle. Avoid, but if she must interact, level them with a frosty attitude and exit the situation.

But Bo's brand of authentic, gentlemanly nice was disarming. Aside from her father, Mariele and her sister, people who were nice to her generally wanted something from her. With vanishingly rare exceptions, the world was transactional.

What did Bo want from her?

Nothing, apparently. He folded the paper that had been wrapped around his breakfast, then tucked the neat square of trash into the bag, probably so he could recycle it later. She sighed. Looking out for others was Bo's code.

She'd be dumb to read more into it than that.

Alex shifted Betty into a higher gear, then massaged her temple. This was different from her usual migraines, and the cloudless sky agreed. Must be because she hadn't slept much, had skipped breakfast and was dehydrated.

"Can you uncap my water?" she asked.

Their fingers brushed as he handed it to her, sending a flutter through her chest. Without thanking him, she swigged the tepid liquid, eager to cage this veering-toward-ferocious headache. Maybe escorting the man on whom she had a hopeless crush to his one true love was to blame for her general blechiness.

Her queasy stomach rumbled.

Bingo. And, hell.

"You sure you're not hungry?" Bo said. His freshly shaven face made him look five years younger. *This* was the face of a computer-based employee who never saw the sun. Much different from the man who'd been tramping across the country with her these past few days. The man who'd caressed her, kissed her, filled her until she barely remembered her name. And yet she found this version just as attractive, like a newly discovered cavern she'd get to explore.

"I'm *fine*," she lied.

She upshifted again.

"Can you slow down? I'd like to arrive alive."

And draw today out longer than necessary? No thank you.

"Don't be a backseat driver."

"Technically, I'm a passenger-seat driver." He leaned over. "All I'm saying is you're going like, thirty kilometers over the speed limit. If you get pulled over, any time we make up will be zeroed out."

"*If* is the key word, because I never—"

A siren *blooped* behind her.

Goddammit. Belize's finest was on her tail. The bright cherry on the dark blue pickup truck's dashboard flashed its red lights.

"This is your fault." She gripped the wheel, then glanced in the rearview mirror. "If you hadn't been distracting me, I would've seen him and slowed down."

"I was *telling* you to slow down."

She chewed her lip. There was an exit ahead that led to a network of roads that would take her deep into the Crooked Tree Wildlife Sanctuary. They'd waste another half day, but...

"I bet I can lose him."

"Um, please don't? It's a ticket. Not a life sentence."

It was also an expense and a hassle she didn't need.

The siren *blooped* again.

"Alex, come on," Bo urged.

"Fine." She flicked on her indicator, then downshifted. "Promise you won't freak out?"

He lifted his shoulder. "Why would I? We'll be on our way in fifteen, twenty minutes."

If her luck held, yes.

If it didn't... No. Today she was choosing optimism. Alex lowered the window, then returned her hands to the wheel.

"Hello, ma'am," the woman officer greeted her. "Do you know why I pulled you over?"

Ugh, she hated bullshit questions. Like she was a naughty child who needed to think about what she'd done. But if she played dumb, maybe the officer would let her off with a warning.

"Was I speeding?"

"Correct." The officer peered at Bo. "Hello, sir."

Bo waved. "Hello. Nice day, isn't it?"

"I didn't mean to speed," Alex said. "My friend here hasn't seen his fiancée in months, and he's here to surprise her with a visit. She's in Ch'ooj Creek, and I want to make sure that we catch the ferry."

"Ma'am, it's reckless to drive one twenty-eight in an eighty-eight, and the ferry runs every fifteen minutes. There's no need for that kind of speed. License and registration, please?"

Shit.

"Yes, Officer. It's in the glove box." She fished out the registration and handed it to the officer. Fortunately the flask was still in Bo's backpack. "My license is in my purse behind my seat. Okay if I get it?"

"Yes."

In an easy, calm motion, Alex withdrew her wallet from her purse, then slipped her license from her wallet. The picture had been taken ten years ago, when she'd first moved to Belize as a fresh-faced twenty-year-old. Back then, she was full of hope and mischief. Today, she was mostly full of regret. Hope still owned a sliver of her soul, though.

She passed it to the officer. "Here you go."

"I'll be back in a moment."

Cars whizzed past while they waited silently. They were *definitely* going faster than 128 kilometers per hour.

Next to her, Bo paged through the pristine Jeep Wrangler manual.

"What are you doing?" she asked.

He lifted a shoulder. "Reading."

"Who reads the manual?"

"Me. I like to know what I'm missing."

"Most people don't do that." Alex shook two pills from the container of acetaminophen she kept in her purse.

"Yeah, well, I'm not most people."

He had that right.

Bo continued to flip pages, reading the print like he held a bestseller. Was he that interested, or avoiding conversation with her? If it was the latter, that was officially a new low for her.

The officer returned to the car.

"Ma'am, did you know your license expired?"

Bo snapped his head up.

Alex feigned surprise. "Gosh, I had no idea."

"You must have received renewal notices." The officer thrust a clipboard at her with a printout of Alex's infractions. "Between that, the reckless driving and your failure to display an insurance sticker, I could arrest you or impound your vehicle."

"Now I know why you were worried I'd freak out," Bo said.

She glared at him, then took the clipboard. Five hundred dollars? She tamped down the urge to complain about Belize's system for license renewals and registrations. No one had time to hang out in the traffic department during the dry season, least of all someone grinding like her.

"Officer, I will take care of the renewal as soon as I'm

home in Azul Caye. My registration is actually up to date. Any chance we can strike out that charge? I had to get my windshield replaced and haven't gotten the new sticker yet."

That was a half-truth. She *might* have received the sticker. The mountain of mail at her house contained an impossible number of depressing bills and paperwork.

"I'm glad to hear it," the officer said. "But the fine is for failure to display. Please sign at the bottom to acknowledge receipt."

Alex's fingers trembled as she signed. Five hundred dollars was a weekend's worth of tips at the resort.

She handed the clipboard back to the officer. "Can we go now?"

"That depends. Sir, do you have a valid license?"

Oh no no no. The officer couldn't order him to drive her precious Betty. She and this car had been through death, breakups and births. Specifically, the nest of baby red coffee snakes that hatched behind the passenger seat last year. This car was like a sister to her.

Which Jules would find offensive.

"Me?" Bo asked. "Yes, but it's from the US. Maryland, specifically."

"May I see it, please?"

Bo complied without hesitation.

The officer inspected the license, tilted it in the sun, then handed it back. "Looks good. Licensed Americans are permitted to drive in Belize, which is fortunate for Miss Stone. If you weren't here, I'd be forced to call a tow truck."

Oh man, the impound lot was the seventh circle of hell. Any escape hatch from dealing with that nightmare was one she would happily dive through.

Bo slipped his license back into his money clip. "Okay, but I don't—"

"Thanks, Officer," Alex said. "He'll drive."

The officer nodded, then touched the bill of her hat. "I'll wait in my car until you're on your way."

As soon as the officer was out of view, Alex rested her forehead against the steering wheel. Bo might grind Betty's gears to dust, but it's not like she had a choice. Alex sighed, then dragged herself upright.

"Let's get this over with." She unbuckled her seat belt, then clicked the button on his.

Bo muttered, "Hope you're a good teacher."

She was not. But what she lacked in patience, she made up for in determination. Julia had been hopeless at first, but Alex eventually coached her through it. She'd be able to do the same for Bo.

Ideally with fewer tears.

As he settled into the driver's seat, Bo adjusted its position to accommodate his longer legs, then fiddled with the mirrors. The passenger seat was comfortable, but strange. Like when she was a kid and had to wear an eye patch after scratching her cornea. Everything was slightly to the right of where it was supposed to be.

"Okay." Bo wrapped his fingers around the gearshift. "What do I do?"

Alex laid her hand on his. He'd deftly worked wonders with her body—he could drive Betty. As long as he relaxed, that was. With knuckles this tight he'd wrench the knob off the shifter.

"Okay," she said. "Lower your shoulders, and take a deep breath."

She'd been joking, but he did it, and the tension in the air eased.

"A manual transmission requires active participation from the driver. You've got to pay attention to the engine's subtle cues for more gas, a higher gear, et cetera. Betty will be honest with you, and if you don't treat her right, she'll give you a fit."

"Sounds like you."

"Ha ha." Alex rolled her eyes. "There are three pedals down there—clutch to the left, brake in the center, gas on the right. The clutch is what you'll use to shift into a new gear. Jam on the clutch a few times to get a feel for its resistance."

"Got it." He pumped the pedal. "So I hold this down when I start the Jeep, right?"

"Yes, but don't start yet." She removed her hand from his. "Want me to signal when it's time to shift? Tap your knee or something?"

He flicked his gaze to hers and held it. "If you touch my knee, I'll run us off the road."

This was not a situation when her heart should flutter, but flutter it did.

"Oh. Then I'll refrain." She gestured toward the gearshift. "The pattern on the knob tells you which gear slot is which. Always start in Neutral, then shift to First. It tops out at about fifteen kilometers per hour, and then you'll shift to Second. That tops out at thirty, then you'll shift to Third, et cetera. We'll end up in Fifth since we're on the highway."

"Is this written down anywhere?" Bo lifted his ball cap, riffled his hair, then yanked the cap back down tight. "I do better with written instructions."

"You can't read and drive. We'd better go or that cop'll wonder what's up."

He glanced in the rearview mirror. "She'll love it when I stall."

"Then don't stall." Alex clasped his forearm. "You can do this, I promise. It's like dancing. You'll get the rhythm of it."

He leaned back on the headrest, then closed his eyes. After a few seconds, he popped them back open, then swiveled his attention to her. More flutters. She hated that her lack of attention to mail had resulted in this, but loved that he was game to try.

"What do I do first, again?"

She pointed to the gearshift. "Put her in Neutral, press the clutch with your left foot, and the brake with your right."

He followed her directions. "Next?"

"Start the ignition."

As he twisted the keys, Betty rumbled to life.

"See? You're a natural. With your feet still on the clutch and the brake, shift into First."

He slotted the gearshift like he'd done it a thousand times. "Like that?"

"Exactly. Ready?"

"No, but I don't have much choice."

"Correct. Take your foot off the brake."

Bo's knuckles blanched with tension as Betty crept forward. "What do I do? Hit the gas?"

"A little. This is the dancy part. Ease off the clutch while you're gently giving her gas."

Betty bucked and lurched.

Alex clutched the grab bar. "Okay, so that was more like a mosh pit, less like a waltz."

So he *wasn't* perfect at everything. Refreshing. But she'd get him through it.

The cords stood out on his neck. "I can't do this."

"Sure you can," she said. "Even if we stall, no biggie. You'll just try it again. It's not like we have much of a choice."

She glanced in her side-view mirror. The cop was still on their tail.

"We need to get to at least third gear before we leave the shoulder. Hear how the engine is revving? That's how you know it's time to shift to Second. Just do the same thing as before—foot off the gas, then press down on the clutch. Once it's all the way down, shift into Second."

"Why is this so complicated?" He glanced down to make sure he was shifting to the correct gear, then returned his gaze to the road.

"It's not, and that was damned near perfect. Time for the clutch and gas pedal dance—ease off the clutch as you ease on the gas."

The gears grunted.

"Sorry." Bo grimaced.

"Don't be. You're doing great. Getting to Third is the toughest shift." She glanced at the speedometer, then crooned in an off-key voice, "Foot off the gas, clutch, shift the gear, ease off the clutch, and on the gas."

"That is a terrible song." His movements were smoother this time, more assured.

Betty picked up speed.

"Nice, Bo. You can merge onto the highway now. Keep giving her gas."

He flicked on his indicator. The highway was clear, so he didn't have to worry about merging with traffic. They were cruising at a decent clip. The high hum of the engine signaled that he should shift again.

Before she could prompt him, Bo hit the clutch and shifted into Fourth, then hit the gas.

"Well, look at you, Bo Ferguson."

"I'm getting the hang of it." He grinned, but didn't take his eyes from the road.

Figures that by-the-book, steady-as-she-goes, dances-a-mean-salsa Bo was a natural. When she learned to drive stick, she'd done everything too fast and stalled. Dad had kicked her out of the driver's seat and lectured her about her impulsivity on their way home.

She covered her mouth as she yawned.

The late nights with Bo were catching up with her. The soothing rhythm of the tires didn't help, nor did the warm Belize sunshine. Behind them, the cop peeled off the highway.

"Hey." She tapped him on the shoulder. "Pull over. Officer Friendly ditched us."

"I've got this." He glanced at her. "Take a break. Eat one of those fryjacks you won't admit you want."

She was done pretending she wasn't hungry. The last stomach rumbles had been louder than the engine.

"You make a persuasive argument." She pawed through the plastic bag for the wrapped honey fryjack. Though it had cooled, its heavenly scent enveloped her as she opened the paper. "But I'll take over in fifteen."

"We'll see," he said.

She didn't appreciate the smarm in his tone and would address it…just as soon as she finished this life-renewing fryjack.

Sixteen

Bo snuck a glance toward Alex. Not the safest choice while driving an unfamiliar car in a foreign country, but he'd risk it. She'd dozed off after breakfast. The curls dancing around her face and hypnotic rise and fall of her chest were more awe-inspiring than a sunrise.

She deserved to rest.

If circumstances allowed, he'd let her sleep all day. Unfortunately, they were nearing their highway exit, and he had no idea where to go from there.

"Alex?" he murmured.

She didn't wake. He rested his hand on her leg, then rubbed his thumb along the outside of her knee.

"Allllex. I need you to wake up."

She startled awake with a snort. "Huh? What? Who?"

"Sorry." He returned his hand to the gearshift. "It's just me. I need you to wake up. We're getting close to the exit."

"The what?" She scrubbed her eyes. "What time is it?"

"Eleven fifteen."

"Why'd you let me sleep so long?"

"You were tired."

She crossed her arms. "Because someone kept me up late and wanted to leave by seven."

"We didn't actually leave until eight, but sorry about the late night." His lips twitched into a grin. He wasn't sorry, not even a little bit.

"Liar." She opened her bag and withdrew a tin of mints. "Want one? These are the nuclear-powered kind that turn your breath to ice."

"I'm good." He eased toward their exit. "Should I down-shift on the off-ramp?"

"No and yes." Her back popped as she stretched. "You don't have to shift while you're reducing speed. Once you've stopped, hit the clutch to put her in Neutral, pull the emergency brake up, and we'll switch back."

"You're not supposed to drive." The words were out of his mouth before he could stop them. "That cop—"

"Is nowhere near here. Look, I appreciate you being a rule-follower and a team player, but you've got limited experience driving stick on a highway. City driving and off-roading require expertise, even if the expert is unlicensed. I'd rather risk a ticket than your safety."

She had a point. He wouldn't want to accidentally drive them off a cliff or run over schoolchildren. At the stop sign, he shifted into Neutral.

"Emergency brake," she said.

"I know." He yanked it up and they swapped seats.

Once she settled behind the wheel, Alex shot from the stop sign—and immediately jammed on the brakes to avoid hitting a teenager who cruised out of an alley on a bike. She was right. City driving was tricky. Cars stopped abruptly to unload passengers, pedestrians ambled across the street, scooters zipped between cars, and Alex handled it all with grace.

He, on the other hand, would've given himself carpal tunnel with all the stops, starts and shifting the crowded streets required.

"Have you been here before?" he asked.

"I've been everywhere." She threaded the Jeep through a narrow alley. "But yeah, I've been to this specific town a bunch of times. This is the pickup point for a couple of Mayan ruin tours."

He folded his arms. It might be dumb, but the fact that she'd been here before nagged at his heart. This past week had been full of adventures and fresh perspectives for him. It'd be sweet if he and Alex could share something new.

"Almost there," she said as she turned.

He wanted to say that this couldn't be a road, but he held his tongue. He'd said that before during this journey, and while he hadn't exactly been wrong, he hadn't exactly been right, either. Roads or not, Alex had taken him everywhere he wanted to go. Just longer than they planned, and that extra time with her had made this the best trip of his life.

So he said nothing, and enjoyed the slow, gravel-crunching ride.

"That's the line for the ferry," she said. "Just up ahead."

She joined a short queue of cars entering a fenced-off area. The roadside was thick with bright green trees, beyond which lay a slice of calm river. As the truck in front of them veered to the right, an official wearing a neon safety vest flashed a palm, indicating they should stop.

"He won't give us a problem about the registration, will he?" Bo tipped his head in the official's direction.

"Gee, I'm not sure." She cut the Jeep's engine. "Let's ask."

"What are you—"

Alex hopped out of the vehicle, then marched up to the man

who'd stopped them. Was she bribing him or—wait, nope, that wasn't what was happening. The official caught her up in a bear hug and spun her in a circle, causing Alex's blue dress to flutter in the breeze.

Who the hell was *this* guy?

Jealousy tightened his gut. *Don't be a caveman. She said she comes here often, so he's basically a coworker.*

Hmph. Bo had never picked up and spun any of his coworkers.

When the burly man finally set her down, Alex gestured for Bo to join her. Great. Just what he needed. An introduction to a ruggedly handsome dude who obviously could handle rough-and-tumble situations. Whereas he could only handle them if Alex was with him.

"Paul," she said as Bo approached, "this is my client Bo Ferguson. And Bo, this is my friend Paul Wickham. He runs the ferry that crosses the Mopan."

Oh, *he* gets to be a friend.

Paul stuck out a meaty paw. "Nice to meet you. Hope she isn't giving you too much shit."

"Nah." Bo clasped Paul's hand in an iron death squeeze. Stupid male dominance nonsense, but Paul was clamping his hand, too. "It's an appropriate amount of shit."

Paul shifted his gaze between them. "I'll bet."

"How's the outlook?" Alex shaded her eyes and fixed her attention to a floating carport connected to steel cables that stretched across the river.

"Clear skies, calm river. Last ferry back's at six."

"Perfect," she said. "I'll be on it before then."

Bo cut his gaze to her. She said that like she was coming back without him. After everything he'd said last night, everything that had happened between them, she still thought he would leave her. Bo flexed his fingers, wanting to draw her in close, reassure her.

"You know the drill, Alex," Paul said. "Drive onto the ferry and your passenger walks."

She saluted. "Aye-aye, captain. Bo, you stay here."

Great. He'd hang out with his new best friend Paul.

Alex hopped into the Jeep, then proceeded toward a different man waving her forward. The metal ramp groaned slightly as she drove over it, but the ferry didn't flinch at the additional two tons of weight. She eased into a gap next to a pickup truck, then cut the engine.

Paul gestured to the ferry with his clipboard. "You'll want to go that way, champ."

Alex cupped her hands around her mouth. "Move your ass, Bo. You're holding us up."

"We better go. You don't want to see her angry."

His back tensed. "Already have."

"Not fun, is it?" Paul gestured to the ramp. "After you."

He didn't love the familiarity Paul had with Alex, and he outright disliked how much a guy like him made sense for her. But he'd be a hypocrite of the highest order if he laid any of those cards on the table since Destiny was a simple hike away.

Bo hitched his pack higher on his back.

As soon as he and Paul were aboard, the other staffer flipped up the corrugated metal ramp and tethered it with a cable. Paul spun a metal crank the size of his arm, and the ferry embarked on its journey across the river. The disturbed water smelled like the Patapsco at home, a nutrient-rich combination of moisture, plants, soil, and an undercurrent of decay.

"This is hand-cranked?" Bo leaned his forearms against the

railing. The ride was surprisingly smooth. "When you said ferry, I pictured the Staten Island Ferry. This is more like a floating carport."

Alex dropped her forearms next to his.

"Engines aren't necessary to get us across thirty meters of calm river. They'd pollute the water and degrade the environment." She bumped her shoulder against his. "Sorry there's no instruction manual for you, though."

He twisted his lips. He didn't *always* need the manual.

Alex exhaled. "Once we're across, the dig site's not far. Are you ready for that?"

"Maybe?" Bo gripped the railing. "I can't believe I'll see her so soon."

"Is that a good thing or—"

The ferry jerked like it had been caught by a giant fisherman. Alex stumbled, and he caught her. The feel of her in his arms, even accidentally, was the most right thing in his world. *Eat it, Paul.*

He kept his arm wrapped around her. "What was that?"

"Probably a giant crocodile." She pushed off him, and he reluctantly let her go.

"Really?" He peered overboard.

"No, Bo. I'm just fucking with you." She pointed at a pulley toward the end of the ferry. "Looks like a kink in the cable."

"Atención, por favor." Paul addressed the eight passengers. "We have a problem with the cable. We need to go back to repair it."

"How long does that take?" Bo asked.

Paul lifted a shoulder. "Not sure. Depends on whether we have to cut and weld anything. A couple of hours, max."

"Oh no, we're not doing that. Hey Paul, catch!" Alex tossed

her keys to him. "We're on a mission with a ticking clock. I'll snag those when we get back."

Bo touched her elbow. "What are you doing?"

"What are *we* doing, is more like it. We don't have any more time to waste, Bo. If I don't make it back to Azul Caye by tomorrow…" She rubbed her forehead. "I need to get back, that's all. We'll wade across the river and hike to Ch'ooj Creek. Grab your gear."

She hadn't led him into danger yet, but his feet refused to budge.

"Don't be scared." Alex opened the driver's door and tossed supplies into a backpack. "Kids tube down this river. There aren't piranha in there or anything."

"I'm not scared of piranha." He peered over the side of the ferry. "I'm scared of bacteria."

She laughed. "The Mopan is one of Belize's sources of potable water, you weirdo."

"Oh." He lifted his cap and scrubbed his hair. "I'm not used to that. If you fall into Baltimore's Inner Harbor, they throw you antibiotics instead of a life preserver."

"Just one of the many reasons I'm thrilled to be living in Belize today." She slammed the driver's door shut, then patted her pocket. "Let's go."

Alex cut through the other passengers.

She'd never held her tongue well. One of the many reasons she and her mother lived on different continents, actually. If a repair forced her to sit still and they picked up their undistracted chitchat, she was sure to admit it sucked balls that she was leading this kind, funny, exasperating man to a person who didn't deserve him.

She obviously couldn't say *any* of that. Not without completely embarrassing herself.

Nope, much better to dive into a river than sit still with her reality.

"Alex, we don't need to wade across the river."

She patted her pocket. Yep, her knife was still there. "We do, Bo. I told you, I need to be back in Azul Caye tomorrow, and you leave in two days, and—"

"I can always change my reservation."

She stopped midpat. Bo, who had plans on top of plans, was suggesting that he could rip up his itinerary. What the what? Something suspiciously like hope curled in her chest, but she wouldn't let herself feel it. Easier not to have hope at all than have it smashed.

Unless…

Damn, Bo was hard to read today. He'd crossed his arms and stood stock still, as inscrutable and frowny as a Mayan royal stelae carving.

"But you're *so* close." She glugged water, then tossed it into her pack. "A three-kilometer hike to the ruins, then another five kilometers to the dig site. It'll take two hours, tops. And calling it a hike is misleading. More like a country ramble along mostly paved roads."

She leaned in to whisper and caught a fresh whiff of his scent. Different today, since he'd used the hotel shampoo and soap to shower, but still him underneath. Getting closer to Bo was dangerous to her self-control, but she couldn't risk Paul hearing her lie.

"These guys always say it'll take a couple of hours, but then they can't get the part or something dumb like that, and suddenly you're fighting a crowd for a hotel room." She patted

Bo on his biceps. "Let's avoid all that hassle and swim across. The river is low and calm."

Without waiting, she slipped over the railing and into the water. *Brrr.* She held her backpack above her head and found her footing in the shoulder-high river. *Onward.* Bo would follow. She was sure of it. He'd shown that his self-preservation instincts disappeared if she led him toward adventure.

She gazed into the clear water.

Crocodiles weren't unheard of around here, but they weren't active when the sun was high and hot. No, the biggest concern this narrow band of the river presented would be incompetent tourists ramming a kayak into them.

She slapped her neck.

And bugs. Lots and lots of bugs.

The water rippled around her as Bo caught up. "Dragging me into a river might seriously reduce your tip."

"Well, joke's on you, because it isn't customary to tip the business owner."

They were midriver now, at the deepest part. The water was now up to her chin. He snaked his arm around her, catching her to him.

"What are you doing?"

He hefted her against his hip. "I'm eight inches taller than you. Wrap your legs around me and hold our bags out of the water."

She thrilled at his warm, solid touch. Bo was support, personified. Even when they annoyed and confused each other, he came through for her.

"I bet you'd like that, wouldn't you?"

"Dry bags? Yes, very much."

"The legs part." She pretzeled her legs around his waist.

"This is weirdly chivalrous of you, but if it gets deeper, I can swim."

"Seems fine, and this way, our stuff stays dry."

He had a point. He also had a handful of her ass.

A giant bird swooped overhead, its shadow skimming the surface of the river. It circled twice, then landed on the shore and dipped its head into the water.

Bo squinted through his water-speckled glasses. "Is that a blue heron?"

"Yeah. Are you an undercover ornithologist?"

"They live in Maryland, too. On the eastern shore." Bo snorted. "Can you imagine if you were a heron from Maryland and you found out you could have been living in Belize all this time?"

"That's true for people, too," Alex said.

Bo shifted his grip on her. "I suppose it is."

"It's hard for some people to change their home base, though. Not me, obviously. But when I moved here my mother acted like I'd shat on the graves of my ancestors. As if four generations ago my California family weren't farmers in Germany. My Belizean half...who knows? Some of my roots could go back a millennia here."

"My ancestors emigrated from Germany and Ireland to Baltimore and stayed there."

"Everyone?"

His shoulder rose under her palm. "Pretty much. Until my dad moved to Vegas."

Bo sidestepped an unidentifiable dark shadow.

"Did he move for work?" Alex asked.

"That's what he'd say, but no." Bo's chest expanded against her embrace. "He's... He's a gambling addict. My mom kicked him out when we were thirteen because he blew our college savings on the Preakness. He caught a flight out West, and he's been there ever since, rolling dice and swearing that his ship'll come in."

"Oh. Bo, that's just… *Oh.*"

All the tumblers fell into place, like Bo had handed her the key to his psyche. When his dad had left and his sister had been ill, his mom must have been focused on emergencies only. This sweetheart of a man had served as a stabilizing force for his family ever since he was a kid.

Risk would have been a luxury.

"That's a lot of ohs."

"You make so much more sense now."

"When did I not make sense?" He shifted his grip, clutching her tighter.

"Since I met you." She slid her hand farther up his shoulder. Purely for non-falling-off reasons.

"I am totally normal."

"Oh, sure, totally. The pathological need to plan things out, to read instruction manuals, to try to predict the future with stats and algorithms. A completely normal level of hating risk."

"Other people do that stuff."

"Not to the extent that you do, Bo. And…*ohhhhh.*"

A lightning bolt of clarity struck her. Bo wasn't desperate to win back Density because she was his perfect woman. Nope. The truth was as clear as this section of the Mopan River. Bo Ferguson couldn't tolerate people disappearing from his life. He'd said he didn't want to get back together with his ex, that all he wanted was closure.

For the first time on this trip, she believed him.

"There we go." Bo set her down in the shallow water at the river's edge.

She clutched the backpacks tight, wishing they were his ex's neck. Density *must* have known Bo's dad ditched their family, that it cost him his childhood, and the ripple effects that impacted his life to this day. How could she do the same thing to him?

Heartless.

The squishy mix of mud and decaying vegetation beneath them tried to steal her hiking boots, but she managed to keep them. Good thing, too, since hiking barefoot for kilometers was not advisable.

Once they'd reached the road, she waved to Paul.

"Is he shaking his head?" Bo asked.

"Yeah. He probably thinks I'm crazy."

"He's not the only one." Bo took his backpack from her. "Which way do we go?"

"Over here." She ducked into a copse of trees. Now that they were out of the water, she could be honest with him. There was *one* thing that worried her about wading across the river above all else.

"Why?" He remained on the path. "That's not a road."

"Nope, but it's semiprivate." She yanked her dress over her head. "Check me for leeches?"

Seventeen

"Leeches?" Brambles crackled under Bo's feet as he approached Alex.

He kept his gaze respectfully fixed on her face.

Tried to, anyway.

But come *on*. There was only so much a gentleman can stand. A gorgeous mostly naked Alex, begging him to inspect her for...

"That's right. Leeches." She retwisted her hair into the bun that had come loose during their crossing. "This time of year should be fine, but better safe than sorry."

He winced. "Gross."

"Don't be squeamish."

"I'm not."

"Then would you please check me for leeches?"

She presented the beautiful column of her back to him. It took every ounce of his willpower not to wrap his arms around her.

"Anything?" she asked.

He cleared his throat. "No."

"Great. Little invertebrate vampires." She delved her hands into her panties and smoothed her hands over her ass. "All clear in the southern territory, too. I'll check you in a minute. Did you pack any sunscreen?"

Dammit, he should have thought of that. "No."

"I've got plenty." She rifled through the bag she'd hung on a tree branch, then squirted a coconut-scented dollop onto her palm. "Catch."

She tossed the bottle to him.

Good thing she'd brought some. Prolonged sun exposure would flame his homebody self until he was the same color as a freshly steamed crab. As he slathered the cream along his face, arms and legs, she shook an aerosol can.

"Mind getting my back with bug spray?"

"Sure." He took the can from her, twisted the top open, then let loose a foul-smelling cloud on her skin. "Jesus, what *is* that?"

"Chemicals that'll stop bugs from eating us alive."

He read the label. "It has DEET in it? Great, we're destroying the environment and courting cancer."

"Don't be such a priss." She took the can from him and continued spraying her arms, legs and torso. "I only use this for long hikes in the woods. Have you ever been attacked by Botlass flies? They're sneaky assholes. You don't notice them until your ankles are speckled in blood, and then by evening you want to claw the flesh from your legs."

"You paint a vivid picture."

"Thank you." She sprayed a pool of it into her hand then wiped it on her face. "Okay, Bo. Your turn for leech inspection."

Respectful gaze, respectful gaze.

He glanced at the tops of the trees. "Do you mind getting dressed first?"

"Am I distracting you?" She cocked her hip to the side. "In my utilitarian bra and bikini briefs?"

She could be wrapped in a full-length parka and he still wouldn't be able to focus. Since they'd met, even when she annoyed him with loud music and bad decisions, he only had eyes for her.

"Very much so."

"Oh. Okay then." She plucked her dress from the broken branch where she'd hung it, then slipped it over her head. "Better?"

No, but yes.

"Yeah, thanks." He reached behind his head, fisted his T-shirt, then yanked it off in one swooping motion.

Alex widened her eyes.

"What?" He surveyed his chest. "Am I infested?"

"No, sorry. I've only seen you when the lights were low, and…" She flashed him a double thumbs-up. "You're good. Leech-free on the front. Turn around?"

He swiveled away from her. His smile was impossible to hide. Clearly he wasn't the only distracted person here.

"All clear," she said.

He stiffened as a cold jet of bug spray swathed his back. "A warning would have been nice."

Now she was hosing down the small of his back, his thighs, his calves.

"I can get my legs," he said through gritted teeth.

"Eh, I'm already back here." She circled around to his front, continuously spraying as she went. The chemical mushroom cloud made him cough.

"There." She twisted the cap. "No bugs are getting through that. Hey, though—check for leeches under your shorts. They especially love ballsacks."

Talk about a boner-killer.

"We couldn't have put the bug spray on *before* swimming through the leech-infested water?"

"Nope. I try not to disturb the hydrosphere."

He could get on board with that, but he still wanted to be leech-free. As Alex crunched over to her bag, Bo cupped his balls. Clear, thank God. None on his ass either. If he'd known about the possibility of leeches and their love of ballsacks, he would've insisted on staying on the ferry.

Definitely next time.

What was he talking about, next time? And it was a good thing he hadn't known *this* time. If he had, he'd still be on the ferry among strangers. He wouldn't be here in the woods with Alex.

The risk had been worth it.

His shirt skidded and clung to the oily residue coating his skin as he pulled it on. He plucked the thin material from his chest to encourage the bug spray to dry.

"Which way do we go?" he asked.

"I'm glad you asked that. I'll make you a deal, Bo Ferguson."

His smile bubbled his cheeks. The last time she'd said that, they ended up naked. "What's that, Alexandra Stone?"

"For the next few hours, we need to be *very* tour guide and client. Snacks, friendly banter, the occasional elbow grab if one of us stumbles. That's it, though, because I like you. A lot." Despite her grin, a shadow passed over her face. "But you need to wrap this—" she circled her finger like a lasso "—up before I'm comfortable with us talking about everything me liking you this much might mean. Deal?"

His chest tightened. This was a different kind of naked. But if Alex could be vulnerable about her big complicated feelings, he could be vulnerable, too.

"Deal, because I like you a lot, too." He shouldered his backpack to keep from hugging her and immediately violating the terms of their deal. "But I still don't know which way we go?"

"Oh, you wanted actual directions instead of metaphorical ones?" She zipped up her bag, then pointed. "Thatta way."

He shouldered his backpack. Years—maybe decades—of leaves and pine needles *shushed* under their feet as they made their way back to the road. The hot beams of the midmorning sun produced short shadows from the thick line of trees flanking the road.

"Do you believe in ghosts?" Alex asked.

He laughed. "Your small talk is so strange."

She lifted a shoulder. "Good conversation makes the time pass. And you, Bo, give good conversation."

"I do?"

"Yes. The only time we aren't talking is when we're asleep or in bed."

Her observation sent a happy ripple through him. He'd spent so much of his life keeping his head down and churn out good work so he could be helpful to his family. He liked that Alex noticed things about him. Observed him.

Got him.

Best of all, she enjoyed him.

"That's funny, because I'm not chatty. Not usually. My sister says I'm in my head too much, trying to figure out the dozens of ways things could play out."

"Are you kidding? There are times when I've wanted to throttle you to get you to stop talking. Why are you different here?"

Because of you.

No way he could say that out loud, though. Confessing

that he could talk to her more easily than anyone else on the planet would be like throwing down a gauntlet. A challenge to all of the rational, logical, well-thought-out reasons that they were a temporary match.

So he went with the next truest thing.

"Everything's new here." He gestured to the trees. "At home we don't have palm trees. There are no hand-cranked ferries, casual strolls to pyramids, red macaws, chocolate made from cacao beans from a farm down the road. There are no jungles, or—"

A low growl thickened the air.

Bo shoved Alex behind him. "What's that?"

"Bo, it's okay. We're fine. It's just a howler monkey. They're not dangerous." She pointed to the top of the tree line. The boughs of the pines dipped and bowed like a seesaw as a small black creature leaped from one thick branch to another. "That noise is the only defense mechanism they have. They won't hurt us."

"Are you sure?" His adrenaline-fueled heart knocked against his ribs.

"I'm sure." She handed him a pouch of water. "So, I was thinking about something."

Was she retracting the whole *this means nothing* declaration? Because hot damn, that would be amazing. The last time she'd used that tone, they'd been at the Sweet Winds Resort and she'd offered him the deal of a lifetime.

"I'm listening." He gulped the water.

She kicked a rock that skittered off the path. "You're about to confront your ex."

His gut tightened. "*Confront's* a strong word."

"And a correct one. What will you say to her? I can't imagine you'll get all shouty and be like, 'Hey, it's me, your tragic ex-fiancé—'"

"I'm not tragic."

"I agree, but my point is, have you rehearsed?"

He had, back in Baltimore. But none of his canned speech applied anymore. Everything had changed in the past week.

"Not much."

"That surprises me." She gestured to the empty road in front of them. "Well, if you don't have a script, whatever you go with needs to be memorable. You could make a joke? Like, 'I dig you.'"

Bo groaned. "No puns."

She couldn't genuinely be trying to help him win Destiny back. He'd clearly done a shit job of explaining that his head had finally caught up to his change of heart. Or maybe... Alex didn't like to admit she needed reassurance, and him saying things to her once wasn't enough.

"Why'd you ditch me?" she suggested. "That's a good one. Use that."

Another joke. They came fast and furious when Alex was on edge.

He wiped his hand down his face. "Alex."

"I'm sorry, I'm sorry." She clutched his forearm. "No matter what, she'll be glad to see you because her career is in ruins."

He laughed despite himself. "You're the worst. Why do you want to help me with this?"

"It's just...you've come all this way, through forests and rivers and rain." She clamped her hands behind her neck. "If she sends you packing, I don't want it to be because your lines are lame. We've got time to kill, and I'm a captive audience. You can practice on me."

"No." He shook his head. "I appreciate the offer, but she deserves to be the first one to hear what I have to say."

That was true, but not the whole truth. If he started talking, explaining his feelings, he'd confess things that Alex didn't want to hear. They only had two more days together, and he didn't want to wreck them.

"I guess I can't argue with that." She kicked another rock.

The sun rose above the tree line, blinding him. He twisted his bag toward his chest and unzipped it. His baseball cap lay against a plastic storage bag into which he'd tucked the velvet necklace box and his passport. He'd wanted to keep them safe from the river.

He grabbed his cap and zipped his bag.

The necklace would have been safer in the glove box of Alex's locked Jeep. He didn't want to risk a theft, though, so he'd kept it with him. He wished he hadn't. He almost wouldn't mind if someone stole it. At this point, the heirloom was more of an albatross than a simple necklace. He'd brought the locket to Belize for the obvious reason that Alex pointed out that first night. He was supposed to give it to his forever-person.

But he didn't want forever with Destiny.

Not anymore. That was as clear as Belize's blue sky. He'd wanted forever with *someone*, and she been his girlfriend. She'd made sense at the time. The *real* question at hand—could he be honest about where his heart was today?

"Hey, Mr. Silent." Alex elbowed him, then pointed at a park sign in the distance. "Let's visit the ruins. That's why I was asking about ghosts. If things blow up with what's-her-face, you can at least brag about climbing to the top of a Mayan pyramid. Your trip to the Jewel won't be a total loss."

This trip could never be a loss.

After all, Belize was the reason that he'd met Alexandra Ruby Stone, the person to whom the necklace in his backpack belonged, whether she liked it or not.

And he only had a day to convince her.

"Sure," Bo said. "Pyramids sound fun."

Fun was an insufficient word. When he'd first touched down in Belize, he had a specific plan revolving around getting Destiny back, or, at a minimum, closure. But Alex's spontaneous itinerary gave him amazing, life-altering experiences, and he trusted her enough to go with it.

This adventure had already changed him forever, in all the best ways.

"Try not to show so much enthusiasm." She bumped her shoulder against his biceps. "Sheesh, Bo, I'm trying to give you the experience of a lifetime."

"Oh, you have," he said.

She bit the insides of her lips, praying he would expound on that statement. They waved at tourists coming from the opposite direction.

"When's the last time you came here?" he asked.

Ugh, any question but that one. Guess they weren't going to unpack that whole *oh you have* statement.

"Six months ago," she admitted.

That was the day Peter ran out on her.

Over breakfast, she'd told him she was ready to expand the business. Stone Adventures had been deeply in the black for two years. They'd built up enough reserves to take the leap. With her father's legacy cemented, she could pivot to caves, cliffs and waterfalls, the types of tours that adrenaline junkies like her craved.

I'll update the insurance policy and the website today, he'd said with a smile.

"Who were your clients that day?" Bo asked.

"A small family—parents and twin six-year-old boys. The boys liked the monkeys better than the pyramids. I was surprised they made it to the top. I was more surprised they didn't topple off and hurt themselves. They reminded me of myself at that age. That's how old I was when I first visited these ruins."

Her dad had brought her on a special daddy-daughter date, their first official adventure together, while her mother registered Julia for preschool.

"I bet that memory's stitched in their DNA." Bo gulped his water, emptying it, then dropped the reusable pouch into his bag. "*My* family's idea of adventure was dinner on the other side of town."

The sweet, clean scent of the mountain air soothed her senses. Her earlier tension headache had dulled, too. Nature was the best medicine.

"Then I'm glad you came to Belize and that I could bring you here. Everyone deserves an adventure."

Bo paused. "Wow, Alex, are you okay?"

"Um…yes?" She raised an eyebrow. "Why?"

"Because that sounded sincere."

"I can be sincere, you jerk." She lightly punched him in the shoulder. "It hurts, but I can do it."

There was a more direct route they could have taken to Ch'ooj Creek, but after their night at Mariele's, Alex had to bring him to this place. These pyramids were special to her.

Sacred.

She'd never brought Peter here. Deep down, maybe she'd sensed he was an asshole.

"Wait, you said you were here six months ago. Wasn't that when you broke up with your ex?"

"Why do you remember *everything*?" Peter was the last topic she wanted to talk about. "And I wouldn't call it breaking up. I came home from this trip to find his clothes and passport gone. He didn't even leave a note."

She kicked another, bigger rock, and fantasized that it was Peter's head.

"You must have been out of your mind. At least I got a text."

"Density still gets zero points." Alex lifted her chin to enjoy a light breeze. "I *was* out of my mind, until after I found the empty bank accounts and hefty credit card bills. Then I was very much *in* my mind, and furious. After I filed a police report, I crawled into a bottle of rum for a weekend. On Monday, I was back to business with a spiky hangover because I was—am—determined to pay my vendors and protect my dad's legacy. The only silver lining in all this is I got out of visiting my mom for Christmas."

The past six months of extra hustle had cut Alex into something new and hard. But the man hiking next to her, trying to hide his startle every time one of the monkeys let a roar rip, had reawakened the teasing playfulness that had gone dormant when Peter took advantage of her trust.

Hmm. Scratch that. He wasn't walking next to her so much as slightly ahead.

"Hey Bo? I'm the one who knows how to get there, remember?"

"Oh, sorry." He dropped back to rejoin her as they rounded

the big bend in the road. "There was a map posted back there…
but you're right. You should lead."

Good. She wanted to be next to him when the pyramids
came into view, which should be right… About… Now.

Bo whistled, long and low.

She agreed.

Four flat-topped pyramids, constructed from mottled black-
and-white limestone, rose toward a cloud-studded sky. Between them lay flat, grassy plazas. Dozens of other tourists
explored the ruins. Good. Buzzy interest in these miracles
warmed her heart.

"There's so much space." Bo rotated a full three-hundred-
and-sixty degrees to drink in the whole picture. "How did
they create this on a mountain ridge?"

Wonder threaded his question.

A thrill bubbled through Alex. She loved it when other
people delighted in these magical places. It was like a contact
high, one that would keep her charged up for days. Her dad's
philosophy, the whole reason he'd started Stone Adventures,
was to bring people to these enchanted destinations so they
could feel the power in them and promote them to others.

A memory of her father calling *hello, old friends* when he
brought her here washed over her. He'd loved this place. Her
smile—and lack of tears—was a surprise. For the first time,
the ghost of his voice warmed her, like she was visiting him
through the pyramids.

Best of all, she'd get to introduce them to Bo.

Alex slipped into tour guide mode.

"They—the Mayans—built this city through a shit-ton of
sweaty labor and precise mathematical calculations. Listen to
this." Her brisk, solid claps echoed across the flat space be-

tween pyramids. "This layout provided great acoustics so the whole population could gather and hear political proclamations or rituals, which were performed up there."

"Rituals?" Bo's gaze tracked the level of the pyramid to which she pointed. "Like ritual sacrifices?"

She tipped her chin up to enjoy the sun on her face. "Yeah, sometimes. They believed that blood nourished the gods. They usually used animals, but for important events like enthroning a new ruler or dedicating a temple, they'd go for a human. Not their own people, though. They usually offered up a high-status prisoner of war."

"That sounds grim."

"Eh." She shrugged. "If you dig a couple of thousand years into any culture's history, you'll find some human sacrifice. Ready to climb the temple?"

She wanted to show Bo the view she loved.

He shaded his eyes. "There aren't any handrails."

"Don't be a weenie." Alex hip-checked him. "Race you!"

She took off, ignoring Bo's call to wait.

The steep stairs made her lungs and legs scream. Bo was close behind her. At the first landing, she stopped to catch her breath.

"Surprised…you…kept up." She braced her hands on her thighs.

"Why…did you…run away?" he asked.

"Because I didn't want to spend ten minutes talking you into climbing up here to see the most amazing view in Belize. I promise you'll never forget it."

He'd never forget who'd *brought* him here, either. Alex straightened, then held his elbow and gently turned him toward the view. If she wasn't guaranteed a space in his heart, she at least wanted to ensure a spot in his brain.

"It *is* amazing." After cleaning his glasses with his shirt's hem, he folded his arms over his chest. Across the plaza, Mennonite girls in purple dresses paused to inspect the friezes carved into the pyramid they just climbed.

She gestured to him. "Come this way."

"There's more?"

"This place has a lot of hidden gems." The stone blocks gritted against the soles of their hiking boots as they climbed. She led him around the corner to another set of carved stairs. Half a steep flight, a twist, a short climb to the top and...

"*This* is the view I'm talking about."

She swept her arm toward the edge of the platform. Before them, the plaza was as flat as a pool table and as green as the emerald tattoo on her forearm. Smaller gray temples lay at exacting coordinates around this ancient city. Beyond the hectare of green trees edging the plaza, blue and purple mountains stretched toward white clouds.

"Whoa," he said. "That's not profound, but whoa."

"I know, right?" She sidled next to Bo, then cleared her throat. "How does it feel to stand in an ancient space reserved for kings and priests?"

This was the question her father had asked her when he first brought her here. She'd been so little, all she'd managed to squeak was *big*. She'd meant that she felt the enormity of the place's vibe, that it seemed to reach across time and space. Her father had understood, laughed, and kissed the top of her head. There was no correct answer, but she desperately wanted Bo to feel the majesty of this place. The eternity of it.

He shifted his weight.

She wouldn't rush this. If she did, he'd spit out a typical response, and not necessarily the real one buried under all of his normal, rational tendencies.

"This'll sound crazy," he said.

Her lips spread in a smile. "Not to me."

She *knew* he'd feel it. He was too pure not to.

"I don't have the right words." He swiveled his gaze across the complex. "The hair on my arms is raised, like the seconds before a static electricity shock. And I have this weird double vision, like I'm seeing the people who are here now, but I can also see the thousands of people who would've gathered here. Which doesn't make any sense. But I guess it's a sense of... wonder. Yeah, that's it, wonder. Awe."

Alex sighed. "That was perfect, Bo."

"Everyone's always chasing happiness, but maybe what we should be seeking is wonder." His chest ballooned with a deep breath. "I get why you prefer these kinds of tours. They make me feel like a part of something bigger. Like we're all blips in time, and we should enjoy today and let tomorrow take care of itself."

He was utterly adorable, and her heart twisted. She may not have him forever, but she refused to lose this moment with him.

"Let's take a selfie." She fished her phone from her backpack, then popped the seal on the plastic bag that protected it from the river. "You can prove you climbed a pyramid."

With their backs to the plaza and the other pyramid in the background, they wrapped their arms around each other. Alex sealed herself to him, indulging in his strength and his sturdiness. As she tapped the button with her thumb, firing off shot after shot, tears prickled her eyes.

What was wrong with her?

She shoved her phone back into her bag. "Sorry. Got something in my eye."

Alex peeled herself from Bo. With her back to him, she sniffed, then dabbed her eyes with the sleeve of her dress.

"Are you okay?" Bo asked.

Argh. *Of course* he asked. With Peter, she could be in the middle of a full-on breakdown, and he would have politely ignored it and given her privacy. She would have wanted that from Peter, too, because her low feelings were best when bottled up like aged rum.

"Just overwhelmed by being up here," she said.

That was close to the truth.

"Here." He held out a handkerchief. "It's clean. Damp from the river, but clean."

"Thanks." She wiped at her eyes. Unfair. This handkerchief contained Bo's scent. She offered it back to him, but he waved her off.

"You can hang on to it."

"Thanks," she repeated as she stuffed the cloth into her pocket. "Might be a while."

By a while, she meant she was keeping it forever. She returned her gaze to Bo. He furrowed his brows under the bill of his ball cap, and whew, if he applied any more pressure to his lips they'd disappear completely.

"Alex, there's something I've been meaning to ask you."

Her knees wobbled. Years ago, a member of a tour group she'd led here had said something like that, right before dropping on one knee to ask another member of the group to marry him. Alex and the rest of their friends had cheered when the bride-to-be said yes.

"What's that?" she forced herself to ask.

He caught her hand—hell, her heart was about to pound right through her ribs—then twisted it slightly to expose the inside of her forearm. "What's the meaning behind your tattoos? When you snapped the selfie just now, it was like they were staring at me."

She slid her hand out of his grip.

Jesus, she was delusional. Had she *really* thought he'd been about to propose to her? The crazy part was—and she would never admit this to anyone in a million years—she wasn't horrified by the idea.

Obviously, she needed to get her head examined.

"Nothing super-deep. The ruby is me, the emerald is Julia and the sapphire is my dad. Those are our birthstones. Our middle names, too, in Julia's and my case. Dad wanted us to always have a stone in our name, even if we got married. Not that I'd ever change my name."

Why would she? Alex Ferguson just didn't have the same ring to it.

Heat swirled her cheeks. Was she fixated on marriage because they were almost at his ex's camp and he probably had that damned necklace in his backpack? Whatever the cause, she needed to stop, because Bo wasn't destined for her.

"So you're Alexandra Ruby Stone," he said.

"That's me." She was grateful he didn't ask why there was no tattoo for her mother. "At your service. What about you? What's your full name?"

"Boaz Jasper Ferguson."

Alex thumped her ass against the sturdy pyramid wall for support. Fate was something she didn't believe in. Luck, chance—sure. But nope to fate. Nobody's story was written, but man, sometimes there were signs.

"Jasper?" she squeaked.

Concern etched his face. "Are you all right?"

"Great. Is Jasper a family name?"

"Nah. My mom likes Jasper Johns, the artist? But since we're from Baltimore, people would assume Johns came from Hopkins. And if she shortened it to John, she thought that would be too common. So she landed on Jasper. Why?"

"Because jasper is a gemstone."

Alex had inherited her habit of christening vehicles from her father. He'd been an amateur gemologist and had preferred to use gemstones for his fleet's names. For the better part of the 2010s, the golf cart he used to scoot around the Caye was known as Jasper.

"Is it?" Bo asked.

She gulped. "Yes. The name actually means 'jewel.'"

She refused to believe that her father had pulled some afterlife strings to send Bo to her. She wasn't even sure she believed in heaven, which was part of the reason she was determined to enjoy the hell out of her life.

"Shall we go?" she asked. Movement would help her shake off the feeling that her dad was looking out for her. "I didn't mean to spend all day here."

He followed her toward the stairs. "Thanks for suggesting we stop. This was so worth it."

"That's what I do. I escort people to awesome sites and force them to pay attention."

He squeezed her shoulder. "Yes, you do."

The sincerity oozed from him. She wanted to lay her cheek on his hand *so* badly, but she wouldn't. The Jasper thing was obviously a coincidence. She was not the one for Bo, and she refused to ruin his fairy-tale return to his true love.

Even if she was pretty sure that person was an emotional troll.

"Let's go," she said. "FYI, it's more harrowing on the way down than on the way up. It's an optical illusion, but take a breather if you need one."

She, however, would not.

The faster she ripped off this bandage, the better.

Eighteen

Ahead of Bo, Alex hopped down the last few stairs. The bounce made her hair fall out of her bun and cascade into the wild, glorious curls that had curtained his face while she rode him last night.

A shiver rippled through him.

He had options. Unlike these pyramids, this wasn't set in stone. They could return, hand in hand, to the ferry, to Azul Caye, and leave Destiny to her dirt.

And then what?

Bo rucked up his forehead. *Hey, Alex, we've known each other for less than a week, but I've lived more in that time than I have in the past ten years. Could we…*

That's as far as he'd get, because Alex would run away screaming. The *whole* time they'd been on this trip, she'd insisted she was done with relationships, that they were simply satisfying an itch that two single consenting people were entitled to scratch.

And if he left now, he'd never find out what had gone wrong between him and Destiny. He *needed* that information. Not so that he could fix it and get back together with her.

No, that wasn't in his head at all.

He wanted to find out what he'd done wrong so he could do

better. Ever since Alex drove into his life in a well-loved Jeep she called Betty, he'd been evolving. Like a blue crab molting, he'd outgrown his shell. This version was still tender, but he liked himself better. He wasn't trying to be who other people needed him to be. He was just himself, and people would like him for it. One specific person might even love him, as long as he didn't screw up what they could have together.

Even though he was worried that he already had.

Bo carefully descended. By the time he reached the plaza's thick carpet of grass, Alex had twisted her curls back into a bun and seated herself on the bottom step.

"Want some?" She held out a pouch of water. "Climbing ruins makes me thirsty."

He took the water. "Thanks."

A quiet minute passed before Alex rose. "We better get on with it. Those kilometers won't walk themselves."

"Yeah" was all he could manage.

The trail's varied vegetation brushed their arms. The pungent, flowery scents emanating from the foliage took him back to their first evening together in the tent. The confessional feel of that small, secret space had been what he needed to talk about feelings he didn't understand. The last two nights had been confessions of a different sort.

Confessions he'd love to make for the rest of his life.

A growl sounded overhead.

"Howler monkey again?" he asked.

"Very good." Alex shaded her eyes and lifted her chin, then pointed. "There."

Above them, a creature leaped from one tree to another. The thick branch bowed under the howler monkey's weight, but didn't break.

"That's so weird that they're just running around up there." Bo craned his neck as another monkey and two smaller ones—kids?—followed the first monkey's path. "I've only seen monkeys in zoos."

"Because you've only spent time in cities. This is the wild, where anything can happen."

Like falling head over heels for someone he'd just met.

Alex reached for the water he still held.

After a sip, she said, "Since you won't tell me what you plan to say to her, which I *totally* respect even though I could gut-check it for you, maybe give you some pointers, can we at least talk about body language?"

He took the water back and guzzled more. "How do you mean?"

"Picture this." Alex spread her hands wide in front of them. "You emerge from the forest at the edge of the dig site. Across the way, over the heads of a dozen minions fiddling with brushes and trowels, you see her—Density."

"Destiny."

"Whatever." Alex dropped her hands. "You lock eyes. She's shocked. Do you run to her?"

Not in front of Alex, he wouldn't.

"The framing isn't quite right. She doesn't do shocked. Surprised, annoyed, mildly amused. But shocked isn't in her repertoire."

"The answer is yes, Bo." Alex ambled backwards while facing him. "Surprise reunions require that you run. Jog, make eye contact, act like you can't believe it's actually her, then *run.*"

"Wouldn't you be scared if someone ran at you?"

"No, because I always have my knife. But if it was *you,* Bo…" Her voice faltered. "I'd be delighted."

His heart stuttered. "You would?"

"Yes." She cleared her throat. "Back to the plan. You run to her. Then what?"

"I say hello?"

"First, you read her signals. If she's smiling and opens her arms, reciprocate. If she's a deer in headlights, approach calmly. Then explain yourself, starting with wanting to make sure she was safe." Alex slapped at a bug on her neck. She glanced up at him. "That's, um, still the case, right? The safety thing?"

The pitch of her voice ticked up a notch, close to a squeak.

Alexandra Ruby Stone wasn't a squeaky kind of person. He got the feeling the question she'd asked wasn't the real one she wanted him to answer. "Yes, but Alex—"

A troop of monkeys scrambled across the treetops overhead. Instinctively, he ducked.

"Don't be nervous, Bo."

Growls surrounded them. "I'm not nervous, I'm just not used to wild monkeys."

"Not about them." Alex chewed her lip. "The dig site is across that meadow."

Alex would rather cuddle a scorpion than finish this hike, but it had to happen.

"The meadow is a shortcut." She left the gravel path. "Cutting through it shaves about ten minutes, and then—Bo?"

He'd stopped at the edge of the clearing, white-knuckling his backpack straps. The poor guy looked like a funnel cloud had ripped away his house.

His voice was low. "You said it'd take an hour."

"I lied. I figured you'd get nervous." She threw her arms wide. "So, surprise! You're almost there."

Bo took a knee, chest puffing.

Oh, shit.

"Are you having a panic attack?"

He nodded.

She knelt next to him. She didn't want him to suffer. His ex's specter shouldn't hold this much power over him. If she could scoop the stress out of him, she would. But the next best thing was to coach him through it as fast as possible and deliver him to Density.

He repeated that his goal was not to get back together. Alex planned for the worst, though, even while she hoped for the best. Adventures were easier that way. Peter had taught her an expensive lesson that she'd be foolish to forget. People lied—sometimes to others, more often to themselves, and everyone else was collateral damage.

"Okay, bucko, tell me five things you see."

He lifted his chin. "The dig site…"

"Not that." She squeezed his biceps. His ex's turf was the last thing he should focus on.

"You." He searched the area around them. "The palm tree behind you…clouds…a macaw. A hot pink spider plant."

"A what?" She followed his gaze. "That's an air plant, not a spider plant. Now tell me four things you can touch."

"Your hand on my arm, the gravel under my knee, my backpack straps…and…"

She clasped his other arm, steadying him.

"Your other hand." He laid his hand over hers. "Does that count? I named you twice."

She swallowed. Every time he put his hands on her, she felt safer, more secure. The world could be spinning out around them, and if he held her hand, it would all be okay.

"I'll allow it. Three things you can hear."

"Your voice. Howler monkeys. Shuffling and scraping at the dig site." His arms tensed in her grip, but his breathing remained calm.

"Almost done. Two things you can smell."

He wrinkled his nose. "The bug spray."

She laughed.

A grin played on his lips. "And you."

"Hey." She lightly punched his shoulder.

"Sorry, I didn't mean it like that. Your lotion or shampoo or whatever. It smells like vanilla and citrus."

Flutters filled her belly. "You noticed that?"

"Since day one." Heat darkened his blue gaze to the color of midnight. "I notice everything about you."

That was equally thrilling and terrifying.

"Last one," she said. "Something you can taste."

His Adam's apple bobbed. "I don't taste anything."

She could fix that. If this was the last chance she had to kiss him, she'd take it. Absolutely stupid, but since when had she thought things through? She licked her lips and leaned forward, pressing her mouth to his. His arms found her waist and tightened, cinching her to him.

"Mint," he growled into her mouth. "I taste mint."

"Nailed it."

He pressed his forehead to hers. "Alex, you're giving me mixed signals."

"Sorry." Her head and her heart were fighting with each other. "But that's it, I promise."

"It doesn't have to be. Can we talk about it?"

She'd love to, but not here. Not within a literal stone's throw of his ex. Any real conversation she'd have with him would involve a ton of humble pie on her part, because this trek across the country had taught her a vitally important lesson—everything she'd said to him that first night in the jungle was a huge crock of shit.

Love wasn't a fantasy, it was as real as the ground under her feet.

"Not now." She stood. "But maybe later? After you handle this reunion situation."

He searched her gaze. She held it as firmly as railings on a rope bridge. She would not break first, because if she did, he'd jump-start a touchy-feely conversation and never march over to that camp to snap the lid shut on his relationship with his ex.

"Got it." He shifted his focus to the location across the meadow.

She blinked to clear the sting from her eyes. "Good."

"Let's go, then. We'll be in and out, and then back home to Azul Caye."

He rolled his shoulders. Gorgeous shoulders that were attached to strong arms that carried her across bedrooms and rivers.

"No, Bo, not us. Just you. It'll be awkward city with me there, so I'll wait here."

Alex's heart twisted, hating the words as she said them. But she couldn't watch him potentially make googly eyes at another woman, and he needed the freedom to say what he needed to say without worrying about how it made her feel.

He shifted his weight. "Will you be safe?"

"Perfectly." She sat, hugged her knees, and gulped her water. "Now go. You'll do great."

He shifted his weight. "I don't know, Alex."

"But I do." She forced a smile. "You should go."

"I don't like leaving you alone."

"I've been that way for a while." Shooing him away might make her cry, but he needed to do this. "Seriously, *go.*"

He sighed. "I'll be back soon. Don't go anywhere."

"Sir, yes sir." She saluted him.

Where *would* she go? It's not like there was a bar in the neighborhood. He crossed the green space in seconds. Sheesh, was he that eager to arrive? She grabbed mini-binoculars from her bag, then trained them on Bo.

He approached a younger guy with a scruffy beard. After a few seconds of conversation, Scruffy pointed toward a huge white canopy nestled at the base of a crumbling ruin. As Bo wended his way toward it, Alex's pulse pounded in her ears.

This was the moment she'd been dreading.

At the edge of the canopy, Bo paused. Tension tightened his body, like that first day when she'd driven backward on the highway. Back then, she'd thought he was an insufferable prick, but she couldn't have been more wrong about this big-hearted, reliable, straightforward man who was game for adventure.

Through the lens, she spied Bo's mouth moving. With whom was he speaking? Alex panned to the left, then gasped.

Density, in the flesh.

And, goddammit, she was beautiful. Tall, lithe and blonde, she could be modeling archaeology chic on a runway in Paris instead of mucking about in the Belizean forest.

Alex, on the other hand, was covered in grit and grime. Her crumpled dress was still damp in places, and her skin was oily from the bug spray.

Yeah, she was a real prize.

Through the binoculars, Alex spied what's-her-name drop

a clipboard on a table covered in sorting bins. As Bo's ex threw her arms around him, Alex felt like Bo's fancy lighter thing. Her frustration started as a spark, grew into a big glob of fire, then erupted into a conflagration.

She'd hoped Density would run away screaming.

But hugging? Happiness?

What right did that woman have to either? Alex would never understand how she'd tossed a treasure like Bo aside. Even if she had a decent reason, she'd dumped him via text like a coward, and *that* was inexcusable.

Alex hurled a pebble.

It plinked unsatisfyingly against a tree.

Knowing Bo, he'd be a gentleman about the whole thing. Alex hurled another pebble. The notion he might let his ex off the hook, that she might not understand how much of an asshole she'd been… That didn't sit well with Alex.

Ugh, they were *still* hugging?

She shoved her binoculars into her bag, then stomped toward the camp. If Bo didn't stick up for himself, make his ex twist a little, she'd do it for him.

Nineteen

A pit widened in Bo's stomach with every step toward the camp. What was he doing? He'd rather stay in the field with Alex, talking about nothing and everything and not knowing what came next. He twisted toward the flat green space, but she was invisible at this distance.

"Sir?" A young bearded guy stopped him. "Can I help you? Are you lost?"

The kid didn't know how right he was.

"Destiny Richards?" Bo asked. "Is she here?"

"Oh, sure thing. Head over that way, dude." He pointed to a dusty canopy under which a half dozen archaeology sorting tables stood.

"Thanks." Bo reluctantly approached the artifact processing station.

There she was, squatting in front of a cabinet, with her back to him. Complicated waves of nostalgia, hurt, and gratitude that Destiny was okay washed over him. They'd been together for seven years—he couldn't shut off caring about her as easily as shutting off a hose.

Missing from that cocktail, however, was desire.

He knocked on a table. "Destiny?"

According to the sudden stiffness in her spine, he was not

a welcome surprise. Her boots ground against the earth as she twisted toward him.

"Bo?" Destiny's trowel clattered on the table and she flung himself at him.

On instinct, he caught her.

"Is it actually you?" she asked. "I can't believe this!"

"Yeah, it's me."

He rolled his eyes. Alex would be disappointed. After all that prep, "yeah" was the best he could come up with.

"I am truly shocked." Belize had tanned her to a shade reminiscent of weak tea. "What are you doing here?"

"I had to make sure you were okay."

Destiny scrunched her forehead. "Why wouldn't I be okay?"

He let her go. "Because you wouldn't pick up my calls. That's not like you."

That's exactly like her. He heard Delilah's voice as though she were standing next to him.

Destiny smoothed her features. "Oh. Hmm. I can see why that might worry you. It's just that I've been working on my boundaries, and I suppose I overcorrected. I had good reason, though—I was worried if we talked, you'd convince me to come back."

His gut clenched. "Jesus, Destiny. I don't want to be with anyone who doesn't want to be with me."

Destiny crossed her arms. "And yet you're standing here. Why would you come all this way if you weren't planning to convince me to come home?"

She had him there. That had been the original plan, but during the journey here, he discovered that he was worth more than that. He couldn't spend his entire life worrying that his person had one foot out the door.

Was there a way to say that and keep his dignity?

"Because," a familiar voice piped up behind him. "He's a good man."

A thrill sizzled through him. He should've expected Alex to barge into this situation since she excelled at not sticking to plans. The characteristic that initially irritated him was now one for he found endearing. Her presence boosted his confidence and saved him from the stilted, unpleasant energy between him and Destiny.

"Hi," he murmured. "I take it you got bored?"

"Very. And the monkeys were too loud for a nap." She bumped her hip against his. To Destiny, she said, "He also needed to know what happened. All your mutuals at home would eventually ask him about you, and what was he supposed to say? That you sent a breakup text and disappeared, but he was *pretty* sure you hadn't been kidnapped or anything?"

Tight frown lines bracketed Destiny's mouth. She shifted her gaze between them, then smoothed her expression and extended her hand.

"Hi. I'm Destiny Richards. And you are...?"

"Alex Stone." Alex's jewel tattoos danced as she squeezed Destiny's hand. "Bo's guide."

"Ah." Destiny nodded. "That makes sense. Bo never trusts himself to find his way."

Her indulgent smile annoyed him. Was that what Delilah had meant when she'd said that Destiny was kind of an asshole? He'd taken those kinds of comments as affectionate teasing, but having been away from it for a while, and having been in the presence of someone without a passive-aggressive bone in her body...

Yeah, he didn't like it.

Alex's shoulder nudged Bo's as she shrugged. "Oh, I don't know about that. He was always game to figure out our next move when things didn't go according to plan."

"Things didn't go according to plan?" Bo joked.

"How long have you two known each other?" Destiny asked.

"Five days," they said in unison.

"Feels like much longer, though," Bo said.

Alex twisted toward him. "Is that a good thing or a bad thing?"

Destiny cleared her throat. "Bo, since you've come all this way, let me take you on a tour. That might help you understand my decision." She tossed a glance at Alex. "You're welcome to come too, if you want."

Without waiting for them to accept her invitation, Destiny pivoted on her heel.

Wow, he had been beyond blind to her rudeness.

"Shouldn't she wait?" Alex murmured.

"She never does." Bo inhaled her blend of vanilla, orange and bug spray. "Thanks for coming, but you don't have to subject yourself to this. I've got it."

"I'm here for you." She squeezed his hand. "But now I am *dying* to know what she's so excited about. Aren't you?"

He was caring less by the minute.

"Come on." Alex tugged his hand. "We might as well."

Alex's presence was a comfort, and her confidence was contagious. As they hurried after Destiny, they hiked past a dozen blue-jeaned people working in carefully excavated sections marked by bright yellow crisscrossed ropes. Metallic tings echoed in the air as the students' trowels scraped against stones and secrets. On the other side of the dig, Destiny's bright yellow shirt was a beacon against the earth tones.

"How is she so clean?" Alex asked.

"Because nothing sticks to her." He hitched his bag higher on his shoulders.

"This way," Destiny called. "We're almost there."

Via paths strewn with fallen leaves, she led them to a shadowed portion of the site. As they caught up to Destiny, the trees fringing the plaza provided a much-needed break from the relentless sun. The air took on an earthy scent, one that reminded him of his first night in the jungle with Alex.

"This dig started in the '80s," Destiny said. "The main goal back then was to date the eras represented in the building styles. The complex was likely multipurpose—spiritual, governmental, residential." The paths were covered by scattered leaves. "This is section N7-16. On my first day, I found cache N7-16-6. It's an exciting, once-in-a-lifetime discovery."

She'd been thrilled when she'd called to tell him about it. It had been a gift to hear the happiness in her voice, a signal that she was in the right place.

"You told me about that one," Bo said. "That you'd probably get a paper out of it."

Destiny caressed a small pillar of smooth stones. "I didn't do it justice. Caches tell us *so* much more about the time period than the buildings themselves. Stones were frequently reused, so it's difficult to date construction accurately. But caches rest undisturbed."

"Until you dig them up," Alex said.

"*Exactly*," Destiny said.

Either she clearly didn't catch the judgy tone in Alex's voice, or she chose to ignore it.

"Caches are time capsules, full of artifacts from a single era and typically well-preserved. Even when everything changes around them, the insides are the same."

Bo stumbled over a tree root. Damn, she could be describing their relationship. The way they interacted with each other as a couple wasn't all *that* different from how they were when they were kids. Just with more bills, pets, jobs and sex.

Destiny hung a left turn. "It's much easier to put together a timeline of changes in the civilization's culture with caches. The ones I found were in north-facing stairs, so we're certain they were dedicatory in nature."

"And you just yanked them out?" Alex pinched the bridge of her nose. "You know, there's probably a good reason that ancient people hid those items in a stone stairwell. Secret portals to vengeful gods and all that jazz."

Bo hid his snort. If he wasn't mistaken, Alex had no patience for Destiny.

"Don't you have a busy imagination?" Destiny led them to a Quonset hut. At the door, she punched in a code. "They *were* a highly superstitious people, it's true, but that doesn't make their fears real."

"What is this place?" Bo asked.

Destiny swung the door open. "This is where we keep the unusual discoveries."

"I've seen horror movies that start this way, Bo," Alex whispered.

"You should be fine, then," he whispered back. "The spunky heroine always survives."

Alex frowned. "Spunky?"

Destiny flicked on battery-powered lamps that flooded the hut with cold LED light.

"The N7-16-6 cache featured large charcoal fragments,

five obsidian lancets, a large jade bead and unbroken lip-to-lip polychrome dishes." Destiny's eyes sparkled. "That they're unbroken tells us the cache was buried prior to the tenth century. I won't lecture you about ancient Mayan mortuary practices in the Terminal Classical Period, but that's what our research is about. We're creating a classification system to make future comparative analyses easier."

"Do you have any Indigenous people on the team?" Alex asked.

That was a *great* question. One that aligned with his approach at work. He tried to balance his team with people from varied backgrounds and experiences. Otherwise, he'd end up coding the algorithms to benefit one slice of the population, and end up excluding others. Destiny hadn't talked about her coworkers or the perspectives they might bring to the table, and he hadn't asked about them in all the time she'd been here.

Destiny crossed her arms. "I am a perfectly capable researcher. Exceptional, even."

Ah, there was her warning tone. At home, he usually dropped arguments with Destiny when that tone showed up. If he challenged her, she'd shift her point, or freeze him out if he pushed too hard. He approached arguments to get at truth, whereas she only seemed to be concerned with being right. All the arguing that he'd grown up with made him strive for peace in his house, and eventually, striving for peace meant letting things go.

But she wasn't a part of his house, and Alex had shown him that arguing wasn't taboo.

In fact, it could be pretty fun.

"No one questions your bona fides..." Bo said. "But couldn't you benefit from the perspective of someone brought up in the culture?"

Destiny shot daggers at him. "I've been studying this for *years.*"

"Have a cookie." Alex shrugged. "Including the Indigenous perspective only strengthens your understanding of the nuances. It would make your research *better.*"

"We're not here to discuss the construction of the research team." Destiny's swallowed-a-lemon pout morphed into her indulgent smile again. "But I'll take that recommendation to the site director. Come look at this plate. What do you see?"

She flicked on another lamp over a covered case.

Before Bo could make sense of the squiggly colors on the pottery, Alex said, "It's a map."

Of course it was a map. He loved how her mind worked, that she'd sifted through a seemingly random assortment of images and clocked the cartography straightaway. That was Alex, always adding to the library of instructions for how to get from here to there.

"You're quick." Destiny tapped on the plexiglass. "We think it's a map to the lost treasure of Ajaw Kan Ek' of Tikal."

"Treasure?" Bo asked. "Don't tell me you've gone full *Raiders of the Lost Ark.*"

"Don't be silly. This—" she hovered her hand over the plate "—is the treasure. I have no desire to follow vague pictograms to locate gold in the Maya Mountains."

"Neither would I." Alex leaned close to the plexiglass separating them from the plate. "Because the lost treasure of Ajaw Kan Ek' is a legend, like El Dorado or Shangri-La. Trying to find things like that is a fool's errand. I have a whole tour built around trying to find Spanish galleons on Secret Beach, but all people find are lost wedding rings. I agree that the real treasure is this artifact. It'll be nice to see it in a museum."

A shadow blocked the daylight streaming through the door. Bo shifted and placed himself between Alex and whomever had arrived. *Cough.* The person filling the door frame had blown a plume of cherry-sweetened tobacco smoke into the hut.

"It's not destined for a museum," said the shadow.

Inserting herself into this reunion was racing up Alex's Top Five Regrets list. If she'd stuck to her plan to drain her flask and nap, she wouldn't be trapped in a hut with Bo's ex and a lunatic who smoked a pipe in the forest during the dry season.

But *nooo*, she'd let jealousy get the better of her.

As the men sized each other up, Destiny barely contained a sigh. This silence was intolerable. Fighting was better than simmering in passive-aggressive quiet.

"Why isn't it destined for a museum?" Alex asked. "Artifacts go to museums."

The man sucked on his pipe, then blew another cloud of toxically sweet tobacco smoke into the air. Great. Maybe she'd pick up a smidge of lung cancer, too.

"I'm not opposed," the bearded man said. He was about the same size as Bo, about ten years older, and sported a fedora. "It could go to any museum that makes a reasonable offer."

This guy clearly wasn't read into the rules about the appropriate handling of antiquities.

"There are laws," she said. "Tourists can't remove artifacts from heritage sites."

"We aren't tourists, and our institution's arrangement with the government predates those laws. Belize, of course, has right of first refusal." He set his pipe in an ashtray in the middle of one of the sorting tables. "Destiny, with whom do I have the pleasure of debating the finer points of our research agreements?"

"This is Bo Ferguson." Destiny said brightly. "And Alexa Stone. Did I get that right?"

"No," she said. "It's Alex."

Big shock that a person with the empathy of an eel misheard her name. Alex relaxed her tightened her jaw. She refused to crack a molar because Bo's ex annoyed her.

The bearded man shot a pitying look Bo's way. "You're Destiny's former fiancé?"

Bo cocked his head. "Correct. And you are?"

"Jack Hedges. I'm the director here."

"Director?" Alex crossed her arms. "Then you should know better than to steal Belize's history."

"We're not stealing anything," Destiny said. "We're studying the contents of the cache. When we've gleaned all we can from them, we'll auction them to raise funds to continue our research. Everybody wins."

The delusion curdled Alex's stomach. "You really believe you're doing something good here, don't you? News flash— you're not. You're mining Mayan history and culture for professional clout, then selling Belize's heritage to the highest bidder. You make me sick."

Destiny raised her eyebrows, then laughed. "That's quite a speech. Did you practice that on your way here?"

Red clouded Alex's vision. What an awful person. If she didn't escape, she'd claw at this woman like a rabid puma. She *thought* she hated Belisle, but compared to this incandescent rage, what she felt for him was mild disdain.

"We're leaving," she said through gritted teeth. "Enjoy your plunder, thieves."

At the door, she glared at Jack. "Move."

He stepped aside.

"Nice meeting you, Alexa," Destiny called.

She paused in the doorway, then flared her nostrils. Maybe she *would* launch herself at Destiny. It would feel *so* good to take all her frustrations out on someone who deserved it, but no. She would not choose violence. Today, she'd choose distance. Her shins protested as she hustled uphill and away from the hut, determined not to give them the satisfaction of her running.

"Alex, wait," Bo called.

"No." She stomped down the trail, kicking rocks and dust along the way. "They are terrible and if I stay here I'll vomit."

He caught her elbow. "Yes, they are terrible, but—"

"There's no but." She whirled on him and thrust her hand toward the hut. "Research to learn about and celebrate the culture is one thing. This is colonizer shit."

"I agree." He hitched up his backpack. "But I… I need more information. From Destiny."

He couldn't make less sense if he were speaking an alien language.

"Like what? Whether they'll sell national treasures on the black market, or if they're courting museums? Ugh." She wiped her hands down her face. "They're worse than Belisle."

"Who?" He wrinkled his brow.

Had she really not told him about Belisle? Her family's history with him was part of her core identity. Bo not knowing this was like him not knowing if she had allergies. Well, she'd warned him if they stayed here she'd vomit—she just hadn't expected it to be word vomit.

"A terrible man from Azul Caye who almost got my father killed thirty years ago." She yanked her hair into a tight bun.

"They went cave-diving and discovered a trove of artifacts, but a rock slide partially blocked their tunnel. Belisle was smaller than my dad, so he got out. But he didn't send help."

"Jesus, that's awful." Bo cupped her cheek, then ran his thumb along her jaw.

She sank into his caress as her breathing calmed. "It took my dad a day to clear enough of the rubble to escape. By the time he hitched a ride back to town, Belisle had already sold their find to a private dealer for a small fortune. Legal, but shady. To this day, Belisle wields his money like a sledgehammer. *He* is the person I owe in Azul Caye, by the way. And I still think he's a better human than those two in there."

She waved her hand toward the Quonset hut.

"They didn't leave anyone to die."

"That we know of." She lifted her head from his palm. "Come on, Bo, let's just go."

He pressed his lips into a thin line. "I get why you're upset, but... I can't help but think there's an opportunity here."

"To smash some skulls?" She lifted a shoulder. "I agree, but the police frown upon that kind of thing."

"Definitely not smashing skulls." He glanced over his shoulder, back toward the hut. "But there could be another tour opportunity, one that helps with your bills."

She knit her eyebrows. "I'm not following."

"You lit up when you saw the map. What if you created a treasure hunt tour? Something easier physically, like Mariele said. I bet Destiny would agree to host people for a fee, let them dig up an unimportant part of the ruins. Haven't we had a great time these last couple of days?" His gaze softened. "Life-changing, honestly. People would eat up adventures like that, especially if it ends with treasure."

Her breath left her. Now she might actually hurl.

Did he not understand that their fun had nothing to do with the trip, and everything to do with the two of them? What had happened between her and Bo *was* the treasure. She couldn't—wouldn't—repackage the magic they'd experienced as immersive X-marks-the-spot theater. That he would suggest such a thing, and wanted to stay and talk to Destiny after everything she'd said in that hut... Alex couldn't deny the truth.

He wasn't the man she'd thought he was.

"I'll take that under advisement, Bo."

She pivoted on her heel and marched away, hiding her tears. Much better to guard her heart and keep him at a safe distance.

Bo fell into step beside her.

"What are you doing?" she asked.

"Walking you to the river."

The obvious, unspoken part thumped her in the chest. He'd escort her to the river, and that's where he'd leave her, too.

"Don't bother. I can get myself across." She used his handkerchief to blot her eyes, then shoved it at him. "Stay and do what you came to do. Win her back. According to plan."

"Alex, come on." He held her shoulders. "That's not what I'm doing."

She shook him off. "Then what *are* you doing?"

"I told you, I need more information." He searched her eyes. "You're comfortable with chasing rainbows based on fifty percent intel and fifty percent intuition. I'm not. It doesn't work for me. And I'm not so sure it's working for you, either."

Anger flared in her gut. "You don't know me well enough to make claims like that."

"Yes, I do," he said simply.

His tone, his eyes, his stance were relaxed. If she flung herself at him in anger, he'd catch her like a safety net. The fucking frustrating thing was, he was right. He *did* know her, and that's why his accurate assessment stung.

"You stay here and sort out whatever shit you need to with those terrible people. I'm headed back to the river. Don't follow me."

Under a chorus of howler monkeys' growls, she left.

Bo, bless him, followed her instructions.

Twenty

Bo flexed his fingers as Alex disappeared around a curve in the trail. He was desperate to chase her, to hold her, to apologize for putting her in this impossible situation.

He glanced over his shoulder, torn.

But this was his last chance to ask Destiny why she'd found it so easy to ditch everything they'd planned together. His annoying brain required this information. Without it, he'd fixate and waste more of his synapses on Destiny's inexplicable choices. He couldn't move on with his life until he started to lock down answers and make decisions.

Everything—his heart, his home, what to do with Lorelai—was up in the air.

With a sigh, Bo headed back to the hut.

When he knocked, Destiny's cheeks bubbled with a smile. "Your tour guide's strong opinions and assumptions must drive you up a wall."

The negative comment about Alex chafed.

Destiny would call it an observation, but that was bullshit. It was a veiled insult.

"I like hearing what she thinks. She's not just a tour guide, she's more like…" A girlfriend, but he should probably talk to Alex about that first. "A friend."

He picked up a rock from a sorting table. Rough around the edges, but there was a mesmerizing shine to it.

"That's funny." Destiny raised an eyebrow. "My strong opinions used to stress you out. Like when I wanted to order Thai instead of Chinese."

"The Chinese place was objectively better."

"Agreed, but sometimes I wanted pad thai, even if it was subpar." Destiny gathered a tote bag hanging from a wall peg. "Speaking of food, it's my lunch break. Want to come with? The mess hut isn't far."

"Yeah, I could eat." He set the rock in its coded square on the grid. "And I want to talk about why you left."

There. He'd laid his cards on the table.

"I suspected as much." Destiny winked at him. "Some things about you haven't changed. But that's fine by me. Relationship postmortem over rice and beans."

She opened the door, then stood aside for Bo to pass by. After shutting it, she tested the door to ensure it was locked. Ironic that they didn't want anyone to steal the loot they'd pilfered from the ruins.

"How do you like Belize?" Destiny asked.

"I love it." He meant it, too.

"Me too," Destiny said. "The job prospects for me are fantastic, the weather is delightful, and best of all, most everyone speaks English."

He winced.

"Only sixty-three percent." Yeah, he'd researched that, too. "Have you traveled much? This country is amazing. We've been through jungles, mountains and rivers on our way here, had a gourmet meal at a chocolate festival, and climbed a pyramid. The wildlife is stunning, too. I've seen toucans, macaws and howler monkeys."

"Ugh, howler monkeys." Destiny led him down a shaded trail. "They're so creepy. Especially when heading to the toilet at night. If I could get rid of them, I would. Have you been to the beaches?"

"Not yet."

"Oh, you must. They are pristine. We went for a weekend getaway when I was desperate for a return to civilization in the form of a hot shower and a massage."

Tension banded around Bo's forehead. After college, Destiny had made jokey back-handed comments about Baltimore, too. Its nickname was Charm City, but she called it a backwater. Belize was apparently receiving that treatment. Combined with her opportunistic attitude toward the antiquities she'd scooped up, he had to admit this was basically her personality—look down on a place and its people, but grab what you can while you're there.

He could kick himself for not seeing that before.

Destiny opened the door to another Quonset hut, and a wall of chatter and savory aromas hit him. Folding tables and chairs were occupied by a variety of people ranging from college kids to grayed retirees.

"Food's this way." Destiny led him to the station where the dig cook had laid out simple fare. As she placed items on her tray, she said, "Grab whatever strikes your fancy. I'll get drinks and meet you at the empty table in the back."

He set a tin crock of stewed chicken with a side of rice and beans on his tray, found a spoon, and ignored the attention of the other people in the hut. As he seated himself, Destiny plopped a tin cup of water on his tray.

"Here you go." She sat opposite him. "Not cold and refreshing, but it's been purified."

"Thanks." He stirred the stew, then scooped up a bite. The tender morsel of chicken fell apart in his mouth. Heat from chilis pleasantly hit the back of his throat. He had no idea how to start this conversation, so he opted to start with truth.

"This is delicious," he said. "What's in it?"

"I have no idea." Destiny popped open her plastic pill organizer and swallowed the collection of vitamins she claimed gave her energy. "If it's too spicy for you, the rice helps."

"I'm good." He scooped up another spoonful of stew. "I could make a joke about spices. But it's not the right season."

Destiny frowned. "What?"

"Season, get it? It's a pun."

"Oh." She smiled. "I'm sure it was."

Wow, not even a pity laugh.

"Tastes like there might be ginger, garlic, cumin, oregano..." He swirled more of the sauce on his tongue. "Maybe thyme, and definitely chilis. I've been learning to cook since you left. I officially use more than Old Bay for seasoning."

"Good for you, Bo. Hobbies are important." Destiny flashed her five-years-in-braces smile. "So, let's get down to business, shall we? Why are you *really* here? Is this some grand gesture? Have you been watching too many romantic comedies again?"

He wrinkled his nose. Everything she said dripped with judgment.

"I was honestly worried. Ghosting didn't seem like you. You've always talked things over with me, teased out all the contingencies. Snap decisions were never your style."

"Well..." She nailed him with her green gaze. "They are,

in fact, exactly my style. Which may have been part of our problem?"

The muscles in his lower back bunched. Obviously, they'd had a problem. She'd secretly applied to a job in another country. Tough to ignore a neon-bright clue like that, but her statement implied something bigger, more pervasive than that one instance.

"How so?"

She lifted her shoulder. "You're the best person I've ever known, Bo. Good to the bone. Everything you've done for your mom and your sister, the way you stepped up after your dad left... The long hours at work, picking up slack and mentoring the new hires... I could go on. You're a saint among men. And I am not. I'm as selfish as they come."

"That's—"

Destiny held up a hand to stop him. "No, it's true. I am. Don't try to talk me out of it."

He hadn't planned to. He'd been about to say that Delilah had described her that way.

"But I don't think of selfish as a bad thing," she said. "It's the only way to guarantee you get what you want out of life. That's why I was always drawn to bad boys. Men who lived on the edge, took chances, who carved their own path. I find them exhilarating."

"I recall." The parade of rebels she'd dated in high school had nauseated him. "Is this going somewhere?"

"Yes. Be patient." She patted his hand. "In college, I was convinced the bad boys had a tender core, something special they'd share only with me if I stuck with them."

No wonder she'd become an archaeologist. She'd spent a lifetime digging for treasure.

"It finally happened with my college boyfriend, but then he cheated on me." She rested her chin on her fist and stared past him. "I was willing to forgive him, but he didn't want forgiveness. He just wanted me to leave. My mother took me in, but on the condition that I try therapy for at least a year. My therapist recommended I try to deviate from my pattern since it wasn't making me happy."

He set his spoon in his bowl. "And that's when you called me?"

"Well, if I recall, you called me."

It was true, he had.

"And Bo, you were so *easy*. There was no secret nugget of niceness. You are simply a kind human, and it's all right there for everyone to see. But you aren't that way *because* the world values it and you're trying to curry favor. That's just who you are. A saint."

He played back the last week with Alex. "I'm no saint."

"Yes, you are." She sipped her water. "But here's the thing. No one wants to fuck a saint."

Ouch. He refused take criticism from her since he wouldn't take her advice either, but that stung harder than a murder hornet.

"That's a shitty thing to say, Des."

"Sorry." She stirred her stew with her spoon. "That came out harshly, but it's how I feel. I tried really hard *not* to feel that way, because when I was with you, I was a good person through the transitive property."

"What?" He'd laugh if her face wasn't deadly serious.

"It's like this. Since *you* were good, and *you* liked me, then *I* must be good too, right? So I never fussed about the ridiculous amount of time and money you spent on your family, or all the extra hours at work. I didn't even blink when you asked if your sister could live with us. I could have balked, but I didn't, and we were fine. Until you proposed."

"A lot of couples who've been together for years get married." This was officially the strangest conversation he'd ever had. "It's the logical next step."

Destiny lifted a shoulder. "I've never needed logic or legal documents to declare love."

"That's not…" He wiped his hands down his face. "Marriage isn't just a legal thing. A wedding allows a couple to declare to the world what they mean to each other, and marriage is where they prove that to each other every day."

Destiny eyed him, sighed, then set down her spoon.

"Bo, what else is there to say? If it makes you feel better, I'm sorry about the way I handled the breakup. In my defense, cold turkey was best for both of us. I'm up against a series of grant proposal deadlines, and I couldn't afford hours on the phone helping you arrive at the conclusion I'd already reached."

He stared at her cool beauty.

He'd been willingly blind to her spiky personality, the mercenary way she'd dealt with people and life in general. According to Delilah, he'd never seen her clearly. He'd crushed on her as a kid, and that had matured to lust, then love. Or so he'd thought… But maybe, during all that time, he'd suffered from a cataclysmic reluctance to be surprised.

It turned out, what he wanted most was to find someone who would help him laugh or fight his way through whatever life threw at him.

Like Alex.

"I have to say, Bo, I never dreamed you'd come after me. But you should know I'm staying in Belize for the foreseeable future. With Jack, actually." Her eyes sparkled. "He has a reputation for breaking hearts, but I have the sneaking suspicion I could be the exception."

His bruised ego transformed into something suspiciously like pity.

"Des, is that a good idea? He's your boss."

"Isn't it deliciously taboo? But there's something I *do* need to come clean about." She massaged her bare left ring finger. "We had a gap in funding, so I had to sell the engagement ring to cover expenses. Consider this your thank-you meal, I suppose? From all of us."

The ring? As if he'd come all this way for a six-thousand-dollar ring that they'd bought at the mall. He'd come because he cared about her, not because he wanted a piece of jewelry back. He wouldn't know what to do with it, anyway. He was happy to be rid of that particular problem. In fact, it was tuition for an important lesson.

He wanted adventure, and he wanted it with one specific person.

"You're welcome," he said, and pushed back from the table. "Have a good life, Destiny."

"Another, miss?" the Sweet Winds bartender asked.

Alex flashed him a thumbs-up as she slurped the dregs of her Panti Rippa. Not the best midmorning beverage, but she was wallowing. She rubbed at the spot on her chest where it felt like Bo had scooped out her heart with Destiny's stupid pointy trowel.

As Alex chewed on her cocktail straw, raucous laughter erupted from the opposite side of the bar. She'd bet they were the destination wedding Mariele told her about when she'd arrived yesterday.

Look at them, all happy and cheerful and in love.

Jerks.

Mariele slid onto the stool next to her. "Ready to tell me what happened?"

"Nope." Alex popped her lips on the *p*.

The bartender delivered her sunrise-colored beverage. As he collected Alex's empty glass, he asked, "Anything for you, boss?"

"An order of fryjacks and honey, please. Thank you, Gabor." Mariele propped her chin on her fist. "How many of those have you had?"

"This is my second one, *Mom*."

"Go ahead, mock me. You arrived here last night soaked in river water and tears, slept in our spare room, snapped at me like a surly teenager, and I don't get a *tiny* bit of the story?"

Alex lifted a shoulder.

Mariele folded her hands over her crossed legs. "I can't help but notice that you're missing a handsome bespectacled American."

"I wouldn't say I'm missing him," Alex mumbled as she munched the wedge of pineapple garnish that she'd plucked from the glass. The tart fruit stung her lips.

"I beg to differ."

"Differ all you want. That doesn't make you right." She wadded the pineapple rind in a napkin. "Our business is done. He wired the second half of the money this morning. I'll leave after lunch to pay Belisle. So I'm better than fine. I'm fantastic."

"Clearly." Mariele gestured toward the fast-draining glass in front of Alex. "Can I make an observation?"

She dropped her head back and groaned. "Can I stop you?"

"Not a chance. Three days ago, you were the happiest I've

seen you since your father passed, God rest his soul. A big part of that joy was a man who is *quite* different from your usual type."

"Wrong." Alex rubbed at the trowel spot again. "My joy was based on getting out from under crushing debt and paying back my friends and neighbors. Not because I succeeded in convincing him we were both single and sex wouldn't mean anything."

"But it meant something to *you*, didn't it?" Mariele grasped Alex's shoulder.

"Don't be nice to me."

"Why, because it makes you cry?"

Alex's throat thickened. Old friends were the best...and the worst. How would she ever get through life without a friend like Mariele?

"Yes." She dabbed her eyes with a cocktail napkin. "I am *so* stupid."

"You're not stupid, it's the flechazo. Love at first sight. That's how you do things, remember? Act first and think it through later."

Alex snorted at that. "It can be flechazo *and* stupid. They aren't mutually exclusive. His ex is so beautiful—"

"And you're gorgeous."

"Thank you, but this lady could've walked out of *Vogue*. She's smooth, put-together, controlled, and I'm like a Muppet on caffeine."

Mariele laughed. "You are *not* a Muppet. And she sounds terrible."

"She *is* terrible. But the worst part is she showed us this amazing collection of artifacts that they found buried in the ruins. When she said they'd auction them off instead of donating the items to a museum, I lost my mind and took off.

But Bo *stayed*. No matter how much I like him, I *can't* associate with someone who supports plunder."

Mariele tilted her head. "Did he endorse their plans?"

"Not explicitly." She lifted the straw from the drink and twisted it around her index finger. "What I *do* know is he didn't leave with me."

"Interesting." Mariele drummed her fingers on the bar. "It's almost like you're making up excuses to nip this relationship in the bud."

She dropped her head back. "Mare, we don't *have* a relationship. We had five days."

"That apparently reduced you to tears and day-drinking." Mariele eased the empty glass away from Alex as the waiter delivered a hot plate of fryjacks and coffee.

"It's been six," said a deep voice behind her. "Counting today."

Alex straightened her spine. She'd heard that voice around the clock, in all sorts of ways, ranging from shouts to moans to whispered jokes. But the owner of that gorgeously timbered voice couldn't be here.

Twenty-One

The tension in Bo's chest eased as Alex rounded on him. He didn't care that her surprised smile faded into a grim slash. He'd found her. That was what mattered most.

When his service had finally kicked in last night, she was the first person he called. When she didn't pick up, he got through to Sweet Winds, and Mariele confirmed Alex had arrived earlier that day. He happily moved mountains over the last eighteen hours to get here.

Alex glared at him. "You have a nasty habit of sneaking up behind me."

"We need to talk," Bo said.

She'd worn her hair down, the way he loved it, and the current churned by the overhead fans played with her loose tendrils. She was back in her typical cargo shorts, tank top and hiking boots. The picture she made was *almost* enough to snuff his irritation with her.

Almost.

"I have to get on the road." Alex crossed her arms. "Can you make it snappy?"

Snappy? He'd been *this* close to bribing a child for their bike, had eaten suspicious street meat from a vendor in Carmelita, and driven through the night, making wrong turn after wrong turn since his cell service dropped out on him more than it stayed connected.

And she wanted to *rush* him?

Bo stepped forward. "Listen—"

"I suggest you two take this to cabana seven." Mariele gestured toward a poolside wooden structure. "No one's reserved it, and it'll give you more privacy. I'd prefer my celebrating guests not witness a lover's quarrel."

Alex waved off her friend. "We're not—"

"Oh yes we are." Bo grabbed her hand. "Shall we?"

She vibrated like a disturbed wasp in his grip. The opening drums and happy bouncing beat of "Three Little Birds" filled the silence.

"Fine." Alex tore her hand from his, then hopped from her stool. "But I can't promise I won't yell."

"Please don't," Mariele called after them. "Ruins the vacay vibes."

Alex marched toward the cabana. Always leading. Not in this conversation, though. That would be his job. They were both guarding their hearts, but one of them would have to take a risk. Jump feetfirst.

For the first time in his life, it would be him.

Apologies were due, but he had some things to make clear, too. Boundaries he had. Instructions for being careful with his heart.

Inside the cabana, a round daybed with a ridiculous number of cushions made it difficult for Alex to find a corner in which to retreat. Good.

He loosened the ties on the privacy curtains.

"Why are you here?" Alex demanded.

Her tone sucker punched him.

"I'm here because *you're* here." He whipped the curtains closed. "You're not the only one who's angry. You ditched me in Ch'ooj Creek."

Her eyes flashed like diamonds. "After you made it clear that you wanted to spend time with your awful conquistador fiancée."

"*Ex*-fiancée." He stayed next to the rack of towels. "And I didn't want to spend time with *her*. I wanted to find out what went wrong between us."

Alex raked her hands through her hair. "Oh my God, *why*? She's a tool, that's what went wrong. Simple. Why do you need more than that?"

"So I can do better."

"With her?"

"No." How was she not getting this? He closed the gap between them. "With you."

"With *me*?" Alex backed away from him. "Bo Ferguson, I have known you for six days."

His heart thumped. He loved it when she used both his names.

He inched closer. "What's your point?"

Alex's legs collided with the daybed, causing her to bobble. He caught her, steadied her, held her.

Respectfully.

"You're ridiculous. You're in a vacation bubble."

"Vacation? If this is vacation I'd hate to see what work is like." He let her go, then folded his arms to stop himself from catching her to him. "I bought a tiny car for three times what it's worth. Then I used up my international plan to find the Sweet Winds resort, which was complicated by the fact that I couldn't remember its name. Once I found it, I made many,

many wrong turns while driving here and trying to read a paper map."

Concern etched her face. "Have you slept?"

"I couldn't. Not until I found you."

"That's the most…" She blinked, and the softness creeping into her gaze was replaced by something icy. "Congratulations, Bo. Mission accomplished. You found me, and I'm fine. Now I have to get back to Azul Caye."

She slinked around him. He could fold, let her win, which would mean letting her slide through the crack in the cabana's curtains. But there was too much at stake, and he had a few more cards to play.

"Alex." He caught the crook of her arm. "I wasn't finished."

Her gaze fixed on his hand. "Weren't you?"

"No." He let her go, then unzipped his backpack. "Not until I give you something."

"Bo, no—oh." She wrinkled her forehead.

He withdrew a slim wooden box from his backpack, then handed it to her. She sat hard on the daybed, clutching the box against her lap.

She traced the lid's grain. "What is it?"

He sat next to her. "Open it."

"I'm afraid to."

"Don't be."

"Okay, I won't." She gentled the lid free, then laughed. "What the hell?"

Nestled inside lay the unbroken plate Destiny had shown them.

"Do you like it?" he asked as he sat next to her.

"I *love* it. Did you steal this?" She clutched his forearm. "*Please* tell me you stole this."

"No, I'd be too paranoid that I'd get caught. I bought it from them."

"But they said they'd auction it." She raked her gaze over him. "Do you have black-market-auction buckets of money? If so, I have follow-up questions."

"I do not." He twisted toward her. "But I'm good at research. Destiny was right—they have an agreement that allows them to profit from their findings, provided they reinvest the proceeds into their in-country research. However, Belize has a robust searchable database of laws and statutes on the appropriate handling of antiquities. There are enough gray areas that a complaint would likely shut down an archaeological dig—and any potential deals—while the authorities investigate."

"You threatened them with paperwork?" She laughed. "How very you."

"They actually didn't care about the paperwork threat as much as they should. But then I waved stacks of cash I withdrew from my wedding savings and made them a generous offer. They took me up on it, and now you can donate it like you wanted."

"Just cash, phew." She exhaled and gently set the plate back in the foam casing. "I was worried you traded your family's locket for it."

"That's not mine to trade. It belongs to the person I want to spend the rest of my days with." As he dug the necklace out of his backpack, he sucked in a lungful of air. This was the biggest gamble of all. "And since that's you, and your style of living means I'll probably meet an untimely demise in a week, the necklace is yours. May I?"

He held the locket out to her. Their fake wedding rings also dangled on the chain.

"Bo." Her eyes glistened, but she didn't back away. "This is too much. I want to say yes, but I... I can't promise you forever."

"All I'm asking for is now." As he brushed his lips against hers, goose bumps fanned across her skin. "We've got today, and then we'll see how it goes."

The past week was evidence it would go exceptionally well. She turned toward him. "But how can you—"

"Alex." He cupped her face. "I love that I don't know. I *thought* I wanted predictability and plans. Gambling and guesswork seemed like the perfect way to lose everything. But this time with you has been more invigorating than the past ten years. I'm a realist. This is fast, but I can't wait for what tomorrow brings, whatever that might be."

"But your house, your job. You can't ditch those."

"I rent." He kissed her, more deeply this time, tasting coconut and pineapple. "And I work remotely. I can live anywhere."

"And your sister, and your mother?"

"Would love to visit the Caribbean." He kissed her again. "I talked to them about it."

She tunneled her fingers through his hair. "What about your cat?"

"I have to fill out an import permit, and then she'll be on her way." He backed away from the trail he was kissing down her neck. "Wait, are you allergic to cats?"

She shook her head. "Nope."

"Excellent." He hauled her onto his lap. "Then I can stay in Belize for as long as I want."

"And how long might that be?" The way she cradled his head as she pressed her lips to his made his heart stutter.

"Let's play it..." He nibbled her earlobe. "By ear."

In the distance, the town's church bells tolled noon.

Alex stiffened in his arms. "Oh, hell."

"What?"

She eased from him. "Much as I'd like to consummate this reunion, I've gotta get back to Azul Caye to pay off Belisle's debt before his offices close."

He caught her hand. "I can be quick?"

"That's not an enticement." She kissed him, briefly but full of passion. "Counteroffer—come with me?"

For the first time in an eternity, he could relax. "Always."

Alex hit the brake and let out a frustrated groan.

They'd made great time along Northern Highway, but the traffic in town was more snarled than her hair after a day at the beach. The sooner this damned traffic light flipped to green and she dropped off Belisle's check, the sooner she and Bo could have *all* the makeup sex. She squinted against the sunshine blasting hot and bright through the windshield.

"Can I borrow your sunglasses?" she asked.

Bo handed them to her. "They're prescription."

"I'll make do." She popped them on, and the world distorted like a low-key funhouse mirror. Perfect. She'd seen the world through Bo's eyes for the past week. Might as well literally see it that way, too. If she didn't get to Belisle's office in time, he'd be a dick about it. Her backup plan was to find him at his favorite watering hole, and if that didn't work, backup plan B was to break into his office and leave the check on his desk.

Bo palmed her thigh. "How far away is this guy?"

"He's in that big building up ahead." She swerved to avoid a goat-sized pothole. "Stop distracting me."

"Sorry." Bo left his hand on her thigh. With his other one, he gestured toward the enormous structure blocking a wedge of Belize's blue sky. "Is that a resort or an office building?"

"Both. It's half resort, half headquarters for his empire. This place was Belisle's first big development project in Azul Caye, the one funded by the stuff he found in the caves with my dad. He carved out a wing for his business operations."

She approached the stately building. Multiple verandas and porches beckoned to tourists, and mature palm trees swayed in the coconut-scented breeze.

"Sorry. Looks like whatever they found could have set you up for life."

"Don't be sorry." She curved around the driveway to the drop-off area. "Their parting was a blessing in disguise. It saved Dad from looking over his shoulder for the rest of his life, waiting for Belisle to stab him in the back."

Bo's forehead wrinkled. "If he's such a snake, why'd you go into business with him?

"*I* didn't." Alex ground her teeth. "Peter did, without my knowledge. I bear some of the responsibility since I completely handed the books over to him without thinking twice, but I *never* thought… All my complaints about Belisle's shadiness, his overdevelopment of the shoreline, overcharging tourists, ignoring the nature conservancy's tour guidelines, littering."

All unforgivable, but man, littering was just a lazy FU to Mother Nature.

"The more you tell me about him, the more I dislike him."

"Peter? Or Belisle?"

He squeezed her knee. "Both."

"Thank you."

"For what?"

"Having my back. Now let's get this over with."

She hopped out of the Jeep, then dug around for her bag. It held the checkbook she'd grabbed from her house when they'd dropped off Bo's tiny rust bucket. She'd already named it Jughead.

Bo met her on her side of the car, then palmed her hips.

"Think this'll take long? We haven't properly celebrated me staying in Belize."

Alex kissed him. "Five, ten minutes tops."

After tucking his sunglasses into the vee of Bo's shirt, she marched over to the empty valet stand. A red-vested man jogged toward them from around the corner.

"Welkom, welkom," he called.

"Heloa." Alex handed him her keys. "I'm not sure you actually need to move my Jeep—I don't expect to be here long. Mind telling me where Mr. Belisle's office is located?"

"Another one of you?" The valet shook his head. "Go on through the main doors, then go left. You'll be waiting, though. Lots of people are here to see him today."

"Okay." Damn. To Bo, she said, "Guess I was wrong about that five minutes."

Bo held the door open for her. "I don't mind."

They crossed the expansive lobby's black-and-white tiled floor. As they headed down the hallway on the left, a low, chattery din grew louder. Periodic peals of laughter cut through the noise, like it was a cocktail party.

Was someone playing a radio?

They rounded the corner. The reception area in front of Belisle's office was packed tighter than a booze cruise during the dry season.

"What's happening?" Bo asked.

"I have no idea." She scanned the crowd.

Her stomach dropped.

They were the vendors—some friends, some like family—to whom she owed money. Were they ganging up on her? Her fee from escorting Bo might be enough to give all of them a taste of what she owed, but not the full freight.

Quietly, she approached one of the women on the fringe. Esperanza lived on her block, had been a good friend of her dad's. She should be a safe person to ask.

She tapped her on the shoulder. "Hi, Espy, it's me."

"Mija!" Esperanza wrapped her arms around Alex. "We've been waiting for you."

"Why? Am I in trouble?"

"Yes." Esperanza held her by the shoulders. "But not with me. Why didn't you tell us you were in trouble with Belisle?"

"It's not like that. I owe him money, that's all."

"And *that* is trouble. He presses his advantage." Esperanza tugged her forward and shouted. "Everyone, she's finally here."

The smiling crowd fell silent.

"What's all this?" Alex clutched at Bo's hand.

"Your rescue party." Esperanza beamed. "Isn't it wonderful?"

A heated tingle swept up the back of her neck and over her face. This was so *embarrassing*. She'd been raised to be independent, to scramble up pyramids and dive into caves. Not to flail for a life preserver.

"I don't need rescuing."

"Oh, child, don't be silly. Everyone needs rescuing at some point in their lives. We protect our own. Have the grace to accept good-natured help from people who love you."

Alex's chest tightened. People who loved her? She'd thought they were all mad at her, that Peter's theft had soured her relationships with her collection of adopted aunties and uncles around town. Bo let go of her hand, then pressed a square of cloth into her empty palm.

The handkerchief from yesterday. Well, hell. Now she really would cry.

"Espy." She gulped, then dabbed at her eyes. "You don't… I can pay some of it back."

"And good for you, but James's daughter won't struggle with this man. Not on our watch."

Esperanza marched Alex through the open doors of Belisle's office. "She's here."

"Hello, Miss Stone." Belisle's pinky ring winked as he sorted a tidy collection of bright bills featuring the British monarch's face. "Your friends have rallied to pay your debt to me."

All of these people…were here…to help her?

On the fringe of the crowd, Bo smiled.

"We don't want you to owe him anything." Esperanza wagged her finger at Belisle. "Your father would never forgive us."

"But I don't understand. How did you know…?" She zeroed in on Bo. "Did you have something to do with this?"

He shook his head. "I wish, but no."

"It was me, actually." Rodrigo stood behind his father with a clipboard.

"You?" Alex's legs wobbled. Bo slipped an arm around her waist, then steered her to a guest chair in front of Belisle's desk.

"When you called last week about my father's—" Rodrigo dragged his bottom lip between his teeth "—offer, I demanded he tell me the story. When I made my distribution rounds, I asked a few of our mutual vendors if they could cut you a break. They were all horrified to learn of the predicament you were in with my father."

"I resent the word *horrified*." Belisle laid the final bill on the stack. "All twenty-five thousand is here."

Rodrigo held a clipboard. "And I have an accounting of what everyone contributed."

"Everyone, no." Tears stung Alex's eyes as she withdrew her checkbook form her purse. "You get all the points for this generous offer, but I can't let you put yourselves at risk. I can pay a lot back to Belisle. Not everything, but a lot. That's why I'm here."

"Put that away." Esperanza tapped Alex's checkbook. "There's no risk. Each of us offered only what we can. Out of respect for your father, we can't let you be indebted to Belisle and his extreme rates. We zero it out today, and you pay us back when you're able, interest-free."

Alex's thoughts flickered faster than palm fronds whipped by a cyclone. Bo had bought that plate, and her whole village gathered around her to pay her debt. Everyone was being so nice to her. None of this made sense.

"Why are you doing this?" she asked.

"Oh, child, that's what friends and family do." The older woman glared at Belisle. "They help each other. They don't steal from grieving people."

"I didn't steal from anyone." Belisle tucked the bills into a zippered pouch. "Keep accusing me, and you'll find yourself on the wrong side of a slander suit."

"Try it," Esperanza said. "It may not technically be theft, but there's doing wrong, Belisle. Taking advantage, and you know it."

Belisle grunted. "We're done here. Shall I call security? Or will you lot clear out?"

"Let's go." Bo held his hands out to Alex, then tugged her away from Belisle's desk.

"We'll have a party to welcome you home." Espy led them through the crowd and out to the lobby. "It will give me a chance to get to know this young man who has hearts in his eyes every time he looks at you."

"I'm Bo," he said. "Bo Ferguson."

"I like the look of you. Will you be staying in Azul Caye for a while?"

"Yes," Alex said, and squeezed his hand. "For a long, long while."

Possibly forever.

Epilogue

Six months later...

Bo's heart skipped a beat. Absorbed in her laptop at the counter, Alex hadn't noticed his approach. As much as she'd amazed him with her skills, talents and know-how when they'd first met, none of it held a candle to the fun, heat and adventure they'd together over the past six months. He loved everything about her, especially her tendency to jump into life headfirst and worry about the consequences later.

"Excuse me?" he said. "Where can I find the finest guide in Belize?"

Without breaking eye contact with her computer, she grinned. "At your service. What do you need?"

"The 11:00-a.m. adventure group is ready to go. Waivers are signed, bug spray applied, and they are desperate to climb some ruins." He leaned over the counter and kissed her. "And your 3:00-p.m. group is full, so no interesting side quests this time, okay?"

"I can't make any promises."

"You're pretty good at making them to me."

Like when she'd promised to make life interesting for him

and Lorelai. He only hoped that she'd let him promise to make her happy for the rest of their lives.

"Okay, okay. I'll have everyone back in time for me to lead the 3:00-p.m. to the Caye." She slipped on the Orioles baseball cap she'd stolen from him. "How's the rest of the week?"

"Great. I tweaked the algorithm so Stone Adventures's ads are being served up to our demographic on social media." He cinched his arm around her waist. "You're fully booked through the end of the month."

She pressed her hands to his chest. "How do you have time to do that while you work full-time for the software company?"

"I'm radically efficient." He fiddled with her curls. "And if I don't bury myself in work, I end up fantasizing about you and then I get absolutely nothing done."

"Thank God we have your special tour booked every day." She clutched his collar and pulled him close. "And that I'm great at taking chances."

He fingered the locket resting against her heart.

"I couldn't agree more."

★ ★ ★ ★ ★

Acknowledgments

The chances of me thanking everyone properly are slim, but I'll give it a shot!

First and foremost, my heartfelt thanks to Afterglow Books, and especially to John Jacobson and their insightful, constructive and often hilarious feedback on *Romancing Miss Stone*. They took an uncut gem and helped to polish it until it gleamed, and I'm forever grateful to them.

A truckload of gratitude also goes to Barbara Collins Rosenberg for her unfailing guidance and belief in my writing. Without you, I'd meander through this business like a hiker without a compass.

One of the best parts of romance publishing are the smart, funny, talented, inspiring and empathetic friends you meet along the way. The writing trenches are real! Thank you to Christi Barth, Robyn Neeley and E. Elizabeth Watson for our regular writing meetups, and to Sarah Storin for your unwavering enthusiasm. I'm indebted to all of you, as well as to Maryland Romance Writers, the group that introduced us to each other and many other wonderful writers.

To my friends and family, who have always supported my writing aspirations—thank you! Especially to my husband,

David, who often has more faith in me than I have in myself. I couldn't imagine walking through life with a better partner.

And lastly, a huge thank-you to everyone who reads, reviews and posts about my books. I see you, and I'm continuously humbled and grateful. I can't wait to share more words with you!